Ginni lies crumpled on the floor. Nikki immediately kneels next to her, watching in horror as blood stains the whole right side of Ginni's lab coat.

Nikki lays her gun down. Then she takes Ginni into her arms. "Ginni? I'm so sorry. Why? Why didn't you get out when I told you?"

Ginni can't open her eyes now. She licks her lips, already feeling parched from the loss of blood. "I...couldn't...leave you," she whispers.

Nikki fights back tears. Ginni's chest wound is dangerously close to her heart. Nikki knows she must do something quickly to stop the bleeding. Instinctively, she lays Ginni back down and grabs a clean gown off the exam table. She desperately presses the folded cotton gown against the wound.

"Nikki..." Ginni tries to talk once again. "The...killer..."

"Don't talk." Nikki touches Ginni's dry lips. "Save your strength. Everything will be okay. You'll be okay. You can tell me everything later."

AGENDA
for
MURDER

JOAN ALBARELLA

RISING
TIDE
PRESS

Rising Tide Publishers
65161 Emerald Ridge Dr.
Tucson, AZ 85739
520-888-1140

Printed in the United States on acid-free paper.

Publisher's note:
All characters, places, and situations in this book are fictitious, and any resemblance to persons (living or dead) is purely coincidental.

Publisher's acknowledgments:
Special thanks to Edna G. for believing in us, to the feminist and gay bookstores for being there, and to the Tucson lesbian community.

First printing: August, 1999
10 9 8 7 6 5 4 3 2 1

         Albarella, Joan 1944 -
         Agenda for Murder /Joan Albarella
              p.cm

ISBN 1-883061-20-2

Library of Congress Catalog Card Number 98-73139

DEDICATION

To Marian, Cuddles, and Ed
And to all the women who served as
military personnel and civilians during
the Vietnam War

ACKNOWLEDGMENTS

I wish to thank Linda Stoddard,
dear friend and first editor, who believed in
me and my work. For her hours of listening
and support,
even in the crazy times.

A special thanks to Vicki McConnell, a
writer's writer and friend, for her guidance,
instruction, knowledge and ability. From her I
learned that the process is most important and
will always parallel life—and so it does.

I am grateful to Lee Boojamra and Alice Frier,
and the community of Rising Tide Press, for
their constancy and dedication to beginning
writers and quality fiction.

To Marian Owczarczak, Daryl Patterson, and
Meg Davis, for their judicious reading, feedback and support.

Also to Karen Whitney, whose talent and
enthusiasm breathed new life and enrichment
into the manuscript.

I also wish to thank the women veterans and
clergy who openly shared their lives and
experiences with me. I hope the book is true
to their impressions and emotions.

AGENDA
for
MURDER

JOAN ALBARELLA

PRELUDE
Vietnam. January 1972.

The bodies are lined up at the 3rd Field Hospital on Cong Ly Street by the Tan Son Nhut Airport. They'll be flown stateside from there. Max wants to stay with Nikki, but she sends him away. She lies, telling the security officer she's representing Chaplain Gambino. She shows her pastoral care ID from the 90th EVAC Hospital. He lets her in. The green plastic bags are lined up on gurneys, waiting for the plane to take them home.

She finds Mo's body and slowly unzips the bag. Someone cleaned the body and put her in a new dress uniform. Nikki wishes it had been her, but it isn't allowed. Mo's face is distorted, her eyes closed. Bruises and fragments of steel and splinters are still visible in the skin on her face and bare arms. Nikki tries to pray, but it's hard to say the words, to bless her goodbye. She touches Mo's face, always so warm and smiling, now cold and vacant.

Nikki finds the small plastic bag of belongings tucked in the side of the green body bag. Opening it, she takes out the ring. This is certainly against regulations, and someone will hear about it when they discover the ring on the list missing. Nikki doesn't care. Mo's ring belongs with her. Both amulets are needed now, if she's to stay safe. If she's to get home. She kisses Mo tenderly on the cheek and leaves the airport.

Feeling terribly alone, she hates them now. For the first time in her life, she lets hate take over her body and her mind. She hates all of them for what happened, and she lets the hate grow. Since she has time coming, she extends her pass to a week's leave. She was saving days for their vacation together. She takes a room in a cheap hotel at the lower end of Thai Hoc Street, then buys five bottles of Jack Daniels from a black-market street vendor. Farther up the street, she buys a twenty-five caliber Browning and ammunition. In her room, she watches afternoon turn to late evening, slowly drinking four glasses of whiskey straight up, letting each swallow burn her throat and insides. This searing liquid joins the festering hate she is carefully nurturing.

At 2400 hours, the street is empty except for the pimps and prostitutes. Nikki walks unsteadily up to a skinny, seedy-looking, thirty-year-old Vietnamese man with a cigarette dangling from his mouth. She asks him to get her a woman, a Vietnamese woman about twenty-two years old, about Mo's age. He protests, saying it's too hard to get girls for women. He can get her a young man. She insists on the girl, presses fifty dollars into his hand and gives him her room number. Then she goes back to the whiskey to wait.

In less than an hour, Trang Trinh, looking younger than her nineteen years, knocks twice on Nikki's door and pushes it open. Nikki is sitting at the edge of the bed. Her limbs feel drunk, but her mind won't allow intoxication. The Jack Daniels bottle she dangles from her left hand is three-fourths empty. Her right hand is under one of the pillows, clutching the loaded Browning.

"Come over here by the bed," Nikki commands in a deep, husky voice as dark as the plan she's been drafting all afternoon.

The woman says nothing but moves slowly and cautiously. Her ninety-pound, four-foot-nine frame makes her resemble a child, but her face and eyes reflect a long, painful life. She's standing beside Nikki, who puts the bottle on the floor and pats a place on the bed next to her.

Trang's suspicion is obvious now. "Are you the woman who wants a woman?"

Nikki pats the bed again, not moving her other hand from under the pillow.

Trang doesn't move either. Suddenly, Nikki grabs Trang's arm and forces her onto the bed. She quickly pulls the gun out from under the pillow, rolls on top of Trang, and viciously shoves the gun into the Vietnamese woman's face. "I'm going to kill you. You killed her, and now I'm going to kill you." Nikki's speech is slurred, and her hand shakes involuntarily.

Trang speaks quietly, not pleading, but appealing to a reason that isn't present. "I didn't kill her. I didn't kill anyone. It's you, the Americans, who do the killing. You killed me two years ago—with no food, no house, night after night of men beating me, using me, laughing...and now...I am dead but can't die, because I have a black baby who needs me. Who is hated and rejected by everyone."

Nikki tries not to listen. Still on top of the woman, she's holding her down even though Trang isn't struggling. Then, Nikki's focus is totally drawn to the grey steel automatic. All she can see is the gun, as if it has a hypnotic power over her. She can feel the body under her. And the vision of the gun and the feel of this woman merge into a different reality. She jerks the gun away from Trang's face and lets her body fall back to a sitting position on the edge of the bed. This time, she dangles the gun at arm's length, as if it is a foreign appendage growing out of her.

Not looking at Trang, she says, "Get out. Just get out." She reaches into her shirt pocket with her free hand, takes out a wad of money, and throws it at Trang, who sits up and gathers the money, putting it in the pocket of her short dress.

Trang sits in silence next to Nikki, not moving or speaking. When Nikki realizes Trang isn't leaving, she gets up from the bed and moves to the dresser where the other whiskey bottles and glasses are. The gun is still in her hand as if they are melded together. "I told you to leave, "she says, as she unsteadily tries to open another bottle with one hand.

Trang stands and faces Nikki's back. "Was she someone you loved?"

This question is too much for Nikki. She slumps to the floor, covering her face with her arm, sobbing and screaming. Finally, she drops the gun, and still crying, crumples into an almost fetal position. When she can't cry anymore, when her throat is so dry she can barely swallow, and her eyes are swollen and stinging, she lies perfectly still. Her face and arms feel the damp wooden floor, and she falls asleep.

When she wakes up the next day, the gun is gone. Trang must have taken it. Nikki doesn't want to drink anymore. She showers and cries, dresses and cries, goes out for food, brings it back to the room and cries while she picks at the vegetables. She has never felt such loss and sorrow. Falling asleep again, she wakes up to knocking at the door.

Trang is back, with soup and green tea in Styrofoam cups. Placing them on a table by the bed, she sits next to Nikki, takes the gun out of her small purse, and puts it on the bed between them. "You gave me too much money yesterday, but I'm keeping it. Here is your gun. Can you keep from shooting yourself?"

Nikki doesn't want to cry in front of this heartless woman and angrily mumbles, "I won't kill myself." She picks up the gun and throws it on the bedside table.

"Good." Trang relaxes somewhat. "I have a proposition for you. Americans love propositions. I want to be your 'Mama San.'" This was what the nurses and soldiers called the Vietnamese women who did their washing and cleaning.

"You're a little young for a Mama San," Nikki says in a weary voice. "Anyway, I work at Long Binh, and I do my own laundry."

Trang is not deterred. Her stare cuts straight through to Nikki and demands attention while she continues negotiations. "I need the job. I have an uncle who lives outside of Long Binh.

He has no legs anymore. He will watch the child while I earn some money."

Nikki breaks their eye contact and stares at the floor. "I can't help you." She looks up again at Trang. "I'm sorry about the baby...but I can't even help myself."

"But, you can help me," Trang insists. "You still have a job, money, and food. My baby needs to live. I can't work the streets anymore. My baby needs me."

Nikki reaches into her pants pocket and takes out some more money. She puts it on the bed between them and again looks at the floor. Trang picks it up. "I will keep taking your money." She puts it into her pocket. "But I would rather earn it. I still have some pride."

They sit in silence again for several moments. Then Trang continues. "My parents sent me to France when I was sixteen to study art. They're dead now, and my brothers and a sister. All I have left is the child. She will be my art, my family."

Standing to leave, she says, "I will be back tomorrow, and you can tell me then when I should begin work. I will need some days to arrange for the ride to my uncle's."

She closes the door behind her, and Nikki, for the first time, feels the total emptiness of the room, the unbearable feeling of aloneness. The next day is the same. Crying and sorrow, nibbling on food because the body separates from the mind and seeks its own nourishment. Trang returns again, but this time not alone. Trailing behind her, in full habit, is Sister Bridget and a Vietnamese nun from the Holy Family Orphanage Nikki often visits.

Sister Bridget had put word out on the street that she was looking for the woman soldier. She was directed to Trang, who, for a price, brought the sisters to Nikki.

"So, look at you." Bridget's Irish accent seems heavier than usual. "I've been searching for you. Was afraid you'd be like this." Trang moves to the back corner of the room by the whiskey dresser. Nikki is still on the bed as if glued to the spot. Bridget stands in front of her like a towering church statue.

"I've paid her ten dollars," she points to Trang, "to bring me here. I'm only staying long enough to have my say. We all get hurt over here, Nicolette. I thought you knew that. I thought you had the faith to face it when it happened to you. Were you just playing with all those dying boys? Telling them about hope and love and not meaning it, not believing it?"

She sits next to Nikki, putting her arm around her. "You have to know, deep inside, that this isn't the last place you'll be. And this isn't the last place Maureen will be. If this world were the only one, we'd have no reason to go on."

Taking her arm away, Bridget stands up. "I want you to pray— that's what you'd tell me. So I'm giving it back. Talk to God, tell Him or Her what's happened. Then forgive yourself, like God forgives you, and get on with the business of life. I'll expect to see you next week for our tea and chat." She motions to the other sister, and they leave as quickly and as quietly as they came. Trang stays.

Nikki knows in her heart that Bridget is the awaited messenger. Her faith is still alive, a shaken faith, a bit fractured now, but perhaps more realistic. She makes a decision to spend only one more day in this odd chapel of a room, mourning Mo. When she leaves this dark night of the soul, she'll go back to her spiritual journey and her work, whatever that might be. Then, she tries to visualize that other world where she'll see her beloved Mo again.

Nikki is lost in thought when Trang coughs. "I can sell this whiskey, and one bottle would be a good gift for my uncle," she says.

"You took ten dollars from that nun." Nikki stands and turns toward Trang.

"I told you. I will take any money that will help my baby. I don't care if she is a nun. She has food and a home, and much more than me."

Nikki knows Trang is right. She's beginning to envy her strength. "I've thought about the job. You can have it. I'm in the WAC compound next to the 90th EVAC Hospital. You can ride down with me, day after tomorrow."

"I don't need a ride." Trang is gathering up the bottles, putting them in a cloth shopping bag she took out of her purse. "I will be there Monday, ready to wash your clothes and clean your hooch. It will cost fifteen dollars a week."

She finishes packing the bottles and starts for the door. When she is next to Nikki, she stops. "I'm glad you didn't shoot yourself. It would have been too bad. Perhaps your God brought us together. Strange things happen in Vietnam lately."

NIKKI SEES TRANG the following Monday. Trang becomes her Mama San, which elicits a lot of unkind remarks from many of the WACs. Trang is approached by several male soldiers for sexual favors, but she ignores everything except her cleaning and her pay, which is more than any other Mama San in Vietnam gets .

Nikki returns to her pastoral care work at the hospital, but something is missing now. A piece of her heart will always be gone. She forces herself to stop grieving and tries to stay only in the moment, no past, no future, no plans, only work. She numbs her feelings like the other women in Nam and vows never to get too close to another person again.

One day several months later, Trang appears as usual for her paycheck. They never share small talk or any talk, unless it's directions. This time, Trang asks for three thousand dollars. She needs it as a bribe to get herself and her child to Malaysia, where she can apply for passage to America.

Nikki's learning not to be surprised by anything Trang does. But she still says, "I don't have that kind of money. And, anyway, how can you trust someone you bribe?"

Trang stands her ground, as she did in the hotel room,

repeating Nikki's words, "Well, I don't have that kind of money, either. It's easier for you to get it."

Nikki still doesn't have the energy to fight, doesn't really like Trang working like a servant, and hopes the plan will work. She decides to call home and asks her mother to send the twenty-five hundred dollars she was saving for a car. The rest she borrows from Max without telling him what the money is for. When she hands the money to Trang, she asks, "And what do I get out of this?"

For the first time, she sees Trang smile. "I will see you someday in America, and I will repay you, or...I will sleep with you until the debt is paid." She turns and leaves and, strangely, Nikki feels another piece of her heart cracking away.

CHAPTER 1
Sheridan, New York. The present.

Nikki Barnes is twenty-five feet from her office door in the musty Hayes Hall basement when she hears her phone ring. She fumbles with her keys, trying several before she gets the right one. Hurriedly, she pushes open the office door, lunges across her paper-strewn desk, and just beats the answering machine. Pausing, she catches her breath before she speaks.

"Hello. Dr. Barnes's office."

"Reverend Dr. Barnes, I'm so glad you're in!" Dean James Haslett, of St. David University, sounds frantic, as usual. No matter how important or trivial the problem, he sounds the same.

"What can I do for you, Dean Haslett?" Nikki relaxes down into her chair.

"It's tragic! Terrible, really! I knew I could count on you even though it's not your night on call at the Medical Center."

Nikki sits up straight, going into professional mode. "You're not being very clear. Try to calm down and tell me what happened. Is something wrong at the center?"

"There's been a murder at the Medical Center!" he finally blurts out. "You're needed there immediately. They're expecting you." This time, Haslett's usual urgency is tinged with panic.

Nikki's body goes on alert. Her mind scans a list of

doctors, nurses, and students she works with at the center. She asks slowly and calmly, "Who was murdered?"

Haslett nervously shoots back the answer. "It's one of the doctors...Dr. Shari Sullivan."

Nikki moves the phone away from her ear. Shari Sullivan isn't just a new friend, she's an emotional memory bridge to Lieutenant Maureen (Mo) Matthews. An echo from years past, from another life in Vietnam, begins reverberating in Nikki's head. "She's dead...She's dead...She's dead..." A past, long buried, begins pushing its way up through layers and years of repression and containment.

"Hello? Are you still there, Reverend Barnes?" Haslett's booming voice can still be heard on the phone, even from arm's length. She brings the phone back up to her ear and in a detached voice says, "I'm on my way."

Nikki opens her lower left desk drawer with her free hand and takes out her black clerical shirt and white plastic collar. Dean Haslett drones on.

"As you know, the Medical Center is not part of the university. It's a private institution, but we do use it as an infirmary for our students, and we do provide security. What I'm saying is, whatever happens there affects us and the good name of St. David University. And even though Sheridan, New York, might seem a sophisticated town to some people, in reality, it is small and very parochial in its thinking. Scandal can easily be translated into loss of student enrollments. And we can't afford any losses."

Nikki isn't listening. She's back in Vietnam. A twenty-year-old college graduate because her accelerated program gave her a three-year bachelor's degree and the title of second lieutenant. Her assignment: communications specialist serving at the United States Army Vietnam (USARV) Headquarters Communications Center, Long Binh.

In the compound are several two-story barracks, housing her and the other WACs. Next to each barrack is a small, camouflaged, green bunker surrounded by sandbags. They have corrugated tin roofs and are six steps below ground level. Totally dark inside, they accommodate two rows of short wooden benches. When the compound is under attack, everyone grabs her flak jacket, helmet, canteen and gas mask, and heads for the bunker.

The WAC compound is located next to the 90th EVAC Hospital. The WACs share their mess hall with the hospital personnel.

It's not unusual for Nikki to work from six in the morning to six at night—long, twelve-hour days, six days a week. She works in the headquarters building in a windowless third-floor operations room. Long Binh is a major center for messages coming from all over Vietnam. The messages include troop movements, surveillance reports, VIP agendas, and casualty reports which need to be sent to the proper service branch.

One of Nikki's duties is typing casualty reports. She sees thousands of faceless names as she types serial number, next of kin, and descriptions of the wounds. Sometimes it's "broken arm," but often it's "pieces of remains not positively identified."

This continuing list of casualties prompts Nikki to go over to the hospital after work and volunteer for pastoral care. Chaplain Gambino is only too glad to have the help. He knows she's trained. She even had her mother mail her certificate from the Newark Emergency Hospital Pastoral Care Training Program. Father Gambino tries to set aside time each week to meet with her and review a few cases, but it doesn't often work out. He's frequently called out to base camps, or is dead tired by the time she's finished with her twelve hours at the Communications Center.

He keeps telling her that she's a natural for the job. He even introduces her to, as he puts it, "a sensitive corpsman" named Max Mullen. Max takes the night shift whenever he can, to do rounds with Nikki.

The hardest times are when the big Chinook helicopters

come in with mass casualties. If it happens on Nikki's day off, she grabs her uncle's old Bible and heads for the hospital. She stays out of the way as the charge nurse does triage. She knows they don't need her for the "walking wounded," or the "immediates." They require immediate attention and surgery. The "expectants" are the ones who need her. They're put in an area behind a screen to die. Nikki can be with them when they beg a nurse not to leave them alone. She can hold their hand until their grip goes slack. She can pray for them and close their eyes once their bodies stop fighting for life...

A CHANGE IN Dean Haslett's pompous voice brings Nikki back to the present. "Remember, Reverend Doctor, you're an official university presence. Try to do damage control and deflect negative publicity to the Medical Center and away from the university."

Nikki cuts him off. "I better get over there. Goodbye, Dean Haslett." Not waiting for a response, she hangs up the phone.

She starts changing her clothes. As she takes off her blouse, her hand goes automatically to the gold ring on the chain around her neck. She slips into her black clerical shirt, but before buttoning the front, she again clutches the ring...

HER MIND IS BACK with the 90th EVAC. Nikki's spending a second night praying with a Vietnamese woman whose newborn baby died of shrapnel wounds that went through the woman's stomach during a mortar attack. Nikki often works with the indigenous women. She sees them as the real victims in this war. They no longer ask for the chaplain, even if they're Catholic. They've heard her nickname and ask for the "Rev. woman," instead.

The woman finally falls asleep, and Nikki, ready to call it a night, starts walking out of the ER. One of the "three stooges" is heading her way. That's what Max calls this particular group of nurses because they're always so upbeat. They continually throw out smart remarks or poke fun at each other, trying to use their adrenaline highs in a positive way. The one called Mo bumps into Nikki with an IV pole she's moving.

"Rev., quitting so early? It's only...," she looks at her watch for effect, "3 a.m. The night's still young. We can find a few more lost souls for you, or how about a Coke in the back? Hey...Sammie heard three new dirty jokes. She'd love to share them with you." Then she grins, and Nikki thinks this woman's entire freckled face is lit up like one of the angels on a Christmas card.

All she can do is smile back, which only encourages the "stooges." Sammie is next to them now.

"Hey Rev, it's a slow night...how about a Coke? You know, all pray and no play makes Nikki a dull girl." Then she starts laughing.

"I've tried, Sam." Mo feigns indignation. "She's afraid to go in the back of the ER with us. Probably afraid you'll tell dirty jokes, and Mickie will take her clothes off."

Just then, Mickie joins them. "And who am I taking my clothes off for?"

Mo answers. "The Rev. She desperately needs a diversion and some R&R."

"Well...," Mickie takes a long look at the silent but smirking Nikki. "My body has never been called a diversion, but it is definitely R&R."

They all laugh at this last crack, including Nikki, who then feels obligated to respond. "I've still got one more day this week at the Com Center. I need the three hours sleep, or I might miss a message."

"Ooooh, very strac. I love that strict adherence to military rules and regulations," Mo mocks.

Sam intervenes. "Okay. Okay. We'll let the WAC go this time. But Saturday, which happens to also be our day off, you are expected to report at 1800 hours to the field behind the mess hall for the grudge game of the century."

"We have grudge games of the century," Mickie interjects, "whenever we can get two softball teams together. You have to play with...them!" Mickie covers her mouth as if she said something bad. The other two do the same.

"I'm not really good at baseball," Nikki says, trying to weasel out of the invitation.

The three nurses surround her. "No excuses, Rev." Mo is on the attack. "You give us your solemn WAC oath that you will be there, or we will throw you on this very floor and tickle the daylights out of you in front of these men who...," she pauses again for effect, "respect you."

Fearing what they are saying might just be true, Nikki says she'll play. The nurses break rank, and she slips away.

She never gets those three hours of sleep though—too restless, too hyped-up. She closes her eyes but keeps seeing Mo. These dreams seem strange to her, but she doesn't stop them, doesn't want to meditate them away. She likes seeing Mo and her smile.

She sees her all the next day, too, in her mind's eye. And she looks for her at the hospital, but an attack at Phan Rang sends a night's worth of mass casualties to the OR. Nobody is really visible. The hospital is a mass of red, pain, and adrenaline swirled together.

THE SOFTBALL GAME is a new experience for the Rev. For most of her life, people thought Nikki was athletic-looking. True, she's not wimpy, but she's no athlete. The WACs are up at bat, two strikes, last inning, and it's Nikki's turn. Mo is covering first base. Nikki is so happy and surprised at managing to hit the ball that she's a little slow getting to first.

"Lucky hit," Mo growls, running her fingers through her short, dark-red hair before she replaces her old Cleveland Indians baseball cap.

The next batter takes a strike, and everyone is screaming at Nikki. "Steal! Steal!" She leaves the base and starts running. When she looks back, Mo is catching the ball from the pitcher. Mo throws it to second, and Nikki whirls around and heads back.

The second baseman catches it and is hurling it back to Mo, who has passed Nikki to catch the short throw. Nikki slides back, safe on base. Cheers and boos intermingle as Mo marches, army style, back to where Nikki is brushing off her pants.

"Pretty tricky, Nikki," she says softly in her naturally raspy voice. "If I didn't know better...," she throws the ball back to the pitcher and moves in close to Nikki. "I'd think you were trying to avoid my touching you...out, I mean." She pats Nikki softly on the back, while electricity flies through Nikki's every nerve-ending.

"I'm going to be watching you, very closely," Mo practically whispers.

Then there's a fly ball, and the pitcher catches it. The game is over. Nikki is frozen on first with Mo still standing very close to her. "No discussion, Tricky Nikki. You have to come to the USO club to celebrate." Mo has Nikki by the arm now and is literally dragging her toward the other "stooges," who finish escorting her to the club.

AS USUAL IN Vietnam, booze is flowing freely. Nikki tries to get into the party mood. She gags on Mickie's stinger, hates Sammie's martinis, and simply refuses Mo's highball. She stays with Coke and, after an hour or so, no one knows she isn't drinking, anyway. Everyone is singing and dancing, and as the guys come in, they join the party.

Nikki realizes how much fun it is partying with these women. She even joins in on the old college and high school gym class stories. Mo sits next to her most of the night, except when she's dancing with the begging grunts in from the boonies. Most of the women feel guilty if they don't honor a request for a dance or a drink. There are so few American women around, and you never know when, or if, the guy is coming back from the next firefight. So, Mo keeps saying yes. She dances, and then begs off, returning to the table where Nikki sits with the other women.

The guys say hello to Nikki. Most of them know her from the hospital. None ask her to dance, and that's okay with her.

At the table, Mo grabs Nikki's arm to make a point, and she puts her hand on Nikki's thigh when she leans in for a joke's punch line. Nikki doesn't hear the punch line. She seems to be losing her hearing. She keeps looking into Mo's eyes and a ringing starts in her ears, and she can't focus on anything but Mo.

Curfew is 2200 hours (10:00 p.m.), so most of the clubs close at 2100. Nikki promised Max, who's working at the hospital, that she'd stop in and see two guys who requested a chaplain. Gambino is out at a camp again and not expected back until tomorrow afternoon. It looks like the club will stay jumping until curfew, so Nikki gets up quietly and heads for the door. Mo is on the dance floor twisting with a Green Beret, his arm in a sling.

Nikki walks outside and down the steps. Without warning, Mo is behind her, tapping her on the shoulder. "Trying to sneak out on me, Nikki?"

"I told Max I'd stop at the hospital before curfew," Nikki says, nervously pushing back her curly blonde bangs.

"You and Max." Mo raises her eyebrows. "I thought he had Rosa waiting for him?"

"He does." Nikki, embarrassed by the insinuation says, "We do pastoral care together, that's all."

The Green Beret is at the door, calling for Mo. "They're playing our song, a rhumba. Come on, let's do it!"

Mo gives him a quick wave and turns to Nikki. "Are you going to the big Van Johnson show tomorrow night?"

Nikki knows about the USO show. Guys are flying in from everywhere to see Van Johnson and his troupe. "No. I'm not

really interested. I thought I'd go over to the hospital or visit with
Father Gambino."

"Gambino will be at the show." Mo sounds like she's
scolding now. "And you should forget the hospital for one night."
The Green Beret is yelling for her again. She turns to go back
into the club, then quickly turns back and whispers, "Meet me at
the bunker next to the hospital tomorrow at 2000. Bring a candle."
Then she's gone, back to the dancing.

Nikki visits the men at the hospital, talks with Max, and
explains she won't be doing pastoral care the next night. He
assumes she's going to the Van Johnson show like everyone else.
She isn't.

THE NEXT NIGHT, she spends time hunting down a
large vanilla-scented candle and a stained-glass holder that diffuses
the light into a rainbow of blues and greens. At 2000 hours, she
puts on her flak jacket and helmet, takes the candle, and leaves
her hooch for the bunker. She knows she isn't going to a drill, but
doesn't know what's appropriate for whatever is going to happen.
Most of the compound is deserted. A makeshift stage has been
erected outside the USO Club, and everyone is there. She can
hear the faint sounds of the music and the crowd as she crosses to
the bunker. As she passes the guard outside the WAC compound,
he waves her on, more interested in the joint he's hiding behind
his back.

Once in the bunker, she lights the candle. A variety of
blues and greens shimmer over all of the walls. "You can lose the
helmet and jacket. This isn't a real attack," Mo says smilingly as
she enters, wearing a short, sleeveless sundress and holding a
canteen and two tin cups. While she spreads a thick green army
blanket on the floor, Nikki takes off the helmet and jacket and
lets the sexual excitement build and move through her body.

"I swear, Nikki, you look like the last virgin in Vietnam."
Mo pours two cups of liquid from the canteen. She hands one to

Nikki, who hasn't moved, has hardly breathed. Mo puts down the cup and takes a few steps closer. Their faces are now only inches apart. Their shadows dance with the blue-green incandescence. Mo whispers, "Are you? The last virgin?"

Nikki can't speak. She's mesmerized by Mo's eyes and hair, and skin, and lips. Before she can reply, they're locked in an embrace. Passionately kissing away the loneliness, the pain, the isolation. Rolling on the blanket, they are touch and heat and climax. And for Nikki, it's knowing why she's different, and knowing what sex and love really are. Oh, she knows this is pure lust. But she's in love—for the first time, maybe the only time—in this bunker with this woman. This is love.

The canteen is full of rum and Coke, a drink Mo is sure Nikki will like. Nikki pretends she does, and it becomes their drink. Whenever they make love, Mo makes sure they have their drink with them...

A TEAR ROLLS down Nikki's cheek as she lets go of the gold ring hanging around her neck. She finishes putting on her black suit and tries to shake off the overwhelming sadness that grips her whenever she has these flashbacks. She leaves her office for the Medical Center.

CHAPTER 2

St. David University seniors Jake Coleman and Carla Miller are giving their second campus tour of the day. Jake is a little punchy as he leads the four incoming freshmen and their parents through the back doors of Sterling Hall onto the quad. "St. David University was built in 1929. That was before you were born. Right, Mr. Eagan?"

Carla shoots him a "not funny, be careful" look, as he continues, "...on ten acres of land donated by Matthew Emerson, a local farmer, who although never married himself, believed strongly that all male children were entitled to higher education. My fraternity brothers and I still hold that belief." Jake starts to laugh, and the two female freshmen giggle along.

He points to the rear entrances of the three buildings that form the front of the campus. "Hayes Hall, Sterling Hall, and Whitney Hall are the oldest campus structures. As you can see, they are typical classroom buildings for their day. Each is four stories, red brick, and ivy-covered. Little has been done to change their facade or update them, except to install newer windows and a modern heating system." He gets a serious look on his face. "Of course, they have been painted and all the lavatories have been cleaned since 1929." Again, he bursts into laughter at his own cleverness.

Carla steps closer to the group, diverting their attention from Jake. "The original, male-only university was not open to women until 1974. At that time, the governing board feared they would lose needed federal funding and voted to admit women."

She points to the twin buildings behind them. "Before the first women arrived, two three-story segregated dormitories were built behind the original campus. The new dormitories were also built of red brick and are now also ivy-covered."

Jake jumps in. "Fraternizing between the sexes was definitely frowned upon back then. And even though we still have separate dorms, all university activities are jointly planned." He pauses. "We fraternize a lot now." He winks at the four new students.

Carla coughs, getting back everyone's attention. She now points to the building they just left. "Sterling Hall is the focal point of the campus. If you will look up, you can see the white, wooden, twenty-foot-high bell tower, which was added to the structure ten years after it was built and which still works."

"The bell tower is interesting for historical reasons." Jake continues the narrative. "It was donated by Matthew Emerson's nephew...," he pauses, "...who jumped off the tower seven years later."

Shocked looks appear on the parents' faces. Jake smiles. "Not to worry, folks. He only broke a leg. Said the sun got in his eyes."

Carla tries to restore order. "Sterling Hall originally housed the dormitory and dining area for the university. Now it is the location of our library, auditorium, and administrative offices. And it has been declared a New York State historic site."

"It may look historic on the outside," Jake chimes in again. "But wait until you see where the big brass works. This place is ultramodern inside."

Carla moves the group toward the end building. "Tucked between Sterling Hall and Hayes Hall is our new student union.

It is only three years old and was built with money collected by our students in a major fund-raising campaign. As you can see, Emerson Union stands out in contrast to the other buildings because it is cylindrical and made of concrete block."

"And...it has no ivy." Jake and the students laugh again.

Carla rolls her eyes upward, then points to the dormitories again. "Another gift from the student body is the newest addition to St. David's campus. Behind the two dorms is a large, paved patio that leads to a man-made circular pond. The pond is stocked with several kinds of ducks and Canadian geese. The paved area is used as an open food court in warm weather." She stops and turns toward the group. "And since this is one of those beautiful May days in upstate New York, we'll be taking advantage of our seventy-degree weather. It's been arranged that we will have our lunch on the patio by the pond. It's a lovely pastoral setting surrounded by open fields and woods. The perfect place to study or just unwind."

"And a great place to take your girl, to...," Jake catches himself this time, "...to...to meet the rest of your study group. Yes, a perfect place to study."

They all walk a little farther, until they are behind Hayes Hall. Jake takes over the commentary. "To the left of the women's dormitory is the Memorial Medical Center, a complete public medical facility and our infirmary. The parking areas and grassy berms separate the center from the university, but that concrete sidewalk cuts through the berm and leads to the front entrance of the Medical Center."

Everyone's attention is directed toward the connecting sidewalk, as Nikki hurries out the back door of Hayes Hall and almost runs into the group. The bright sun bounces off her flaxen hair and causes her to shield her eyes with her hand. Jake sees an opportunity to impress the parents. "Professor Barnes, would you like to meet some of our new students and their parents?"

Nikki is preoccupied with getting to the center, but knows

the importance of reassuring the parents of new students. "Hello, everyone. Welcome to St. David. I wish I had more time to talk, but there's an emergency at the Medical Center, and I'm needed right away." Waving, she turns, squints her grey eyes again in the bright sunshine, and quickly makes her way down the short sidewalk to the front foyer of the Medical Center.

Once inside the foyer, the unusual layout of the building is apparent. The octopus-shaped building has five separate hallways, or tentacles, running off in different directions from the main entrance area. Each hallway leads to a different suite serving a different medical specialty.

Groups of white-jacketed workers are huddled together, some crying, some staring into space. Some faces show fear, others look confused or helpless. Nikki passes each group slowly, her instincts and experience telling her to listen, to touch, to try and console.

The security guard recognizes her and silently points toward Suite B. She walks the hundred-foot hallway, passing a hematology lab, adjoining halls, and a glass-enclosed registration/billing area.

As she passes the closed registration/billing area, Nikki sees her reflection mirrored in the glass enclosure. Hard to recognize herself sometimes. Her curly blonde hair now has a white streak above her forehead, on the left side. When she brushes her short hair back over her ears, she notices a little more white than blonde on the sides, too. And where did that extra weight come from? One hundred and twenty-five pounds isn't bad for someone five foot three inches tall, but she was a hundred and fifteen for so many years. The muscles and tone are still there, but her face is fuller. Her deep grey eyes complement the white clerical collar, and her vanilla ice cream complexion looks lighter because of the black shirt and jacket. This is part of who she is now, an Episcopal priest.

The muffled sound of voices in the suite gets her attention, and she moves down the hallway. Two uniformed police officers guard the entrance.

"I'm Professor Barnes from pastoral care. I was told I'd be expected," she says to one of the officers.

He nods her into the suite. "The sergeant is over there."

More uniformed officers are gathered in small groups. Nikki recognizes a suite secretary and nurse standing in one corner, talking to a dark-suited man taking notes.

A loud voice from another corner catches her attention. "Just what is being done? I don't want the media here. They'd have fun with this one. Who's monitoring those barracudas? I don't want any of them milling around."

Nikki sees only the back of the man speaking. She doesn't recognize him, but she knows the woman leading him away from the exchange. It's one of her students, Lisa Holt.

Nikki's attention is pulled back to a trio of men standing behind her, close to the suite entrance. As one of the men exits, he says, "Thanks, Sergeant. Mullen."

The man being addressed turns toward her. He stares, his eyes widen. "Nikki...Nikki Barnes?" He steps toward her. "Rev...Can you believe this?" He thrusts out his hands.

Max Mullen is heavier now, and his face is a mass of healed scars. His nose looks like it was ripped off, rebuilt, and reattached. The voice is familiar though, and those deep, blue, kind, and smiling eyes haven't changed at all...

VIETNAM PLAYS AGAIN in Nikki's head like an antique newsreel. The dirt road on the way to Xuan Loc, the hundred-degree heat, Max driving, his rifle next to him in the jeep. She with her forty-five automatic, even though women are not supposed to be armed in Nam. Suddenly, Viet Cong come out of nowhere...cracking rifle fire...grenade explosions...screams... screams...

With great effort, she pushes the memories away and moves in closer. "Max? It's really you!"

She skips the handshake and attempts to hug him. His rotund belly prevents her from getting too close. He bends down, and they semi-embrace. She kisses his cheek.

"Nikki Barnes? How've you been, Rev? I can't believe it's really you." Tears begin to gather in the corners of Max's eyes. He attempts to blink them away. "Thought maybe you bought it. Ya know, like some of the other guys—survived the war, died in the peace. Then I read where you made the old nickname real. Got yourself ordained with those other Episcopalian women in Philadelphia. Saw your picture in *Time* magazine. Ya don't look any worse for the job."

Slightly embarrassed, Nikki steps back from him, shakes her head in disbelief. "I can't believe it's you...here, I mean, after all these years. It's a little scary...coincidences, I mean."

Max tries to put her at ease. "Told ya years ago, ain't no coincidences. Everything has a reason. You look good, Rev."

"You look good yourself." Nikki tries to stop staring at him. "You haven't changed much, except I don't remember you being so, so..." She hunts for the right word, remembering his sensitivity. "You look taller than I remember."

Max laughs, his deep baritone starting from his feet and working its way up. "It's not height. I've gained a few pounds. It's my wife, Rosa's, cooking. Remember Rosa? I showed you her picture every day, in-country. Hell, I showed everyone her picture, all the time. Kept me going. Anyway, she cooks like a restaurant, and I'm the result."

Nikki tries to recall Rosa and is flooded with more memories...all the photographs, charms, and drugs, all the hopes that kept people alive. Her mind winds back to the 90th EVAC Hospital after a mass casualties night. She's helping the nurses tag the bodies and put them in the green plastic bags. All the personal items the soldiers carried are itemized and bagged too—

their dog tags, religious medals, beads, photos, and all the charms and amulets they hoped would keep them alive. She sees the booty, too. The prizes they carried to remember their victories. Human ears on a key chain or dried fingers—reminders of how they lost their humanity long before their lives.

She remembers Mo and the Basque Restaurant on Tu Do Street, where they exchange their amulets, their hope for protection from all harm. They give each other identical, thin, gold rings. Nikki wears hers on her pinkie finger; Mo wears hers on a chain around her neck...

MAX'S CARING FACE pulls Nikki back into the present. "So, Max, what are you doing here? How long have you been a cop?"

"Eighteen years now, a sergeant. Hell, that's higher than my army rank! Didn't know what to do when I got out. Went back to school for awhile but felt too old. Rosa's brother was on the force, so I joined up, too. Familiar territory, all that rank jazz."

Nikki stares at Max's face again, his involuntary badge of war. He keeps on talking. "Wasn't surprised when Haslett said he's sending a university rep. We've worked with that windbag before. Was gonna tell him to forget it, but he says it's the pastoral counselor, Reverend Nikki Barnes. How many could there be? So, we meet again in another hospital. It's destiny, don't you think?"

Nikki isn't sure. She's ill at ease with the chance events unfolding and triggering her flashbacks.

"Did ya know the victim?" Max moves into a professional tone. "Name's Dr. Shari Sullivan. She's an ob/gyn doctor in this suite."

There's a catch in Nikki's throat as she answers. "I didn't know her well. I've only been at the university since September. Part of my job is to alternate weeks on call as pastoral counselor here at the Medical Center Student Clinic. Dr. Sullivan was the first doctor to call me during my night rotation. A student miscarried and requested a counselor. When I got here, Shari met me and explained the procedure she performed on the girl. It helped give me the medical connection to the girl's depression.

"I encouraged the student to call her parents and go home for a few days. After she was transported to the hospital, Shari and I went for coffee." Nikki realizes she's rambling. "After that, whenever we worked together, we went for coffee."

Nikki doesn't tell Max that the first time she saw Shari Sullivan, she thought she was seeing Mo again. Shari was the same size and height, had the same color hair worn in a short, tapered cut like Mo's, and had the same raspy voice. And when they had coffee that night, Shari said to Nikki, "Getting her to call her parents was pretty tricky, Nikki." That was Mo's favorite expression from the softball game years ago. With those words, Shari had dislodged a jagged, broken piece of Nikki's heart and sent a cutting pain through her psyche. It left Nikki thinking that perhaps it was time to heal, to reach out to someone, open up and take a chance again. But now...Shari was dead, too.

Nikki forces her thoughts back to Max's question. "I only worked on three specific cases with her this school year. Had coffee a couple of times."

"What did you think of her?" Max takes out his pocket notebook and pen.

Nikki pauses briefly before giving a professional response. "She was very compassionate and concerned about people."

"Know anything about her personal life, friends, family?" Max asks as he writes notes.

"To tell the truth, Max, I was just getting to know her. Most of our conversations were about student patients. I wanted to know her better, but now it's too late." Looking up into Max's eyes, she says softly, "I'd like to see the body."

Max walks behind the reception desk and into the hall

leading to the examining rooms. "It's not pretty, Rev, but you've seen worse."

He motions to a man dusting fingerprints off the door frame of the first examining room to move out of the way. He and Nikki enter the small examining room just as the photographer bounces a flash off a stainless steel sink.

Nikki sees yellow dots for about thirty seconds while the photographer leaves. When the dots fade, she sees the body of Shari Sullivan lying on the floor as if taking a nap. She is on her stomach, arms stretched upward, face turned to her left side. The only difference is her eyes are open, and a letter opener with a decorative handle formed by the carved words "Memorial Medical Center" sticks out of her back. Dark red blood pools around the wound, soaking the back of her white coat. Nikki takes a deep breath, lets it out slowly, then bends down to the body. She reaches over to touch Shari's face.

"God! She looks like Mo Matthews! Never noticed it," Max exclaims in sincere shock. "Sorry, Rev. I didn't realize she looks just like Mo..."

NIKKI IS BACK at the EVAC hospital in Nam, impatiently waiting for Max to finish his shift. He's going to drive her into Saigon. It's about a twenty-mile ride from Long Binh, and she doesn't want to be late. Mo got a ride earlier in the morning so she could meet her friend Beverly, from Special Services, for lunch. She wants to borrow Beverly's apartment for the night.

Nikki twists the ring on her little finger as she thinks about the rum and Coke Mo has already prepared. She's sitting in the back of the empty triage room when Max and Jack come in. *What's Jack doing here*, she asks herself. *He's supposed to still be working at the Com Center*. Then she sees it in their eyes, before they say anything.

Something bad has happened, something prayer can't help. She's already choking as they tell her. A sapper, this time a child pretending to sell flowers, went into Le Fleur Restaurant on Nguyen Hue at lunchtime. The restaurant was filled with reporters, servicemen, and Special Services personnel. The sapper was carrying high explosives. The restaurant was destroyed. Everyone inside was killed. "Lieutenant Maureen Matthews is dead," Jack says quietly.

The words are hollow and reverberate over and over again in Nikki's brain. "Mo's dead...Mo's dead."

"I have to get to Saigon, Max. Will you drive?" She can't cry. She can't scream. She can't pray. She shuts down her feelings like everyone else in Vietnam...

THE FEEL OF Shari Sullivan's cold cheek brings Nikki back to the present. "I'd like to help you catch this murderer," she says, standing to face Max. "As much as I can, I mean. I've felt so helpless about Mo's death all these years. I shouldn't have let her go into Saigon without me. I know intellectually I wasn't to blame, but I need a chance to...to do something. Can I help, Max?"

"I know, Rev." He lightly touches her shoulder. "We go back a long way. I'll work something out, so you can help."

Nikki touches his arm, then takes a small prayer book out of her jacket pocket and moves to the body. Max moves next to her. Both are back in Nam with body after body of male warriors, and women, and children. Now, another victim links Nikki and Max to their shared past.

Bending down again, she blesses the dead woman. Max quietly leaves the room as she silently reads from the prayer book. Nikki touches Shari Sullivan's face again. "I'm going to help this time...for you, Shari, and for you, Mo. This time I can help."

CHAPTER 3

Nikki finds Max by the reception area desk discussing his notes with his partner, Detective Henry Ostrow. Henry is tall and slender, a marked contrast to Max, but he wears a similar off-the-rack brown suit.

"I've taken some statements." Henry's slow cadence is also a contrast to Max's clipped style. "Seems business was going on as usual while this happened."

Shocked by this revelation, Nikki asks, "You mean, they were seeing patients while this happened? No one heard anything? No one tried to help?"

Henry replies, as if reading from his notes, "No suspicious noises, nothing out of the ordinary. Not even a long amount of time for her to be with a patient. She was seen going into the room with a Ms. Marlene Smith at one o'clock. No one thought to check on her until one-thirty, when her next appointment arrived. That's when the nurse from the desk found her."

"Sounds unlikely." Max looks around the area as he speaks. "Hard to believe no one heard anything. What happened to this Ms. Smith?"

"She was sent by the deceased to the lab down the hall for a pregnancy test and came back around two o'clock, just as we got here." Henry pauses and nods toward a young woman nervously pacing at the back of the room.

"I don't think she's a viable suspect," Henry continues. "The team nurse verified the length of time for the test. It was also normal procedure for Dr. Sullivan to discuss the preliminary results with her patients."

"Better talk with her." Max ends his discussion with Henry. He and Nikki cross to where Marlene Smith is now sitting. Her eyes are red and puffy. She alternates wiping them and wiping her nose. She's wearing jeans and a St. David sweatshirt. A half-filled book bag is on the floor next to her. "Can I go now, please? My partner will be very worried. If it's on the news there's been a murder here...I should have been home an hour ago."

Max is kind but firm. "Might have to ask a few more questions. We'll get a phone, so you can call your boyfriend. I'll check with one of the officers, let you know."

He walks back to the desk where Henry's speaking to a uniformed officer. Nikki stays behind. "I'm Nikki Barnes with pastoral counseling here at the center." She sits next to Marlene. "Is there anything I can do for you?"

Marlene starts to sob softly. Nikki takes a clean tissue out of the supply she keeps in the pocket of her suit jacket. She hands it to Marlene. "Have you known Dr. Sullivan for a long time?"

Marlene stops crying, again wiping her nose. "I've been coming to her for almost two years. I've been trying to get pregnant."

Nikki leans toward Marlene. "Did you like her?"

There's no hesitation. "Yes. She was like a friend. She was the only one in this town who would help us." She looks directly at Nikki. "Are you really a minister?"

Sensing the distrust and discomfort her clerical clothes bring out in people, Nikki tries to be reassuring. "I'm an Episcopal priest, but I teach Literature of the Bible and Moral Ethics here at St. David." She smiles as she adds, "I'm on a leave of absence from my church duties."

Marlene relaxes a little with Nikki's warm smile. She looks at the balled-up tissue in her hand, then back to Nikki . "I want to tell you something in strict confidence. I don't know who did this, but I think I know why."

She has Nikki's full attention as she continues, "A lesbian can't always get good medical treatment...especially when she's trying to get pregnant." She looks for a reaction and gets only continued attention. "It didn't matter with Dr. Sullivan. She was happy for us. She usually let my partner come with me for the exams, but Alicia had to work today. Dr. Sullivan's delivered babies for at least three other lesbian couples I know. And if I know about it, so do people who don't think it's such a good idea. You know what I'm saying? It's a little scary."

The tears Marlene is holding back start to flow again. Nikki reaches over and holds her, letting her cry. A good use for her broad shoulders.

Max's return breaks the comforting embrace. "You can go now, Ms. Smith. We'll call if we need more information. Don't leave town without letting us know." He hands her one of his cards.

Marlene, anxious to leave, grabs her book bag. She puts her hand out to Nikki, who stands and gives her a hug instead. "Don't worry," Nikki says quietly. "Just take care of that baby." This brings a small smile to Marlene's face as she hurriedly walks away.

Max sits next to his old pal. "Never could understand why these girls don't get married. A kid needs a mother and a father. Say, Rev, did I tell you? I got two kids...both boys."

Nikki smiles at this revelation and his remarks. Max's views could be very narrow. That hadn't changed, but it was time for some updating. "Max, do me a favor—don't call me Rev anymore. Okay? I outgrew that nickname, and I'm officially on leave from the priesthood. I like my friends to call me Nikki."

"Leave? Sounds serious." Max's tone changes slightly. "Pretty funny. Just get used to a woman who's a Father, and you go on leave. Thought you always wanted to be a priest. All you talked about was the underground group and seminary when you got out."

Nikki pushes her watchband up and down as she tries to explain. "That was what I wanted. But when I got back to New Jersey, my family seemed different, the whole world seemed different. No parades for us. No one even wanted a Vietnam vet around." Her grey eyes are sad.

"I went to New York and moved in with one of the women in the Underground Ordination Group. Even got a paid position in pastoral care at the Queens County Vet Hospital, and that supported me while I attended the New York Theological Seminary. They started allowing women to take classes because their numbers were down, and they needed tuition to make expenses. They never realized we had other plans." She pauses. "Then, in 1975, sixteen of us were ordained priests in unsanctioned services in Philadelphia. It took another year for the House of Bishops to approve."

"What about the leave?" Max wants her to continue.

"I was curate—assistant pastor, at St. Simon's Church in Albany for fifteen years. During those years, I went back to college and got my doctorate in English Lit. My vicar died in 1990, and I didn't get along with the new one. So, I got an assistant's job at St. Paul's in Rochester and decided I needed a leave." She intentionally leaves out some details.

Max's scarred forehead wrinkles. "I hear you, Rev...I mean, Nikki. We should talk more, catch up on old times."

Detective Henry Ostrow walks over, interrupting the reunion. "The Medical Center staff wants to leave. I doubt we'll get much more out of them this afternoon. Might even be better if we read their files before we talk to them again."

"Good idea," Max agrees. "Get appointments set up and let 'em go."

Nikki notices the dark-haired man she saw earlier with her student. He's leaning against one of the hallway entrances leading into the reception area. He's in his mid-thirties and wears an expensively tailored, double-breasted Armani suit. His goodbye kiss with one of the nurses looks like the cover of a romance novel. He's handsome enough to be a model, with perfectly styled hair and wingtip shoes as shiny as his manicured fingernails.

She leans over to Max and quietly asks, "Who's that?"

"Sheldon Peterson Jr., MD. His father's the major shareholder in the Medical Center. Junior's chief of family medicine. Haven't you met him yet?"

"I haven't met many of the doctors," she explains, trying to loosen the plastic clerical collar by tugging on it. "The center hours are nine to five. I'm called over mostly at night. Only the emergency clinic is open, and they work with limited staff."

"Well...time to meet the boss." Max leads her toward Peterson. When he's close enough, he says, "I'm Sergeant Mullen. This is Reverend Barnes. Like to ask a few questions."

The doctor takes control immediately. "Let's go to my office."

His office is rich with dark walnut. As Nikki and Max enter, they face his desk, which practically runs wall-to-wall. Behind the desk, full-length double windows allow a panoramic view of the older ivy-covered buildings of St. David. He takes his place behind the desk and nods to Nikki and Max to sit in the two matching chairs opposite him.

Nikki ignores the numerous degrees and service citations on the wall. Instead, she's drawn to the sparse, organized surface of his desk. The desk appears too clean. There's only a small appointment book, an out basket containing about three letters, and a letter opener identical to the one used to kill Dr. Sullivan.

Dr. Peterson breaks the silence. "I can't believe a murder— right here. My father is very upset."

"You've already told your father?" Max takes out his little

notebook with the pen clipped to the pages.

"Of course! You must realize what something like this could do to a medical center. Medicine is based on trust and confidence. A murder during office hours does not evoke confidence." His annoying laugh exposes his feelings of superiority.

"Any idea who might have wanted to harm Dr. Sullivan?" Max cuts to the important question.

"No, Sergeant. I have no idea who might do such a thing. Dr. Sullivan was a respected member of our profession. She was well-published in her specialty—high-risk pregnancies—even before we hired her. And, she was an excellent doctor." Peterson ends his obligatory speech.

Max tries to fill in the missing pieces. "She have any enemies, personal problems, habits, associations?"

Peterson takes a long pause, measuring each word. "As the executive officer for family medicine, I know a great deal about my employees, but you must realize that our doctors have a personal life. Dr. Sullivan was always professional, but...how shall I put this? She was a bit of a maverick at times."

"And what does that mean?" Max asks.

Peterson pushes his palms together as he replies. "I warned her several times about the possible outcomes of some of her choices."

"Can you be specific?" Max keeps writing.

Peterson leans back in his leather executive chair. "There are political ramifications for much of what a doctor does. Dr. Sullivan did abortions, something the center will no longer be doing. I and several board members found a strange dichotomy existed between her high-risk work and her abortion work. I spoke to her about it, but she felt both had a place here. She tended to be more emotional than politically wise."

Max looks up from his notebook. "She ever threatened because of her work?"

"Anyone who does abortions today is at risk. Just read

the newspapers," Peterson snaps.

"Know of any specific threat she got, or the center got?" Max shoots back.

Peterson is sitting up straight again. "No. We've never received any threat or any negative publicity. But the Board did agree abortions could be done elsewhere. The center doesn't need to invite any criticism from certain groups."

Now, Max pauses before speaking. "You think Dr. Sullivan's death has anything to do with abortions?"

Nikki can't sit quietly any longer. "Dr. Peterson." She lets his name hiss through her clenched teeth. "You've presented a rather narrow picture of Dr. Sullivan."

"And, just what is your concern in this, Reverend Barnes?" Peterson asks condescendingly.

Max intervenes. "Reverend Barnes was a friend of Dr. Sullivan's, and she's here for Dean Haslett as the university's official representative."

"As a PR person, you mean. My father has already taken care of things. Our ad agency is on it. They'll have people thinking of this as nothing more than Dr. Sullivan dying of something like a heart attack. She will get understanding sympathy, and then it's business as usual. So, you can leave now and tell the dean everything is under control."

Max makes eye contact with the doctor. "Reverend Barnes will be assisting me with the case. The police department likes to use all available resources. We like having a good relationship with the university." He turns to Nikki. "Anything else you want to ask?"

Nikki takes Max's lead. "Does everyone at the Medical Center have a letter opener like that?" She points to his desk, her grey eyes carefully watching for Peterson's reaction.

"All staff and the doctors were given one for the sixth anniversary of the center. I guess that creates about one hundred and twenty suspects." There's Peterson's smug laugh again.

"Hmm...one hundred and twenty suspects. Okay, might as well start with you. Dr. Peterson, where were you at 1:30 p.m.?

Sheldon Peterson holds his head high, smiles, and says, "In my office, and feel free to check my alibi."

Max stands. "You can count on it. I'll have more questions for you later." He offers his card and requests that Peterson not leave town.

AS THEY WALK down the small hallway back to the reception area, Max reads Nikki's thoughts. "One more to go, and it's quits for today."

The reception area is now empty except for one doctor. She's sitting in a corner writing notes into a patient's chart. Another stack of charts is on an adjoining chair.

Dressed similarly to Shari Sullivan, the doctor wears sensible heels and a tailored shirtwaist dress under a white lab coat. However, the resemblance stops there. This woman is a slender five foot, eight inches tall. Her skin is a bronze tan, and her light brown hair is streaked with red highlights. Nikki has seen her several times in passing at the center. And each time, a voice inside her head, which she tries to ignore, has said, "Isn't she pretty? Maybe more than just pretty?"

"Dr. Clayton?" Max's voice startles the woman. She jumps slightly and looks up quickly. Large green eyes assess Max and move to Nikki. Her forehead wrinkles in concern, then she takes off her reading glasses and relaxes.

"Sergeant Mullen of the Sheridan P. D. And this is Reverend Barnes, the university representative working this case with us. Like to ask you some questions." Max doesn't sit down. Nikki wonders if he's somewhat intimidated. She knows she is.

"How well did you know Dr. Sullivan?" Max begins his questions.

"We worked together, and we lived in the same building." She speaks quietly and answers flatly.

"Any idea who did this?" Max continues.

"I can't think of anyone who'd want to hurt Shari. Her patients liked her and the staff respected her." Her expression is tight again, and no hint of emotion escapes in her speech.

Max nods and goes on. "You see Dr. Sullivan this afternoon?"

"I spoke to her just before she saw Marlene Smith. Shari was anxious to get the results of the pregnancy test, and she said she'd share them with me. I had another patient waiting." The doctor maintains eye contact with Max, but her voice is now almost a whisper. "I never saw her after that."

Max continues the questions. "You hear anything unusual? See anyone out of the ordinary in here around that time?"

"My hands were full with a noisy seven-year-old and his doting mother. I didn't hear anything..." She pauses, green eyes glaring. "Don't you think I'd have gone to see about Shari?" Her voice cracks with emotion, but she quickly regains composure. "We have new patients every day. This suite specializes in family medicine, so people of all ages come here. There's always heavy traffic and strangers, and that includes staff."

"Staff?" Max focuses on this remark.

Resting her long, slender fingers on the folder in her lap, she quietly explains. "We use several doctor's assistants, lab technicians, nurses, and student receptionists. They change frequently. Most of them are strangers to me."

"Dr. Peterson assign the staff?" Max asks.

Her face tenses again. "Yes. He's head of the suite."

Max jots in his notebook and turns to Nikki. "Want to ask any questions?"

Nikki is suddenly tongue-tied. "No, ah, not really," she stammers. "No questions. No."

Max offers his card. "Thanks. Please don't leave town. We'll want to talk to you again."

"I have patients." Her voice reveals her tiredness. "I'll be right here."

Nikki and Max make their way back to the entrance of the building. "Getting pretty late," Max says. "How about coming to the house to meet Rosa and the kids?"

"Thanks Max, sounds nice, but..." Nikki wants to avoid hurt feelings. "I've got a late dinner meeting with one of my students. Then I have to read and correct about three hours' worth of student papers. How about a rain check?"

" Live alone?" Max tries to keep the parting cheerful. "No one with kids can do that much reading at home."

"I'm not totally alone." Nikki feels she needs to justify her life again. "I live with Fluffy."

"A cat, right? Single women always have cats. Treat 'em like babies," Max adds.

"Not me." Nikki disregards his apparent cat ignorance. "Fluffy was a stray when we met, all black fur except for white at the neck, which looks like a clerical collar. How could one priest turn out another?"

Max laughs his wonderful, cavernous laugh again. "Okay. We'll do it some other time, maybe Sunday. Sunday's lasagna day." He doesn't wait for a refusal, just squeezes Nikki's shoulder and heads for his car.

CHAPTER 4

Nikki arrives early for the farewell dinner with her tutorial student. She orders a cup of coffee and lets the warm steam caress her face. As she sips the hot coffee, she remembers the phone call last January from Dean Haslett requesting her help as a tutor...

"Reverend Barnes." Haslett clears his throat loudly. "Douglas Fairburn, CEO of Fairburn Enterprises in Buffalo, has contributed the most money to the university endowment fund for the last five years. He won't be pleased if his daughter fails her College Composition course."

Nikki's not familiar with any student named Fairburn. She patiently waits to hear her place in this elaborate story.

"The composition course is a problem." He sighs loudly. "To be honest, she's alienated three professors so far. She's a young lady with a severe attitude problem but, according to her entrance tests, very capable of achieving. That's why I thought of you. Your counseling background and ministerial work are just the skills needed to help her. Of course, your background in English will also be helpful. I'm sending her over this afternoon."

"Attitude problem" proved to be an understatement. Nikki remembers the quiet office. As she sits reading papers at her desk, Barrett Fairburn throws open the office door and literally stomps in unannounced. She's a foreboding figure at five foot, eleven inches, and one hundred sixty pounds. Her shiny black hair is long, parted on the side, and hangs straight to her shoulders. Her skin is English white, and her brown, almond-shaped eyes give her the look of a Native American. She's a muscular twenty-one-year-old, who obviously spends a great deal of time working out with weights.

She ignores the fact that Nikki is working and plops in the chair next to the desk. Her hairy legs are accentuated by short green argyle socks and high-top sneakers, which go nicely with her baggy jeans cut off just above the ankle. The rest of her unconventional attire consists of a bright yellow Hawaiian shirt under a red-and-black-checked hunting jacket. Nikki feels a lot of care and planning went into this getup. Clearly, Barrett wants to be noticed.

Unsure of the game or how to approach this woman, Nikki opens. "Can I help you?"

"I'm Barrett Fairburn," she growls, picking at a hangnail on her thumb.

"And?" Nikki attempts contact again.

"And you're Nicolette. My new tutor." She leans into Nikki's face.

"It's Professor Barnes, or Reverend Barnes," Nikki corrects her.

Barrett counters with, "Titles build barriers. I never use 'em."

"Titles show respect and professionalism." Nikki's temper is rising.

"It's Nicolette—or I walk," Barrett stubbornly states.

Nikki sits back in her chair and consciously relaxes her tense shoulders. How should she play this hand? Be the teacher and let the girl walk, or try to see why this girl's so angry. "Okay." She goes for the challenge.

Barrett is taken off guard. "Okay? So I walk, or so it's Nicolette?"

Nikki shrugs, trying to appear indifferent, then takes a clean yellow pad out of her drawer. "Now, what seems to be the problem with your composition class?"

Barrett's insecurity shows in the scowl on her face. She's staying for now. "The problem is I want to be a chef not a writer. I applied to the Culinary Institute and got accepted. But my mother, the Dragon Lady, won't let me be a 'common cook or cleaning woman' as she calls it, until I get a business degree from this stinking hell hole."

"You want to be a chef? I think that sounds interesting," Nikki says sincerely.

"Why does it sound interesting?" Barrett's suspicious now, throwing up the wall again. "We trying to focus on a topic of interest to break the ice?"

Nikki doesn't hesitate. "No. I love eating—so cooking interests me."

"Oh—cool." The wall is coming down slowly.

The tutoring starts with more informal conversations in Nikki's office. They meet once a week at first. Then the sessions increase to two or three times a week. Barrett begins each Monday session trying to shock Nikki by talking about the wild house parties she goes to on the weekends. How she gets drunk, gets into a fight, or ends up sleeping in her car on some deserted side street.

When Nikki doesn't respond as expected, Barrett resorts to stories about her family. She's very close to her African-American half-sister, Celine. Barrett repeats her cheerleader description of Celine at least once in every discussion. "Celine is black, beautiful, and brilliant."

The Dragon Lady wants Celine to go to business school too, but Celine, "who isn't afraid of anything or anyone," doesn't listen to her mother. Barrett says, "Celine is super cool, really rad." She speaks a new language for Nikki.

Barrett explains. "Celine ran away from home for six

months last year, and five hired detectives couldn't find her. One day she just calls the Dragon Lady and says, 'I'm coming home. I'm not going to school.' And she did just what she said. She's designing jewelry now. Boy, I wish I had her ovaries. I wish I had the Dragon Lady's ovaries."

The sessions begin with Barrett's anger, but usually end with laughter. She even does some writing for her comp class, as long as she can read the compositions aloud to her captive audience. Nikki's honest in her criticism and instruction. But she lets a lot of things pass because she enjoys this young rebel. Barrett is distinct from the other students, not complacent or traditional. She likes the attention that looking and thinking differently from the other students brings her. She's a likable contrast and a needed diversion for Nikki.

After six weeks of meetings, the gifts begin. Barrett mentions a dish she cooked the night before. Nikki shows interest. It appears at her office the next day. They discuss favorite flowers and brandy. Both appear the next session. Some days, Barrett loiters around to personally deliver her tokens of appreciation. Nikki knows the exchange is escalating, but thinks she's firmly in control. She's just met Shari Sullivan, and she's letting a lot of feelings creep out of hiding. Her self-analysis tells her Barrett's visits are filling her need for attention, too. So, Nikki asks herself, who has the problem here?

"HI, NICOLETTE. I see you're wearing your death suit." Barrett's deep voice tugs Nikki out of her trance and back to the restaurant.

"Still being irreverent about my clerics and my name," Nikki says in a light tone as she notices Barrett is wearing an attractive grey Liz Claiborne slack suit. Barrett has never looked so mature or conservative. Nikki half-apologizes for the clerical clothes, realizing how special the dinner is to Barrett. She briefly explains her call to the Medical Center and her reason for wearing the suit.

Barrett doesn't show much interest in the murder. Instead, she insists on ordering for the two of them. They start with two glasses of Merlot. Next, the salads arrive.

Nikki never expects dinner to include Barrett's ardent endearments. The spontaneous revelations ruffle the very leaves of her spinach salad. They abruptly shake her out of her preoccupation with Shari Sullivan's murder.

"But, I love you, Nicolette. I love you!" Barrett speaks loud enough for the other patrons to hear and turn their heads.

Nikki nearly chokes on a crouton. She quickly sips some water and tries to appear calm. She speaks quietly, overly controlled. "You can't love me! I'm your...your...professor. What I mean, Barrett...," she stumbles for a way out, "is...is...that students and teachers need to maintain a professional relationship. I'm not just a professor, but a priest."

Nikki shivers, aware that the priest line is an obvious cop-out. It's only been a year since she's really worked on integrating being a lesbian with other aspects of her life, like being a priest. It wasn't until her last parish that she openly came out to her vicar. He asked her to please not share that information about herself with anyone else.

Nikki was painfully aware that the Christian Right was very active in Rochester, NY, and people from all denominations were attending rallies and prayer meetings. Conservative members of her own parish were condemning gay life-styles based on the Episcopal teachings, which prohibit sex outside of marriage. The House of Bishops was threatening to make a Presentation of the Rochester bishop for heresy because he wouldn't fire a popular priest who was openly gay. These events, and the vicar's unacknowledged but clear shunning of her, is what led Nikki to ask for the leave of absence. She admits to herself, she's still working on the integrating.

Barrett's forced laughter jars her back to dinner. "I don't care about a professional relationship. I love you!"

"Barrett, please keep your voice down," Nikki barely whispers now. "Where did you get such an idea?"

Barrett reaches over and puts her hand on Nikki's, freezing it to her fork as if paralyzed. Barrett lowers her voice slightly to sound romantic. "Nicolette, I thought you felt the same about me?"

Nikki stares at her hand being crushed by the weight of Barrett's athletic strength. Calmly and deliberately, she says, "I don't love you, Barrett."

A waitress appears with entrees. Nikki's reflexes return, and she slides her hand out of Barrett's hold, fork and all.

Barrett, never one to be interrupted when she's driving home a point, continues. "What about the letters?"

The waitress coughs. "Will there be anything else?" She places the food on the table. Barrett gives her a dangerous look, and the waitress quickly leaves.

"There's been a miscommunication." Nikki nervously runs her fingers through her short, curly blonde bangs, pushing them to the side. Having survived war and the seminary, she certainly can undo a sexual misunderstanding. "What letters?"

Barrett is relentless. "The beautiful cards and letters."

"Those were thank you notes," Nikki says, exasperated.

While Barrett tries to grasp the difference, Nikki wonders how she got into this jam. Had she needed something to distract her when she started working with Barrett?

"Nicolette, I thought you felt the same," Barrett says, breaking through Nikki's ruminations.

"I'm sorry...I don't love you, and I apologize for any behavior that made you think I did." Nikki's back in control. "Don't you realize if anyone at the university heard this conversation, my job could be in jeopardy? I could get fired."

Barrett lowers her voice. "Why? It's none of their business."

"I learned a long time ago, better be discreet if you want to keep a job. This is a bad misunderstanding. I was offering what I thought was professional help and, maybe, friendship."

Nikki is almost pleading.

"We are friends." Barrett now speaks softly. "And I want to go to bed with you."

"I think I better leave." Nikki stands up abruptly and practically throws her money on the table. She turns and walks quickly out of the restaurant.

Barrett is right behind. Her muscular body brushes against Nikki's as they both squeeze through the doorway at the same time.

Nikki turns to Barrett, addressing her curtly. "I'm going to my office."

"I'll go with you." Barrett is still next to her.

"I'm going alone." Nikki continues walking.

Barrett blocks the sidewalk with her body. "So, what are you angry about?"

Nikki shakes her head. "I'm sorry Barrett. I really am. I'd like to be a friend, but now I'm not sure it's such a good idea. I think we should keep the relationship professional. I don't want any more personal discussions."

"No! No!" Barrett's hand is outstretched like a crossing guard ordering cars to stop. "I know what I want." She gives Nikki a calculating smile. "I'll wait. Someday, we'll be in the right situation, not here, but alone together." Stepping back, she says in a softer voice, "I don't want you to lose your job. But someday you'll be my woman." She turns and walks toward the university's main parking lot.

Nikki watches her for a moment, flabbergasted. How did she allow such a misunderstanding to occur? Maybe it's raging hormones. That's what Max always blamed back in Nam. Meeting Shari, beginning to open up to her, had caused her to let down her guard. Her hormones must be running again, and she's not even aware of who they're running to. She smiles at the craziness of her thinking, but she needs the comic relief. Turning, she walks the two blocks to her office.

CHAPTER 5

The exterior campus lights flicker on as Nikki enters Hayes Hall. The hallway is black except for the red exit signs. She inches carefully through the second doors of the entranceway and feels the wall for the light switch. She's used to returning to her office after dark, but tonight feels uncomfortable. Murder does that to the psyche. Turning on the hall lights, she waits, listening for something, anything. There are no sounds except the usual old creaks and the buzzing of the fluorescent lights. The office doors are closed; the hall is empty.

She walks the length of the hall, reassuring herself that her uneasiness is related to the events of the day—Shari Sullivan's death, the argument with Barrett. She fumbles with her office lock, then stops just before pushing open the door. She listens again. Nothing...but something. The first thing she sees after entering the dark office is the blinking red button on her answering machine. Once the lamp is on, she goes to the machine and pushes the Play button.

"I know we're meeting for dinner, and I'm really excited about it. But anyway—shit, I hate talking on these things. Anyway, you know that double Dutch apple pie I told you about? Well, I baked one for you. I'll bring it tonight." Barrett's voice is loud and clear.

Nikki is about to protest to the machine when the left side of her head explodes with excruciating pain. An all-consuming light fills her vision, and the floor comes up cold like a cement pillow.

"NICOLETTE, CAN YOU hear me? Wake up. Open your eyes."

Through a blurry fog, Nikki sees Barrett yelling at someone.

"Well, where the hell have you been!" Barrett booms. "I called for help ten minutes ago."

Something cold and wet touches Nikki's forehead, as she's lifted onto a gurney. She hears Barrett's garbled sounding voice. "If all the hospital emergency rooms are full, you butthead, take her to the Medical Center. Just make sure a doctor's there to help her."

Nikki feels the gurney pop up and roll. She wants to say something, but her head hurts and she's too sleepy to put the words together.

NIKKI WAKES UP surrounded by bright lights and stainless steel. The room looks familiar. Suddenly, a sharp beam of orange light moves into her line of vision. "Follow the light please." The voice is familiar, too.

Nikki swivels her eyes with the light, trying to identify the voice. A terrible headache interferes with coherent thinking. The orange light goes out and the serious gaze of Dr. Clayton moves into the center of her pain.

"Can you tell me your name?" The doctor's quiet, deliberate tone sounds almost condescending.

Nikki struggles to form words. The entire left side of her face feels swollen, and the pounding headache now has a noticeable rhythm. "I'm...Father...Nikki...Barnes." She forms each syllable separately.

"Father?" The doctor moves out of her gaze but can still be heard. "Doesn't she mean Reverend?" she quietly asks Max.

"She's an Episcopal priest, Ph.D., Reverend Doctor...professor...at the university." Max leans over Nikki, looking at her upside down. She'd know him from any angle. Dear Max, trying to simplify the situation by making it more complex.

"I'm...on...leave...call...me...Nikki." These slow, equally paced words bring Dr. Clayton's green eyes back into Nikki's view.

Nikki pushes through the pain and moves into a sitting position. Her baggy slacks almost cover her shoes. The world swirls like a manic merry-go-round. Max supports her back, while Dr. Clayton steadies her shoulders. Nikki feels like slipping into either pair of arms and going right back to sleep.

"The pain medication is already working," the doctor says, releasing her hold, but Max continues to steady Nikki.

"How many fingers do you see?" Dr. Clayton holds up two fingers in the victory sign.

"Two fingers, no wedding ring." A goofy smile comes over Nikki's face.

The doctor tries to be reassuring. "You're going to be all right. You have nine stitches and a slight concussion. You need to go home now, but please try to stay awake for a few hours. It would be better if you weren't alone."

Nikki sees her give Max a questioning glance. Nikki quickly wants to clarify their relationship. "We're just good friends."

The doctor looks back at Nikki and again speaks slowly and deliberately. "I'll give you something for the pain. And be sure you don't get your stitches wet. Do you understand what I'm saying, Professor?"

"What the hell happened?" Nikki uncharacteristically blurts out, rubbing the back of her aching head.

Max comes around the table. "Someone was waiting for

you at your office, did a number on your head."

Nikki swings her legs around to the side of the examining table and begins to step down. "Why'd they hit me?"

"Don't know, but we're gonna find out," Max says firmly.

Dr. Clayton reenters, handing Nikki a small, white paper cup with a couple of Tylenol. "Feel free to wear the hospital gown home. Your clothes look pretty hopeless."

"She's not goin' home." Max is in command, while Nikki studies the white gown she's wearing over her slacks. "She's coming home with me."

Nikki realizes what he's offering and quickly looks up. "Max, thanks. But, I don't want to meet Rosa this way. I'm fine, really. I'm all right."

"You heard what the doctor said." Concern is in Max's voice. "You can't be alone. Rosa won't mind."

"No, Max. I just wouldn't be comfortable with the kids and all. I think I need quiet tonight." She looks to the doctor for help and, to her surprise, finds it.

"She really needs to rest quietly tonight, Sergeant." The doctor's professional tone is perfect. Nikki likes this woman.

Max reluctantly gives in. "Guess it could be stressful meeting Rosa and the kids. Talked about you so much, I'm sure Rosa would want to meet you. Another time, Rev."

Dr. Clayton quietly interjects again. "Absolutely no food until morning. Concussions can cause nausea and vomiting in some patients." She directs her next question back to Nikki. "Should I have the sergeant send in your friend?"

"What friend?" Nikki's fuzzing out again.

Dr. Clayton's emerald eyes seem to be twinkling now. "There's a young woman with a pie in the waiting room. She came in with you and the paramedics."

My God, Barrett! Nikki attempts to explain. "She's a student."

"She seems concerned." The doctor lets a small smile escape.

"She's over-concerned," Nikki addresses Max. "I'm spending the night with another friend. Please tell her I'm fine, I can't eat pie, I've already left. And Max, you ought to be getting home, too. It's getting late."

He nods hesitantly and gives her shoulder another goodbye squeeze. She knows he'll run interference for her with Barrett.

A short time passes as the doctor cleans the countertop and washes her hands. Nikki attempts a weak thank you to her back. "I guess I'm lucky you were still here."

Getting no response, she asks, "Is there a phone I can use to call a cab?"

The doctor turns around slowly, a questioning look on her face. "A cab? Can't your friend pick you up?"

Nikki's stuttering returns. "The other friend...is my cat...Fluffy...good company...when I'm sick."

Dr. Clayton doesn't raise her voice but puts her hands on her hips. Irritation is obvious in her voice. "Didn't you understand my directions? I said you shouldn't be alone tonight. Now the sergeant is gone and so is your student."

The snippy tone quickly clears Nikki's head. "I'll be fine." She takes several shaky steps toward the door. "I'm very resilient."

The doctor is not impressed. "You're still my patient, and I'm responsible for you."

Nikki wants to protest, but her limbs feel like cooked noodles.

"Come with me, please." The doctor leads Nikki down the hallway. She walks slowly, her lithe body trying to match Nikki's sluggish rhythm, her arms close enough to brace Nikki if needed. They stop at the last room, the treatment room. It contains the crash cart, EKG machine, and an adjustable hospital bed.

"I think you'll be comfortable here. I'll leave the door open and check on you. I'll be next door in the common room doing some paperwork." Her voice seems softer now. "Raise the bed to a sitting position. Rest, but try not to fall asleep."

Nikki sits on the bed, then gingerly rests her head on the pillows. Dr. Clayton takes a blanket from one of the supply shelves and covers her. "If you need anything, just call." The doctor leaves.

"Must stay awake," she mutters to herself. A minute later Nikki sits up, slips off her shiny loafers, and bends over to remove her socks. This proves to be a difficult task. "Must get my socks off." She is dizzy and her head whirls for a few moments. She doesn't know if it's from the concussion or the doctor's attention. Exhausted, she closes her eyes for what seems like just a second.

A mysterious woman floats into Nikki's fantasy, wearing stethoscope, earrings, and a silver negligee. Nikki feels danger and tries to pull herself away from the image by counting her toes, visualizing each one as she counts. Just as she is about to reach eight she hears the doctor's soft voice. "I was afraid you'd get too relaxed and fall asleep." The slender Dr. Clayton is standing next to the bed.

"Hope you don't mind." Nikki's voice seems detached from her body. "I've taken off my shoes and socks."

A soft, warm hand is on Nikki's arm. Dr. Clayton is smiling. "I don't care what you take off, Professor Barnes." The good doctor continues to smile.

"I need to count my toes." Nikki's words are slurring. "Whenever I was in the bunker for a long time, during incoming fire, crowded and hot, no room to even stand, I would count my toes in multiples of nine. Nines are always distracting."

"I'm sure, and I'll keep that handy piece of advice in mind." The doctor sits on the edge of the bed. "The center's pretty slow tonight, so I'll keep you company for awhile."

The doctor's body brushes against Nikki's leg as she continues. "You have quite a few titles. Are you Professor or Father? Is anything you say really true? Or is that Tylenol not the first drug you've ever taken?"

Nikki tries to sound indignant. "I don't do drugs, never have. Saw too much of that in Nam. Saw it destroy a lot of lives.

Besides, how could I do drugs and be a professor of ethics?"

A seriousness takes over the doctor's expression. "Are you really a priest?"

Nikki thinks she hears genuine interest. "Yes, but I'm on a leave of absence."

The doctor's smile returns as she softly says, "Good. I never liked priests—too judgmental and sanctimonious."

"Even women ones?" Nikki is smiling now.

"Never met a woman one before." For no reason that Nikki can figure out, the doctor abruptly ends the conversation and gets off the bed. She looks at her watch. "I think you've been here long enough, and I'm ready to close up. Why don't you put on your socks and shoes? I'll be right back."

A confusing ten minutes pass while Nikki struggles to sit up and put on each sock and shoe. Dr. Clayton returns, wearing an indigo trenchcoat. She hands Nikki her black blazer with the bloody lapels and says, "I'll give you a ride home. Do you feel steady enough to walk or should I get a wheelchair?"

Nikki bristles at the suggestion and replies, "I can walk just fine."

Nikki puts her blazer on over the hospital gown and begins weaving toward the door. The doctor switches off the lights behind them and takes Nikki's arm, gently guiding her out of the Medical Center.

BETWEEN BEING HIT with a blast of fresh air and trying to concentrate on her walking, Nikki never realizes they've crossed the parking lot and are getting into the doctor's teal-colored Honda Accord. Nikki sits down in the matching upholstered interior, leans her head back against the headrest, and feels as if she has slipped into a cool forest stream.

She has little recall of how they get to her house, but does remember Dr. Clayton, with her arm around her, helping her select the right key for the front door. She also remembers a suggestion that she call the doctor Ginni. Finally, Nikki gratefully eases herself into bed with her friend Fluffy at her feet.

Within seconds, sleep enfolds her.

CHAPTER 6

Morning arrives with Nikki nursing what feels like a terrible hangover. She growls to herself during coffee and growls at the delivery man from the drugstore. The only time she doesn't growl is when she catches a reflection of herself in the bathroom mirror. Then she moans. A small patch of hair has been shaved and the bald spot is surrounded with caked blood. The shaven section reveals nine black silk *x* marks, and she also sports a purple-tinged black eye.

"Shouldn't I have a bandage on this?" she moans to the unresponsive mirror. "No, but try not to get your stitches wet," she answers herself, in a mocking imitation of the doctor. The phone rings and pulls her away from the mirror.

"Hello. It's Dr. Clayton...Ginni." The soft voice has a nervous hesitation to it.

"Oh, hello." Nikki stops growling but is reticent about using the doctor's first name.

"I called in your prescription." Her voice relaxes a bit. "It should be delivered any time now. I didn't want you to go too long without the pain medication."

"They've already arrived. Thanks. You certainly take good care of your patients...Ginni." There—she called her by name.

"Not all of them get this much attention," Ginni answers

in a hushed tone. "I also wanted to remind you of your appointment with me tomorrow. I'll need to check your head wound and the stitches. I wasn't sure if you remembered everything from last night. So, let's see...come to the Medical Center around five. This way, you'll be my last patient."

"I may see you before then." Nikki is regaining strength. "I'm helping with the murder investigation. We'll be at the Medical Center today to ask some more questions."

"Today, you should be resting, and that's doctor's orders. I'll see you tomorrow at five." Ginni Clayton hangs up.

Nikki is still smiling when she answers her ringing doorbell and lets Max in. "So how're ya feeling this morning, Rev, oops, I mean, Nikki?" he asks, concern written all over his face. Nikki reassures him that she's okay. Max saunters through the hall to the kitchen saying, "Nice place." Only Max can think a hallway paneled in fake wormwood and a kitchen built in 1949 is a nice place.

He sits at the kitchen table and flips open his small black notebook, ready for business. "Five St. David students work in Suite A. One's a physician's assistant, did a stint in the army. Two are nurses, one's a guy. Another's a maintenance technician, janitor. And one's the private secretary to Peterson. Haven't ruled out doctors or staff yet. But with the attack on you, looks like a student to me." Max looks up from the notebook. "Remember anything from last night? Something you saw or heard?"

"I never heard a thing, that's the trouble. The whole building was quiet, too quiet and dark. I never heard a door open or footsteps, nothing." She lets out a low groan as she sits down.

"Should've listened to your instincts. That's what kept us alive in Nam, Rev." Max puts away the book. "Trust your instincts. Wasn't that your motto?"

"I guess I've forgotten it for awhile. Out of battle, out of mind." Her instincts have been turned off, another way of surviving in another kind of world.

"Looks pretty nasty," Max says, nodding sympathetically toward her black eye. "Hurt much?"

"It looks worse than it is. More embarrassing than anything." She stops talking for a moment, resting her arms on the table. "I'm so angry, Max. I can't believe I let someone get that close to me and didn't hear him. I'm going to get this bastard," she says, as she carefully runs her fingers along her stitches.

"That's the spirit!" Max pauses. "But, I don't think you should do it today. Just hang around the house, take it easy. I'll keep you posted. Got enough food? Rosa makes delicious lunches, homemade meatballs on thick Italian bread and a slice of that crazy student's pie. I'll get it for you." He stands up, walks toward the door.

"I don't really want the lunch. When I'm sick, even the smell..." Her mind clicks and focuses. "Max, I remember something."

He turns back. "From last night?"

"Yeah. I remember a faint smell of perfume. I think my attacker smells of perfume or aftershave. I know that sounds crazy coming from someone who can't tell the difference." She stops. "Maybe these pills. I'm not sure, but I think I smelled it."

"Trust your instincts. You smelled perfume, focus on it. Maybe you'll be able to identify it. Meantime, I'll put the lunch in your fridge. Check you later," Max says as he leaves.

Nikki joins Fluffy in the darkened living room, relaxing in the overstuffed chair that came with the furnishings. She closes her eyes and sleeps. A few hours later, a sharp knocking on the front door wakes her. Checking the peep hole, expecting to see Max again, she opens the door to Barrett Fairburn, who is carrying several brown paper sacks.

"Nicolette! You've got a shiner bigger than Nebraska." Nikki reflexively touches her eye. Barrett doesn't wait for an invitation, simply pushes into the house and bounds for the kitchen. "I've made some Jewish chicken soup, guaranteed to help healing."

"I'm not hungry," Nikki says coldly.

Barrett's not listening, just keeps busy unloading several bags. "Soup's not a lot to eat. Why don't you try it? You'll feel better."

Nikki cautiously sits down, realizing she is hungry. Barrett almost spoon-feeds her lunch and at one point gets a good look at the stitches. "Oooh, uncool! They look disgusting!"

"I need to wash my hair without getting the stitches wet," Nikki says dejectedly.

Barrett, still shaking her head, says, "I know just the place. Mr. Ivan."

IVAN IS A strong name for a slender beautician who wishes to be called a hairstylist.

"Oooh, they look disgusting, dear!" Ivan's a close friend of Barrett's.

"I know it's disgusting," Nikki says, gritting her teeth. "I need to wash it without getting the stitches wet."

"Why?" Ivan asks.

"Why what?" A communication problem.

"Why not get them wet?" Ivan asks again. "What's gonna happen?"

"I don't know," Nikki says, feeling silly. "Maybe they'll shrink." She laughs, but her remark is met with expressionless stares from Barrett and Ivan. She tries to explain the importance of following doctor's orders, but her words are lost as the two friends exchange a variety of hairstyling ideas and lead her to the sink.

Nikki's head is washed, blow-dried, and styled several different ways without much luck. Ivan is frustrated.

"It's no use!" He throws up his arms for effect. "Whoever shaved your head is a butcher. Someone with no respect for appearance, for style."

"I think I was bleeding heavily," Nikki says nonchalantly.

"Style may not have been the first consideration."

"Let's try some mousse." Barrett's trying to help.

Nikki now has spiked hair, her second pill is wearing off, and she remembers she was never fond of beauty shops. She's had enough. "I have to go. I'm not feeling well. Thank you, Ivan. I don't feel disgusting anymore."

NIKKI'S HEAD AND hair feel better, and out of a sense of indebtedness she lets Barrett drive her home and invites her in. She also lies and says Max is on his way to take her to his house.

"I hate cops." Barrett almost stomps her foot. "He ordered me out of the center last night, and he took your pie. I don't think you should hang out with cops. Did he give you the pie?"

"Of course. I loved the pie." Lying to Barrett is getting easier.

Her head now requires less attention, so Nikki can feel all the other bruises on the rest of her body. Barrett offers a gentle massage for her neck, which seems to be helping...until she breaks the relaxing silence. "Nicolette, I still love you."

Nikki flies out of her chair and faces her. "But I don't love you. You'll have to leave, please."

"But Nicolette..." Barrett comes around the chair, getting closer.

"Max will be here any minute." Nikki is desperate.

"I don't believe you." Barrett towers over Nikki. "You wouldn't hang with that cop."

"You never believe me, and you should." She's backing out of the room, when suddenly the doorbell rings. Nikki dashes for the door.

Is it possible to have prayers answered before they're formulated? Nikki grabs Max by the arm and almost drags him into the kitchen. "You remember Barrett? She's just leaving. And I'm ready to go."

Barrett grudgingly picks up her things and goes to the

door. "I'll bring more soup tomorrow."

"Don't bother. I'm working with Max tomorrow and spending the rest of the week at his place. Good night." Nikki practically pushes Barrett out the door.

"What's with that young woman?" Max asks.

"I think it's an age thing," Nikki jokes.

"Are you spending the week at my place?" Max asks, smiling.

"No. It's a lie." Nikki feels guilty about what she said and crosses her arms, searching for some comfort. "That young woman makes me lie."

Max is confused but still tolerant of Nikki's explanations. He briefly discusses his day's investigations and courteously leaves, knowing Nikki needs rest. Turning out all the lights, so it looks like no one is home, Nikki finally makes it to bed. Her dreams are filled with women, past and present, alive and dead. The images are sad and troubling, leaving her melancholy and confused. She sobs in her sleep, hugging lost loves goodbye.

CHAPTER 7

Nikki wakes to morning sunshine and renewed motivation. She still feels self-conscious and tries to comb her hair over the stitches. It doesn't work. So she places an old, black beret over them, hoping it will draw less attention.

While they drive to the Medical Center, Max reports on yesterday's interviews of staff and student employees. Two students were off work the day of the killing; their whereabouts confirmed by witnesses. Of the three on duty, two were students in Nikki's ethics class.

Max agrees with Nikki that she can talk to them informally. As he puts it, "Chat 'em up. Get your own take on 'em. We'll check the personnel files. Sometimes a clue shows up."

THE PERSONNEL OFFICE at the Medical Center is crowded with file cabinets and several desks. The fluorescent lights hum incessantly and a phone rings nonstop. The secretary cheerfully agrees to clear some desk space for the reverend and Sergeant Mullen. Nikki sits for two long hours reading files, then finally decides to take a walk to the waiting area and stretch her aching body. A voice from behind startles her.

"Hello, Professor Barnes. Sorry to hear you were assaulted."

She turns, facing a short, slightly built man in his early twenties. He's wearing dark blue work clothes and carrying a wastebasket. Edmond Long, a religious fanatic, "born-again something," is smiling at her. He says he's Christian, but Nikki finds nothing familiar in his beliefs.

"It's really bad, what's happening around here. I tried to tell you once, Professor. Satan is alive, running loose on this campus, and this is the result." His face turns the brownish red color of his hair and eyebrows. "God has turned His back on this place."

The preacher in Nikki slowly comes forward. "We can't blame God for what humans do, Edmond. Although there is the idea that some people become Satan." She isn't really in a philosophical mood, but he brings it out in her.

He gestures with the wastebasket, raising his voice again. "Satan is everywhere, just waiting his chance. Where sin is, he is."

She isn't surprised Edmond assumes God and Satan are both males. "I worry more about man than Satan, and my present concern is with the murder of Dr. Sullivan." Having said that, she walks away from Edmond.

As she passes Sheldon Peterson's office, she sees Lisa Holt sitting at the computer. Lisa's dark brown hair rests softly on her shoulders. While in Nikki's class, Lisa always wore provocative miniskirts which accented her attractiveness. Here, she is more conservatively dressed in a blue business suit. However, her blouse is still low cut and the skirt still a mini.

"Professor Barnes." She gives Nikki a slow, sexy smileand purrs, "Nice hat."

Lisa always sounds like she's flirting, Nikki muses, remembering how she used to tease her many male fans. An intelligent student, she was one of the few business majors who took Modern Moral Ethics as an elective.

"I didn't know you were working here," Nikki says as she enters the room.

"I'm completing an internship," Lisa explains. "I started in the reception area, but Dr. Peterson needs extra help and asked for me."

"Do you like it here?"

Lisa drops the smile. "Are you asking as my professor or as some kind of special investigator? I heard you're working with the police on the Shari Sullivan murder."

"Both, I guess. Teachers are always interested in talented students." She hesitates. "Did you know Dr. Sullivan?"

"Not really." Lisa breaks eye contact as she rummages through papers in a folder. She stops and looks directly at Nikki. "You're going to find out eventually, and knowing you from class, I don't think you'll be shocked. I don't know anyone here very well except Sheldon—I mean, Dr. Peterson. Sheldon and I have been seeing each other for almost three months. It isn't what you think, Professor Barnes. We're in love."

Nikki tries not to react to this new information. She shifts her eye contact from Lisa to a family portrait on Peterson's desk. "Does it upset his wife?"

Lisa laughs, slightly embarrassed. "I don't think so, at least she never mentioned it to me. I think she has a special interest of her own." Lisa knows she has Nikki's attention now but gets busy with the papers again.

"Interesting! Thank you, Lisa. I'll leave you to your work." Nikki smiles and turns to leave, but has another question. "Oh, by the way, do you have one of the Medical Center letter openers?"

"You mean like the one used to kill Dr. Sullivan?" Lisa replies smugly. "I did, but frankly, I can't stand the tackiness of that advertising stuff. I threw it away when I received my sterling silver letter opener, see?" She holds up the expensive letter opener. "It was a Christmas present from Sheldon."

Nikki half-smiles and leaves the office. Returning to Max and the personnel files, she agrees to talk to Eugene Blake, even though he wasn't one of her students. His file indicates he was an army paramedic during Nam, but lucked out and served his full stay in a Texas army hospital. He's listed as six foot, two inches and weighs about two hundred pounds. He's also listed as a certified physician's assistant, who works under the supervision of Dr. Peterson. Nikki knows this allows him to see patients, prescribe drugs, and do referrals. She also notes he's taking some pre-med courses at the university.

Nikki goes to look for Blake and finds him in the doctors' common room, standing with his back to her. He's a large, full-bodied man whose size reduces everyone else to Lilliputians. When he turns around and faces her, he is indeed a Gulliver-like giant. His white lab coat is too short in the sleeves and too small to button.

"Can I help you?" His voice is deep and loud, and his bushy black hair needs a trim. His eyebrows move up as he speaks, drawing attention to his deeply pocked skin.

"I'm Professor Barnes. I'm helping investigate Dr. Sullivan's murder."

He speaks too loudly. "I know who you are, but you don't remember me, do you?"

Nikki is sure she'd remember meeting this mountain of a man, but her face reveals her doubt.

Blake booms again. "Dr. Levy introduced us in your office. I was carrying the ficus."

Nikki unconsciously pats the white streak in her hair as she tries to remember. "Of course, the ficus."

Dr. Levy's office is next to hers. He likes to interrupt anyone whenever he can and talk about flora and fauna. She remembers the large ficus being introduced to her one day. The tree didn't look as if it would fit in his office, but Levy was having a student bring it in to join the twenty other plants he harbors.

In addition to remembering the leafy interloper, she also recalls that Levy often gave students his office key, so they could water his precious plants when he's out of town. "Didn't you take care of the plants for Dr. Levy during semester break?"

"Yeah." He sits heavily on a nearby sofa, which causes all three of the cushions to sink. "I watered them before, during, and the week after break."

This would have given Blake an opportunity to make a copy of the office key and use it whenever he wanted, like the night she was attacked. She moves to stand next to the sofa and casually watches Blake open some mail with a pencil while he ignores her.

"Aren't there any letter openers in here? I seem to see them everywhere." Nikki tries to be casual.

"You mean like the one stuck in Sullivan's back?" he answers sarcastically. "Remember, I was there. I worked that day. No, there aren't any letter openers here, but mine is at home if you'd like to see it."

Nikki changes the subject. "Did you like working with Dr. Sullivan?"

He doesn't hesitate answering. "I couldn't stand her. She was a bossy bitch. Never let me assist at exams or deliveries and refused to assign her patients to me when she was out. I can truthfully say we hated each other. Our arguments are notorious...but I didn't kill her. I've probably thought about it, but I didn't do it." He stands up, gathering his mail.

"I'm going to be a doctor. We uphold life. It's our sworn oath. Killing that bitch would go against the rules. I have to go now, Professor. I have patients waiting."

He brushes past Nikki while she tries to reach inside and trust her instincts. "One more thing...," she almost shouts.

He only half turns back.

"That's nice aftershave you're wearing. What's it called?" she asks awkwardly.

Blake gives her a bothered look. "It's Cool Water—for men, Professor Barnes." He walks away down the hall.

She rejoins Max and goes over her observations. They

agree Eugene Blake was in the vicinity, had opportunity, and readily admits to hatred of, and long-standing arguments with, Shari Sullivan. But, Max suggests, there might be others with similar motives or a missing link that they haven't yet discovered.

"What about the wife?" Max asks.

Sometimes it's hard for Nikki to follow his detective's logic, but she tries. "What wife?"

"Peterson's wife. He plays around with the student, Lisa Holt. Maybe he also fooled around with Shari Sullivan. Think tomorrow we'll visit the wife."

Nikki's relieved to hear they'll save the other interviews until the next day. She looks at her watch, it's almost 5 p.m., and remembers she still needs to keep her appointment with Dr. Clayton.

NIKKI FINDS GINNI Clayton in examining room A. Her long, slender body is bent over as she sits on a low, stainless stool, rubbing her weary jade-colored eyes.

"You look tired." Again, Nikki avoids using Ginni's name.

Ginni looks up and smiles. "Hello, Reverend Barnes. I like your beret." Her voice is muted.

"You don't like it?" Nikki says lightly. "I just thought it made me look less conspicuous."

"You're probably right." They are staring at each other now. "With a hat like that, no one will notice your black eye." Nikki recognizes a sense of humor she hadn't noticed before. "Sit up on the table, please, and I'll look at those stitches." Ginni rises from the stool and moves to the examining table.

Nikki obediently follows Ginni's directions. She sits and takes off the beret. Ginni leans over and takes a close look at the sutured wound. Nikki is acutely aware of the fragrance Ginni is wearing.

"Several people told me it looks disgusting." Nikki tries to make small talk.

"Disgusting?" Ginni takes a step back and reaches for the blood pressure cuff. "Who said it was disgusting? It's some of my best work. You won't even see the scar...and then you can get rid of that hat."

She puts the cuff around Nikki's arm, pumps it up, and listens with her stethoscope. As she bends over slightly, Nikki notices the red strands in her dark brown hair; they sparkle under the fluorescent lights.

Ginni looks up at Nikki. "Your pressure is a little low. Have you had anything to eat, today?"

Nikki comes back to earth. "I had some lunch."

"What did you eat?" Ginni returns the stethoscope to a counter and picks up the ophthalmoscope. She flips off the overhead lights; the room is dark. Dr. Clayton presses the On button of the scope. She is almost nose-to-nose with Nikki. The silence in the room is overwhelming. The two women stop breathing.

Nikki is very conscious of the proximity of Ginni's body, of Ginni's lips, and timidly offers, "I had a bite of Max's sandwich and a Coke...I think." Nikki is trying to treat the question as part of the medical exam.

Dr. Clayton looks at Nikki's other eye. "Not a good lunch, but it gives me a good excuse." She slowly steps back from Nikki.

"Excuse for what?" Nikki suspiciously asks.

"An excuse to ask you to dinner." The doctor's voice is still quiet and matter-of-fact. The room remains dark. Dr. Clayton turns off the ophthalmoscope.

Nikki doesn't expect this. "I don't know. I really don't want to be seen looking like this..."

"Priests do not live by Coke alone. Isn't that biblical?" Ginni smiles and flips the light back on, but her expression quickly changes to serious. "You do need a good meal. I know a place where the food is wonderful, and no one will see you. And...I could use some of your pastoral counseling. I'm having a hard time with Shari's death. I need someone to talk to."

CHAPTER 8

As the women drive along the coast of Lake Ontario making small talk, Nikki realizes how easy it is to be with Ginni. A red sun is dipping below the horizon as Ginni pulls the Honda into the parking lot of Hernando's, a restaurant hidden behind a lonely pier. Nikki notices only a dozen or so parked cars.

A giant stone fireplace in the center of the dining room is home to a roaring fire. The women are seated at a table facing a row of drafty, water-stained windows looking out onto the lake. The wind howls and rattles the windows, and the waves kiss the shoreline.

As they finish dinner, Nikki wipes her mouth thoughtfully and places the napkin back in her lap. The candlelight flickers and dances in Ginni's eyes. Nikki hears but doesn't absorb what Ginni is saying. She is looking for a way to change the conversation. Finally, Nikki sees her opening.

"We're so close to the water's edge. The rhythm of the waves puts me in touch with life's rhythms: birth, life, and death." Her pale grey eyes move from the water to Ginni. "Did you want to talk about Shari Sullivan?"

Ginni sips her Merlot as tears form. "Shari had gotten into the habit of stopping over at my place almost every night lately. She was unhappy at work because of her problems with Sheldon Peterson. One night, several weeks ago, she confided she was romantically involved with someone and needed to talk about the relationship." Ginni clears her throat, almost whispering, "God, I miss her. Shari was sweet and good and didn't deserve to die so violently." Thoughtfully, she swirls the Merlot in her wine glass.

Nikki measures her words, wanting to say the right thing. "Everyone at the Medical Center seems to feel the same about her."

"Not everyone. Someone didn't like her; someone killed her." Ginni lets the anger pass. "Shari liked most people; babies were her passion. Her main goal in life was to help every woman who wanted a baby. She even created a technique for delivering high-risk pregnancies. She put a lot of love and energy into her work...didn't really leave much time for a personal life."

Nikki sees the grief in Ginni's eyes. "She was an intelligent woman, but lacked self-confidence. One compliment from the right person could win her over immediately. She was strong when fighting for the babies, but quickly lost perspective in her private life."

Nikki hates acting like an investigator but wants more details. She puts her elbows on the table and rests her chin on her interlocked finger, then asks, "What about Eugene Blake?"

Ginni looks up. "Shari despised Blake. She caught him yelling at one of her patients for gaining too much weight." Her voice still low, she smiles briefly. "Now, I would have found that conversation funny, Eugene talking about weight. But Shari saw herself not just as their doctor, but as their protector. They followed her advice because they knew she really cared about them."

"Blake hates her too much for that to be the only reason they disliked each other," Nikki says offhandedly.

"Oh, Blake told you about the fights?" Ginni pauses. "You see, Nikki, Blake wants to specialize in ob/gyn He has some hidden agenda, but Shari never told me what it was. She strongly believed women need to control their bodies."

Ginni stops speaking and looks around the restaurant. Some late diners are being seated nearby. The fire sputters and sparks in the large granite fireplace as one of the waiters stokes it. Ginni continues in a soft voice.

"She was definitely pro-choice and even performed some abortions. All I know is she didn't want Blake assisting her. She even refused to let him see her patients and threatened to file a formal complaint with the state board, if Peterson didn't get rid of him. She even asked staff members to call Peterson and recommend Blake's dismissal."

"Did Dr. Sullivan ever file the complaint?" Nikki asks, sitting back in her chair.

"Not to my knowledge. But Peterson did let it be known that Blake was a valuable member of the Medical Center staff. In fact, he's the one who sponsored him. Personally, I didn't have anything to complain about. No one wants my patients." She looks through the window at the water, white caps against a moonlit sky. "I feel like a traitor for not supporting Shari." She purses her lips together, wetting the pale mauve lipstick. Ginni motions to the waiter for the check, finds her American Express card, and pulls on her coat. "I need some air. Can we get out of here?"

Nikki follows her out of the restaurant to a wooden deck overlooking the short sandy beach. Ginni's perfectly still, as she stares out at the water and wraps her coat tightly around herself, almost like a blanket.

"Shari's death isn't your fault." Nikki's next to her now.

Ginni begins to cry, body-shaking sobs. Nikki moves closer and wraps the tall, slender woman in her arms. Ginni hugs back, resting her head on Nikki's shoulder while she cries all the tears held inside for days. A few minutes later, Ginni slowly pushes away from Nikki, wiping her tears with her hand, trying to regain some composure. She walks down the wooden steps to the beach. Nikki follows, pulls the collar of her coat up, and shoves her hands in her pockets. Two silhouetted figures alone on the beach.

They walk, listening to the waves lapping the beach and watching the water wash debris onto the shore, as if the tide is sweeping out the remnants of winter. Nikki finally breaks the silence. "I want to thank you again for the other night. I'm really grateful for your help."

Ginni stares into the warmth of Nikki's eyes, nods. "If you sincerely want to thank me," she is still struggling to recover her demeanor, "have dinner at my place on Saturday. It's my first day off in two weeks. I want to share an experimental stir-fry with you."

Nikki hesitates, searching for a reason to decline. "I'm afraid I can't make it. I have the benediction at Saturday's graduation."

"What time is graduation?" Ginni is soft-spoken but persistent.

Nikki nervously looks at her feet. "At four, but I'm sure the ceremony'll last until at least six. And by the time I..."

"Good, let's make it for seven." Ginni looks up at the brilliant night sky and smiles. "That way I'll have most of the day to figure out the directions for preparing the vegetables."

She quickly pulls a small pad and pencil from her bag and ends the conversation by writing down her address, then handing it to Nikki. She cuts off any possible objections by turning and heading back to the car.

Ginni drives them back to the Medical Center, where Nikki has parked her car. "Pretty creepy at night, isn't it?" Nikki says, getting out of the car.

"The center never seemed that way until the murder." Sadness shadows Ginni's eyes.

"Then I'll see you Saturday." Nikki smiles weakly, giving in to the moment.

Ginni smiles back, nodding assent, and drives off.

NIKKI TRIES TO put her thoughts in order as she drives home. Eugene Blake seems to be holding his position as number one suspect. There are also lots of unanswered questions. And... there's Ginni. Nikki's feeling something so strong, she quickly pushes the emotions away. Instead, she concentrates on a warm bath and the as-yet-unwritten benediction she is scheduled to deliver at graduation.

CHAPTER 9

While driving to their interview with Mrs. Peterson, Nikki has a strong urge to confide in Max about her Saturday dinner plans with Ginni. But she's hesitant. Too much revelation might make them both uncomfortable. She does tell him about her previous night's meeting and what she learned about Shari's murder.

They pull up to the Peterson's upscale house which sits on a perfectly manicured lawn. Max checks the street out and explains the possible connection between Peterson's extramarital affairs and the murder of Dr. Sullivan.

"The murderer is sometimes a wife done wrong." He parks and stares at the front door thoughtfully. "Or, based on what Clayton says, Shari Sullivan caused waves, gave Peterson too much trouble, could hurt business. The number one priority for him and his father is his career."

They ring the doorbell, and Mrs. Peterson answers. Nikki notices that she looks only slightly older than Lisa Holt. Her deep brown skin and East Indian features take Nikki off guard. There was a different woman in the family portrait on Peterson's desk. Children's voices make playful noises in another room, as Max and Nikki are shown into the living room. The house is spacious. Expensive porcelain vases, Oriental rugs, and gilt-framed paintings adorn the near-empty room.

They sit on a white brocade sofa with Mrs. Peterson on a matching loveseat. The entire room is white, including the walls and curtains. In contrast to this sterile decor, Mrs. Peterson's delicate features complement her dark skin. Her black hair, long and silky, is tied loosely in back with a dark, blue flower-patterned scarf. She sits on the edge of the loveseat, the lower part of her legs crossed, her face and entire body reflecting a pervasive mourning.

Nikki unbuttons her blazer and sits back on the sofa. She's first to speak. "I thought I saw a family portrait in your husband's office..."

"I'm the second Mrs. Peterson." She enunciates each word, giving her speech a fluid rhythm. "Obviously, I'm not the woman in the photo. Sheldon insists on keeping the picture of his first wife on his desk."

Only Max's eyebrows react. "What happened to the first Mrs. Peterson?" He takes out his notebook and pen.

Mrs. Peterson makes eye contact with Nikki as she replies. "They were divorced four years ago. Ann received a large settlement, left her baby daughter with Sheldon, and moved to California, where she is happily remarried."

"So you're raising their child?" Nikki's interested in the baby's welfare

"I married Sheldon a year after his divorce." She looks at Max and continues, "I was a nurse at the Medical Center when I met him. Later, I legally adopted Sabrina. She's four, and our son, Jason, is one."

Max moves to the question of murder. "Did you know Dr. Shari Sullivan?"

Mrs. Peterson's expression doesn't change. "Yes. We worked together at the center before I was married. We became friends after...," there is some hesitation, "after Sheldon began his affair with Lisa Holt."

"And when was that?" Max needs facts.

"About six months ago. I stopped at the center unexpectedly. We had a yelling scene in Sheldon's office...very upsetting. Shari was in the hall. She was concerned and very understanding. As time passed, we became friends."

Max keeps writing. "Your husband have any other girlfriends?"

Mrs. Peterson does not change her expression. "He may have. I only know about Lisa Holt."

Max looks up at her. "And what about Dr. Sullivan? Did your husband have an affair with her?"

"No! I assure you, Shari never slept with him," she says quickly.

Nikki feels a need to ease some of Mrs. Peterson's obvious discomfort and pain. "Were you close friends?"

"Yes. Shari is...was very easy to like." Her shoulders sink slightly. "From the beginning, my marriage has been one of convenience. I accept this. I have a nice home and would never want to fight Sheldon for custody of the children. My life would be totally empty without them. I stay in the marriage, but we share a house only, nothing more. Besides, Sheldon's father would never tolerate another divorce. If I filed, Sheldon would be desperate, and he's dangerous when he's desperate."

Noting this last comment, Max asks, "Can you tell us any more about Dr. Sullivan?"

She sits back slightly in her chair. "Shari brought me home that day." She pauses as if picturing the scene again. "She made me a cup of tea, and I asked her to come back when she finished with her patients. My nights are lonely after the children are in bed. Shari loved the children, and they loved her."

"When's the last time you saw her?" Max asks.

"The night before her murder...before she died." Her voice lowers.

Max pushes. "You see her here?"

"No. I went to her place. We met there sometimes." Mrs. Peterson looks at the floor.

"How'd she seem? Upset over anything?" Max asks quickly.

"She didn't seem any more upset than usual. We had an agreement—when we were together, we wouldn't talk about work or Sheldon. So, if she was upset about either, we wouldn't have talked about it. She seemed happy. We talked about our vacation. The children and I were going with her to Disney World. She was excited and looking forward to all of us being together."

Nikki feels the deep sorrow in Mrs. Peterson's voice and senses there's more to this relationship. Interrupting Max, she asks, "Did you speak to her at all on the day of the murder?"

"No." Her answer is directed now at Nikki. "Shari was coming here for supper. Sheldon had plans for the evening. He often stays at Lisa Holt's house. I waited for about an hour after her last scheduled patient. When she didn't call, I got worried. It wasn't like her to be late without calling. Then Sheldon called— not to tell me what happened to Shari—but to warn me to be discreet when the police called."

The Peterson children come racing into the room to check out the company. They run into their mother's arms. She hugs and kisses both of them while Nikki does another double-take. The girl is fair-skinned with light brown hair. The boy catches her attention. Nikki wasn't an excellent biology student, but she does remember something about recessive genes. Jason is a blue-eyed redhead, with no resemblance to either parent, and certainly no hint of East Indian parentage.

Nikki intercepts another glance from Mrs. Peterson. "You have beautiful children. I love red hair."

Mrs. Peterson quickly lifts the boy into her arms and stands up. "If you don't have any more questions, the children need some attention." Her tone strikes Nikki as overcautious.

Max gives her his card while she shows them to the door, clearly relieved they're leaving.

BARELY BACK IN the car, Max turns to Nikki. "Didn't Mrs. Peterson say the boy was hers? He sure doesn't look like either of 'em."

"Maybe he's adopted," Nikki says, pulling on her beret.

"She didn't mind saying the girl's adopted," Max offers.

Nikki agrees. "You're right. She does seem to be hiding something. Let's go rattle Peterson's cage. It seems he left a few things out of his story."

CHAPTER 10

Dr. Peterson takes a long time answering the knock on his office door. His usually impeccable appearance is betrayed by a crooked tie and some unbuttoned shirt buttons. As Nikki and Max are shown in, Nikki notices Lisa Holt is also disheveled.

"Nice to see you again, Professor," Lisa purrs as she leaves the room.

"What can I do for you, now?" Visibly irritated, Peterson motions for them to sit.

Nikki demands attention with her steel-eyed stare. "We've just talked to your wife," she says coldly.

"Well, my wife is not supposed to be talking to you." He starts tapping the desk with his index finger.

Max can't resist. "She said some interesting things about..."

Peterson cuts him off. "About dear Dr. Sullivan. My wife just couldn't keep her mouth shut, could she? Doesn't care who she embarrasses. I thought she'd have more concern for the children. If she's not careful, she is going to lose those kids."

Max and Nikki are both surprised by his outburst. They look at each other, and Nikki plays her hunch. "How long were your wife and Dr. Sullivan lovers?" Max twists a little in his chair.

"I think lovers is too nice a word for a couple of deviants." Peterson keeps the same angry tone.

Max coughs, makes a note in his book, and asks, "Anything else you want to say about Dr. Sullivan?"

"Yes." Peterson spits out the words. "She was a perverted bitch, who got what she deserved." Wham! Peterson slams his fist down on the desk to emphasize his point.

Nikki maintains her temper. "According to your wife, Dr. Sullivan became her...," she pauses deliberately, "lover...after you took up with Lisa Holt."

Peterson's face flushes bright red, as he realizes they know about his affair. "As I told you before, Dr. Sullivan and I had some differences of opinion about our work."

Max nearly smiles. "Like?"

"We only performed four abortions at the Medical Center last year. Most of them for St. David students. Sullivan and I were the only doctors who did the procedure. I thought it best to change our policy regarding abortions, and she didn't. The stubborn bitch was so damned close-minded."

Max persists. "How did you want to change it?"

"I want to stop the abortions altogether. I want this suite to be an alternative choices suite." He sits back in his plush chair.

"What are the alternatives?" Nikki is curious as to why a woman like Shari Sullivan would not consider alternatives.

"The usual." Dr. Peterson calms down, returning to his smug mode.

"You'll have to educate me." Max can be smug, too. "What're the usual ones?"

"There will be counselors on staff to direct patients toward keeping the child or placing it up for adoption," Peterson curtly explains.

"I must admit," Nikki tries her hand at smug, "when I first met you, you didn't seem so conservative in your thinking."

"Well, appearances can be deceiving, can't they? Look at

my wife and Sullivan. They didn't look like dykes." He pauses, staring at Nikki. Then he dismisses her and addresses Max. "I have always supported adoption. My son, Jason, is adopted. It's unfortunate that Dr. Sullivan died, but it does give me the opportunity to change our policy on abortions."

Max continues the questioning. "So you were angry at Dr. Sullivan?"

"Yes, over the policy, but I didn't kill her. As for the affair with my wife, Susan was looking for a way to get back at me. There's been no sex in our marriage for years. I stay for the sake of the children." Peterson offers a self-righteous smile.

This remark puts a knot in Nikki's stomach as she asks, "How did you find out about Dr. Sullivan and your wife?"

"That wasn't easy." He now plays the man betrayed. "I usually come home late, so Sullivan was always gone by the time I got there. That's how it went on for a long time. Even the weekend visits to Sullivan's apartment occurred when I was away. Susan actually took the children there. That's what I call sick."

He grimaces for emphasis. "Their affair could have gone on forever, but I came home early one night to get a different suit for the theater. There they were, going at it on the living room rug. Disgusting! Imagine—on the living room rug!"

"What'd you do?" Max asks, with an expressionless face.

"I called them pervert sluts...and they laughed. They looked at me and laughed. They were shameless and didn't even try to get dressed or apologize. They told me to have a nice evening." His face is crimson now. "If I had a gun, I would have killed them."

"But, you didn't, right?" Max drops his tone.

Realizing the seriousness of his last remark, Peterson calms down. "Of course not. That's just a figure of speech."

Max wants to know more. "Would you say Dr. Sullivan had enemies here at work?"

Peterson is quiet now, measuring every word. "None that

I know of. I told you, she was well liked."

"How was your work relationship after you caught her with your wife?" Max asks.

Peterson is practically textbook now. "We were always professional to each other. We are trained physicians. We didn't let our personal feelings interfere with our work."

"Anyone else in Dr. Sullivan's life we should know about?"

Peterson thinks for a moment. "She didn't have many friends. You might talk to Dr. Clayton. They worked together at times. Although, they did seem rather competitive. What I mean is, there aren't many promotions in a medical center like this one. Both Dr. Sullivan and Dr. Clayton would be logical choices for any promotion. So they were competitive to a point."

Max wants to pursue this more but realizes he's pushing his time with Peterson. He has one last question. "Where were you at the time of the murder?"

Peterson's indifference returns. "Right here in my office with Ms. Holt. She'll be glad to verify it. Now, if you'll excuse me. I am a very busy man."

AS THEY LEAVE, Max and Nikki notice an open door next to Peterson's office. Nikki walks to the doorway and looks in. Inside is a private kitchen with microwave, sink, and minirefrigerator. At the counter is Lisa Holt, preparing a small tray of crackers and cheese. Lisa turns as Nikki enters. "We missed lunch, so I've fixed a snack. Would you like some?" She holds out the tray.

"No, thanks. But I did want to ask you something rather personal," Nikki says quietly.

"What is it, Professor?" Lisa looks at her questioningly.

"I wondered what the name of your perfume is. I might get some." Nikki tries to sound casual.

Lisa stifles a laugh. "I'm glad you like it. It's called Cool Water. But, I have to warn you, it's very expensive. Sheldon buys it for me."

Nikki counts off suspects again. "Your perfume reminds me of an aftershave with the same name: Cool Water for Men."

Lisa feigns a pout. "Well, you can get the aftershave if you prefer. They're both made by Davidoff. Of course, the aftershave is more masculine."

Nikki ignores the innuendo and rejoins Max, who heard everything from his spot next to the doorway. They watch Lisa return to Peterson's office.

"Now we've got two sources for the smell," Max says. "Blake's back in the action, and we can add Holt. Instead of eliminating suspects, you keep adding."

"Right." Nikki looks at Peterson's door. "But the same people keep turning up with motive and opportunity."

"Jerks aren't always murderers. Peterson might be a jerk, but why risk reputation and money with murder?"

"He hated Shari Sullivan," Nikki answers.

"He hated anyone who spoiled what he wanted. Didn't kill 'em all. What about his wife? Why didn't he kill her?"

"No guts, Max. No balls, no brains, no guts. So, who do you think did it?"

"My best suspect is Blake...," Max hesitates, "...but I can't figure out why Peterson wants him hangin' around."

Nikki continues his reasoning. "Exactly! There's something that doesn't fit here."

"Right, Rev." Max rests his hand on her shoulder. "And when it does, we'll have the murderer."

CHAPTER 11

The outfit Nikki has chosen for Saturday's graduation ceremony consists of a baggy black pant suit with an oversized jacket, a lavender clerical shirt, white collar, and the now-familiar black beret. She sits on the dais praying silently for Shari Sullivan and for a speedy end to "Pomp and Circumstance." The prestigious guest speaker is so confused by his own remarks that he cuts his speech short. So Nikki arrives early at Ginni's apartment, carrying flowers.

A smiling Ginni answers the door wearing jeans and a white river driver shirt with all five buttons unbuttoned. Nikki notices how the cotton top clings to her body like a leotard. Ginni's smile, however, turns to mild surprise when she sees the large silver Khi Rho cross Nikki is wearing.

"Good, you're early." Ginni sounds slightly preoccupied, as she stares at the cross.

"I hope you like flowers." Nikki holds out the bouquet of large yellow and white mums, hoping to break Ginni's gaze. The bouquet doesn't work, so she tries something else. "Like my shirt?"

Ginni laughs. "There's something about a woman in uniform, even a priest's uniform, that's so appealing." She takes the flowers and leads Nikki into the kitchen.

A four-foot-long butcher block counter is stacked with neat little mounds of every vegetable imaginable. The other side of the room holds a small table and two highback chairs. A skylight over the table lends a dusk-like light to the area.

Nikki moves to the counter. "Everything looks great."

"I'm still in the experimental stage, but I've spent all day studying the book...and thinking of you. Take off your jacket; make yourself comfortable."

Nikki isn't sure she can be comfortable, but takes off the jacket, collar, and cross. Then she unbuttons the top of her shirt.

Ginni gives a quick glance of approval as she stir-fries vegetable number one. "That looks much better," she says, smiling.

THE EXPERIMENT IS a success, the wokked meal delicious, and the conversation light, like the white Zinfandel. As Nikki helps Ginni clear the table, they chat about movies. After the last dish is put away, they move into the living room to watch a rerun of *Annie Hall* on cable.

Nikki is beginning to feel very comfortable with Ginni and is moving closer to risk-taking. Her guard is coming down, and her loneliness is an ache needing solace. She notices how close they're sitting next to each other and makes no attempt to move. The movie is not as interesting as she remembers, nor as stimulating as Ginni's shoulder touching her own. Nikki longs to feel Ginni's body pressed against hers.

"Nikki?" Ginni whispers.

Slowly, Nikki turns to face Ginni. Their eyes scream with desire, and their lips meet in a long, hungry kiss. Nikki's arms wrap around Ginni as they move closer. Long moments pass. Then something fearful comes forward in Nikki's mind. She panics and quickly pushes away from Ginni, practically jumping off the sofa.

"What's wrong?" Ginni's still seated on the sofa. Her voice is soft but concerned. "What's the matter, Nikki?"

Nikki's feelings are whirling out of control. She is

frightened and angry, without knowing why. "Is this what you did with Shari Sullivan?" She regrets the remark as soon as it is said.

Ginni's face hardens. "No. I never did this with Shari." Each word hits Nikki with deserved shame and guilt. "I haven't done this with anyone for a long time." She stands. "I think you better leave."

Opening the closet door, she quickly retrieves Nikki's jacket and hands it to her. The large cross falls out of the pocket. Ginni bends down and picks it up. "I shouldn't have tried to seduce a priest. I knew nothing good would come from this. I told you when we first met—I don't like priests."

"Why?" Nikki asks quietly, pushing the fear back to where it hides. "Why don't you like priests?"

Ginni pauses, but then decides to answer. "When I was a sophomore at St. Mary's College...a good Catholic girl, planning to be a medical missionary...I spent most of my free time with my friend Sarah, collecting money for visiting priests. Just before summer, Sarah asked me to help her get an abortion. Father Gabel, one of those visiting priests, paid for the abortion. But first, he told her she'd committed a terrible sin by seducing him. And she believed him."

Nikki takes the cross from Ginni. "You didn't seduce me. You didn't have to. I'm just not a good choice." Her voice cracks. "The priest thing isn't in the way. I'm scared of what I'm feeling, of what I might feel. The problem isn't you... I'm sorry for the remark about Shari. I don't know why I said that."

Each word seems to stick in her dry throat. "I got scared and took my fear out on you. I'm sorry I ruined the evening."

Surprisingly, Ginni gives a half-smile, revealing a subtle dimple on her right cheek. "And my only Saturday off this month."

Nikki starts for the door. Ginni touches her arm, stopping her. "I didn't know you scared so easy. You know, being a priest and soldier and all." Her voice softens again. "We just went a little too fast. You know, something was bound to happen."

This last remark makes Nikki smile too. Her throat relaxes.

Ginni comes closer. "I can understand how you got the idea about Shari and me, but we were friends, not lovers. I don't quite understand what happened tonight, but what do you say? Can we give this another chance? I'll try not to scare you."

Nikki feels like a small child. The icy wall she threw up minutes before is melting a little in the comfort of Ginni's understanding. "Like I said, I'm not a good choice." The hurt child is getting scared again.

"You're my choice. Please stay." Ginni's right next to her now, her hand on Nikki's arm.

"I can't...I have to go." Nikki starts for the door but turns back. "But I'd like to see you again, if you don't mind a neurotic Vietnam vet." This admission takes all her courage. Her heart struggles to vanquish the fear.

"I'd like that," Ginni answers in a soft tone. "How about Monday, after work?"

This time Nikki feels the pull. She leans into Ginni and kisses her. Not long and passionate, but soft, with deep supplication...like an apology and a wish, all in one.

Nikki closes the door behind her. She feels the old ache. Instincts from Nam are telling her: don't love anyone, you might lose them. A deep caution grew somewhere inside her since she lost Mo. This fear is the unbearable pain of that loss.

ON HER DRIVE home, Nikki's mind is pulled into the past, into the torment she thought was behind her. Once home, she prepares a hot cleansing bath and sinks into the steaming water. As the water flows over her body, she begins to cry, feeling the emptiness no longer tolerable. Memories of nameless soldiers dying in her arms play over and over. Unnamed and unclaimed bodies of men, women, and children strewn along Vietnamese dirt roads keep calling to her. Again, she sees the faces of VC soldiers, killed while trying to stay alive. Faces frozen in portraits of agony. Pressure builds in her chest and even tears can't ease it. Only screaming can. Alone in the ebbing water, she screams as loud and as long as she can—pushing the weight off her chest and pushing away the nightmares and the sorrow of lost love.

CHAPTER 12

Two days pass and Nikki, feeling the strain of their separation, is anxious to see Ginni again. She walks quickly down the corridor to the empty waiting area of Suite B. Ginni is waiting at the entrance to the examining rooms in her white lab coat. "Come back to the common room. I'll get my coat."

Her soft voice leads the way, while Nikki watches the subtle curves of her lithe body moving down the hall. The voice, the body, something's happening. Nikki's breath gets a little shallow.

Ginni turns, slowing her pace so Nikki can catch up. There's that look, that smile. "I only have time for a quick dinner," Ginni says, sounding disappointed. "I have a consultation at Mercy Hospital at seven. They sometimes last a few hours."

Nikki smiles. "Dinner's fine. There's a nice Italian place a few blocks from here, Checkered Table."

"Not worried anymore about being seen?" Ginni asks.

Nikki removes the beret, raking blonde strands over the stitches. "Not enough to miss the opportunity of being with you."

Ginni's smile widens. "My coat's right here." She enters the common room with Nikki, takes her coat off a wall rack, and gets her purse from a locked file drawer. Then she stops at the work table in the middle of the room, picks up a stack of pamphlets, and throws them into the wastebasket.

"What's all that?" Nikki asks.

Ginni scowls. "Same old standard gory photos of bloody fetuses and dead babies, sick antiabortion propaganda shit." Frustration is apparent in her voice. "Every night a stack shows up, and every night I throw them away. It's a little game I play with Mr. Edmond Long, a slithering fundamentalist worm."

"A little game?" Nikki furrows her brow.

"Yes." Ginni hastily slips on her trenchcoat. "I told him he's wasting his time on me, since I don't do abortions. But I did make the mistake of saying I believe in them. Now he's trying to save my soul, I guess."

Nikki's mind is checking off suspects again. "Did he play this game with Shari Sullivan?"

"Probably. But Shari just ignored the pamphlets. She'd leave them on the table. I'm the only one who throws them away." She finishes buckling the belt on her coat.

This new information distracts Nikki momentarily. Trying to fit it into the murder puzzle, she suddenly makes eye contact with Ginni again. Then, all she can think about is Ginni. She moves closer, puts her arms around Ginni and kisses her softly. Ginni kisses back and quickly, but reluctantly, pulls away. "Not here. I wouldn't want anyone to see us, especially Long."

Realizing her faux pas, Nikki stammers, "I'm sorry. I...I don't know what I was thinking."

"I know exactly what you were thinking..." Ginni's eyes sparkle as she grins. "And I'm glad. But it could be awkward if we're seen."

THE CHECKERED TABLE smells of real food, delicious meals cooked to order. The two women sit in a dimly lit back room with checkered red-and-white tablecloths, eating antipasto and hot, crusty garlic bread, while they watch the candle melting and dripping down the sides of an empty Chianti bottle.

Nikki sips some wine, looks into Ginni's eyes, and says, "I'd like to start this relationship over again, if that's possible."

"Are you sure?" Ginni reaches over and gently squeezes Nikki's hand, while she stares longingly at her.

"But I need to go slowly. I'm cautious and don't really trust myself or anyone else since Vietnam. But I think I want to. I'm trying to learn how again," Nikki stammers.

"I understand, Nikki. I'm also cautious, ever since med school. Believe me, I've had my share of relationship troubles, too." Ginni reaches over and pats the soft pale skin of Nikki's cheek. "So, I guess we just learned something about each other." Suddenly, Ginni looks at her watch, stands, and pulls on her coat. "Amazing, I don't know where the time has gone, but I have to get over to Mercy."

As she reaches into her purse, Nikki says, "I have it."

Ginni throws a kiss. "I'll call you soon." She walks past Nikki and pauses for just a moment to touch Nikki's shoulder. Nikki places her hand over Ginni's. Her touch fuels Nikki's mounting desire. This emerald-eyed woman might be someone she could share her painful past with. And maybe someone to share her future with.

FEELING ENERGIZED, NIKKI decides to walk back to the Medical Center. Her spirits are high, with dozens of questions buzzing through her head. She wants to ask Edmond Long a few more questions. Like just how far he would go to make a point about abortion.

She stops at the security desk, takes out her ID, and places it on the desk. "I'm Reverend Barnes. I'd like to talk to Edmond Long."

The security guard looks up from his newspaper, "Sorry, just a sec." He removes the Walkman headphones from his ears and lets them hang around his neck. "Okay, now what can I do for ya?"

Nikki rolls her eyes heavenward, once again identifies herself, and asks for Edmond Long. She can clearly hear the heavy metal music emanating from the Walkman. "Young man, do you realize you'll be stone deaf in a few years if you keep listening to that stuff?"

The security guard ignores her remarks and checks a clipboard, which is sitting next to the sports page. He smiles, looks at his watch, and points down the hall. "He should be in Suite B, probably the common room, Reverend." He replaces the headphones.

Nikki makes her way through the building to the Suite B waiting area, noticing how empty the Medical Center feels. She stops and listens to the lonely hum of the fluorescent lights. Part of her wants to run back and ask for an escort, but she puts that thought aside. Instead, she goes past the waiting area to the common room. She announces her visit with a firm knock on the partially open door. "Edmond? It's Professor Barnes... I'd like to talk to you."

She gets no answer and cautiously enters the room. Nikki jolts, when she sees Edmond Long's body. Still in a kneeling position, he's slumped over a wastebasket with his head pushed down inside the basket. Blood pools in ever-widening circles onto the back of his dark blue shirt.

Nikki doesn't need to go near the body to know Long is dead. She learned to recognize dead bodies in Nam. Eyes wide, scanning right and left, Nikki backs slowly out of the room, then turns and races back toward the security post. Just as she makes her way around the reception desk, a deafening gunshot resonates in the hall. A bullet zings past her face, so close she can feel the whiz in the air.

Nikki begins to scream, "Guard! Guard! Help! Someone help me!"

She darts across the room. Seconds later another gunshot rings out behind her. This propels her into a side hallway screaming, "Incoming! Incoming! Help! Help me!"

She's terrified. Adrenaline surges through her. She races down the hall, her heart pounding out of her chest. Nikki, afraid to turn around, anticipates the killer's bullet entering her back. She can hardly breathe, but her legs carry her another twenty feet. Suddenly someone grabs her by the arm and yanks her into a connecting hallway. A hand clamps her mouth shut. She struggles furiously to pull the hand away. She needs air.

"Nicolette? It's me, Barrett!" Barrett pulls her along and in a hushed whisper blurts, "The security guard's dead. Someone stabbed him. We gotta get outta here! I think the killer's probably still in the building. Follow me! There's an exit door at the end of this hall."

They race to the exit and, together, push through the double doors. With arms pumping, they sprint across the parking lot to the campus security shack. Panting and gasping for air, they explain what's happened to the guard. He quickly punches in the number for the Sheridan Police.

Barrett leans against the brick guard shack, trying to catch her breath. Nikki, angry and gasping for air, looks at Barrett. "What the hell were you doing at the center tonight? And don't lie."

Barrett answers between gasps. "Looking for you...because...I baked another pie. It's in my car. I know that cop probably didn't give you the last one."

"I don't want any more damn pies, Barrett. I thought you understood. I don't want to see you." Nikki's frustration is apparent.

"But, Nicolette, I don't want you mad at me," Barrett pleads. "I want us still to be friends."

"How'd you know I was at the center, that I'd be there?" Nikki growls.

Barrett takes a small step closer to Nikki. "You're always at the Medical Center lately. When you didn't answer your phone at home or in your office, I knew you'd be at the center. I went in to ask the guard if he saw you, but he was slumped over the desk and bleeding bad. Then I heard you screaming for help, so I rushed to find you." She lowers her voice. "I don't want to talk to any cops, Nicolette. I don't want to be involved. This is scary shit. I'm gonna leave now. Will you be okay?"

Police cars with screaming sirens screech to a halt near the Medical Center, followed by an ambulance.

"You can't leave. The police will need to ask you some questions." Nikki's obviously perplexed. Barrett could be involved with the murders, but, on the other hand, she did save her life. She tempers her voice. "Please, you may be able to help. I'll be right here when they question you. Barrett, I think you can help."

Barrett smiles and takes Nikki's arm. "As long as you'll be here, I'll talk to 'em. Does this mean we're friends again?"

With Barrett all but hanging on her, Nikki thinks a moment before speaking. "One thing's for sure, Barrett, our paths seem to constantly crisscross."

CHAPTER 13

Max jumps out of his car. The red and blue swirling lights of the squad cars create an uncanny circus-like atmosphere in the parking lot. Max deploys the men quickly, asks Nikki and Barrett for the details, then escorts them both back to the Medical Center. As they approach the building, they see the injured guard being lifted into an ambulance for transport to Sheridan Memorial Hospital. Detective Henry Ostrow meets them at the entrance and reports that the building is secure.

"Guard's in pretty bad shape, sliced and stabbed," he comments dryly.

He hands his notes to Max, who reads and listens at the same time. Ostrow goes on, "Edmond Long's been shot twice in the back and half-stuffed into a wastebasket."

Max returns the notebook. "Henry, talk to Ms. Fairburn. Get her side of the story and then send her home."

Detective Ostrow takes Barrett aside to ask her a few more questions. He makes notes as she talks. Satisfied, he tells her she can leave, but she refuses to go. Only Nikki's acceptance of the new pie will convince Barrett to go home.

The exchange of the pie, from Barrett's car to Nikki's hands, takes a few more minutes. Nikki, feeling a little foolish, is left studying the pie in her hands. Max walks back to her and says, "What's with that woman and her obsession with pies? She all right or what?"

"I told you, she's my tutorial student from the university." Nikki raises her eyebrows and shrugs her shoulders. "And I hear she bakes a great pie." Nikki doesn't really answer Max's question.

Max doesn't smile. "I don't know, Rev, she seems to turn up whenever you're being assaulted." He softens slightly. "Pies are damned good. Henry'll put it in the car. We need to look at Long's body." He pauses, looks again at the pie. "Just to be safe, Henry'll do a background check on Barrett Fairburn."

CRIME LAB TECHNICIANS swarm about, taking photos of the crime scene and dusting for prints in the common room. Edmond Long's body lies sprawled on the floor. Nikki kneels next to him and says a prayer.

"Almost feels like Nam around here," Max says, remembering their time together at the 90th EVAC Hospital. As a corpsman, Max accompanied Nikki whenever she visited the Intensive Care Unit. They would go bed to bed, praying with, or over, each soldier. Then they'd move to the hospital morgue and pray over the bodies waiting to be flown home.

Now, Max sweeps the common room with his eyes, as he pulls out a pair of latex gloves from his pocket and puts them on. "Killer used a gun on Edmond Long but slashed the guard. He's good with a knife, but why not shoot the guard?"

"Did you see the pamphlets in the wastebasket?" Nikki asks, standing up and brushing the dust off the knees of her pants. "Some lurid antiabortion propaganda."

Max moves the bloody papers with his pen to better see the cover of one. Nikki continues, "Long was fiercely opposed to abortions being performed here at the center. He left these pamphlets for the doctors. Every day one of the doctors threw them out, and the next day a new batch would reappear."

Max wipes his pen on a tissue. "What's the killer trying

to say? He's pro-abortion? Doesn't jive with the Sullivan murder."

"Right, she performed abortions. So why kill her?" Nikki finishes the thought. "Maybe this murder is a ploy to get us off track?"

"Don't think so, Rev. We're probably looking at an important clue and just not seeing it." Max flips back a few pages in his notebook. "Let's deal with the facts."

Nikki makes a mental checklist. "The murderer is someone with access to a gun and access to the Medical Center after regular hours."

"We'll know more when we find out what kind of gun was used. Should get the report on the bullets tomorrow," Max interjects. "Anything else?"

"It's incredible, Max, I didn't hear anything. No gun shots, no cries from the security guard. Nothing. This guy operates like a pro." Nikki takes her beret off and fluffs up her flattened blonde hair, raking it again with her fingers, careful not to disturb her head wound. "And this time, I didn't even smell anything. With the popularity of Cool Water in this building, I think that clue is pretty useless."

"Nothing's useless." Max pauses, then adds, "I'm worried 'bout you, Rev. Can't help thinking your luck's about to run out. You might be a target, too."

"Nah...I just came back to the Medical Center at the wrong time." Nikki looks again at Long's body. "The murderer wanted Long, not me. I hardly knew either victim."

Max bends down to take another look at the body. He pokes through the dead man's pockets. "You knew him as a student. Fairburn's a student, too, and you know the students who work here. We keep coming back to them."

"I don't know them well," she adds quickly. "And I can't remember any who hate me enough to kill me. I think I was convenient for the first attack and stupid for the second. No one knew I was coming back to talk to Long."

"Don't say no one." Max gets her attention. "We know

Barrett Fairburn figured it out. And what about the friend you had dinner with? Mighta said something there."

Nikki doesn't look at Max. Instead, she studies the leather tassels on her loafers. "I had dinner with Dr. Clayton. I've seen her a couple of times socially," she says guardedly.

"I don't wanna discuss it here. We'll talk later." He speaks softly, so no one else in the room can hear. Nikki grows uncomfortable, wondering what he wants to discuss.

Max brings his voice back to normal. "Any other connections you can make?"

"Not really." The priest in Nikki surfaces again. "Has Long's wife been notified?" Nikki's concerned about the young woman waiting for Edmond to return home and being greeted with this news instead.

"Been taken care of. She called some people from her church who'll go with her to the morgue. I'll talk to her later. There's still questions that need answering." Max puts his notes away. "Don't think there's any more for us here."

Henry is in the entrance area talking to several officers. Max leaves Nikki at the double doors and walks over to the group. Henry and Max briefly exchange information, and Max returns. "Henry's finishing up. I'll drive you home. Maybe come in for a piece of pie."

MAX SITS AT Nikki's kitchen table rambling on about how he can drink coffee all night and still sleep. He sips a fresh-brewed cup while petting Fluffy, who sits purring in his lap.

Nikki stays with herbal tea. Too many sleepless nights dissuade her from coffee. She doesn't like being alone with herself in the middle of the night. After serving the pie, she encourages Fluffy off Max's lap.

"Pie's delicious." She'd forgotten Max's habit of talking with his mouth full.

"Barrett can bake, can't she?" Nikki wonders what they're

really talking about.

"Looks like a javelin thrower." Max sprays some crumbs as he speaks.

Nikki laughs in agreement. Barrett does look like an athlete. "She's a little unusual, and overly attached to me. I know better than to get involved with students, but I didn't see this coming. I thought I was helping her."

"I guessed, from the way she hangs around." Max takes a second piece of pie and, with a full mouth, continues, "Pie reminds me of my mother's—a real pie." He gestures with his fork for emphasis.

Nikki can't tell if the conversation is going in the right direction or not. "Barrett's a little mixed up, lonely. You know, looking for someone to share things with. I guess she thought because I was understanding, it could be me."

"Uh huh." Max is ready to get to the point now. "Is that the story with Dr. Clayton? You're lonely, she's nice to you, someone to share things with?"

He's right-on this time. Her grey eyes grow larger as she shoots back, "What's the problem, Max? We had dinner a few times. I know it's awkward because of the case, but she's not really a suspect. I enjoy her company. It's rare when I meet someone I can talk to, and Ginni seems like someone I can trust."

"Oh, Ginni already?" Max sits back from the table.

"I don't need this bullshit, Max." She feels defensive. "What's bugging you? Is it Barrett or Ginni? Or is it just me?"

"Relax. Relax. You think I never get overly involved in my cases? You still think I'm a choirboy? I don't care who you choose to spend time with. I was over there, too. I know what it does to the head. Never told anyone, but when I got married...I couldn't do anything in bed. Kept thinking of all those corpses. Felt guilty I was alive having fun." He pauses briefly. "Still gets me sometimes."

Nikki calms down. "I know, Max. As soon as you think

you've put it away for good, it comes back."

Max smiles. "When I saw you again, all I thought about was you finally became a priest. Thought you should be like in the movies—holier than most, not far from heaven."

"Then you woke up and remembered the real world, right?" Nikki smiles, too.

"Yeah. Woke up and remembered Nam, and what a joke a uniform is. No offense, but behind every one of those clerical collars is a human being with faults and a sex drive. I understand, really."

Nikki isn't sure Max understands everything, but he's at least getting closer to reality. "So it's okay I have this crazy student chasing me with pies, and I'm seeing Ginni?"

"No. Neither one is okay, "Max says flatly.

Shocked by Max's seriousness, she asks, "Why? What's the problem, Max?"

"Two people been killed in less than a week, and you've almost been killed twice yourself." Max takes a breath. "Everyone is still a suspect. Henry's checking out Fairburn. She might be crazy enough to be involved in these murders, and Dr. Clayton is very much a suspect."

"How's she a suspect?" Nikki protests, slamming her hands on the table. "They were friends. There's no motive for her to kill Sullivan."

"Seems there is." Max pushes his chair away from the table. "Learned more about Clayton after interviewing the staff. Seems when Peterson changes over the suite, he'll move into a strictly administrative position. And guess who'll be the new chief of family medicine, with the money and prestige to go with it? Virginia Clayton! Would have been between Clayton and Sullivan, if Sullivan was alive. Yeah, I think that's a possible motive."

Nikki twists her watch band back into place again. "How do we know she's even aware of the promotion? She never mentioned it. Besides, it hasn't happened yet."

Max changes direction. "Where's Clayton tonight? She

know you were still hanging around the Medical Center?"

"She was with me at the Checkered Table 'til almost seven. Then she had to be at Mercy Hospital. You can check it out."

"Count on it, Nikki." Max is in professional mode. "And, that's not all. The nurses told me Clayton and Sullivan had big arguments. Maybe over Sullivan's relationship with Susan Peterson. Could point to jealousy—always a good motive for murder."

Nikki finds the information about Ginni's promotion and the arguments with Shari puzzling. Why didn't Ginni mention them? Nikki unconsciously taps the side of her shoe against the sole of her other shoe as she continues Ginni's defense. "How would that explain Edmond Long's death? What did jealousy have to do with that?"

Max leans forward. "Don't have all the answers yet, just questions. And some are for Virginia Clayton."

"I don't think the questions are justified." Nikki feels an involuntary need to protect Ginni.

"Sorry you feel that way." Max takes a deep breath. "But just as well, you won't be asking them. I'm questioning Clayton tomorrow...alone. I don't want you to see her or that Barrett Fairburn until I check them both out."

"What are you talking about?" Nikki wonders if she's off the case altogether.

"I'm talking about your life and the danger you're ignoring. I don't want anything happening to you. You may not have noticed...but I'm real fond of you. I can assign an officer to you—just a little extra protection. If you don't want this, then you got to do what I say. Including staying away from a certain woman 'til she's cleared."

Nikki hears everything Max says, but she wants him to understand her feelings for Ginni. "No Max, no bodyguards! Now what about tomorrow's interview? Don't you think I want to know how Ginni answers your questions?"

"I'll tell you how." Max softens. "I don't want you there

'cause she'll hold back, maybe bend things a little if you're there."

Nikki gets the picture. "Like I just did. Right?"

"You got it." Max smiles again. "You know I'll tell you everything. I figure we'll meet for lunch. Henry should have a few reports back by then."

Max gets up, ready to leave. He walks over to Nikki and puts his arms around her.

She walks him to the door while he scans the living room and checks the door locks. "Think your place is safe? Don't know what to expect from this case. You can come to my place, even bring the cat."

"I'm sure this place is okay. The Medical Center seems to be the target. Hardly anyone at St. David knows where I live. The faculty office doesn't give out professors' home addresses." She touches his arm. "Thanks for the offer, Max. Not many people are willing to take both me and Fluffy."

He leaves, firmly closing the door behind him. She double locks it immediately and reassures herself that she's safe. After all, the only two people who know where she lives are Barrett and Ginni. She knows what Barrett wants and can stop her. She wishes Ginni wanted the same thing.

NIKKI GOES TO bed feeling apprehensive. In her dreams, a naked Susan Peterson is lying on top of another naked woman on a white rug. Walking up to Susan, Nikki strokes her ebony back. Susan turns and smiles. Under her is Ginni, lying on her back, holding out a hand, beckoning Nikki down with them. Nikki turns away and starts running in slow motion. She comes to a large church door and struggles to open it. Pushing it just wide enough to get through, she slides into a brilliantly lit giant kitchen filled with oversized pies of all kinds. Barrett is cooking at a giant stove. She turns, stretching out her arms. Nikki quickly tries to go back through the church door, but it disappears.

Another sleepless night.

CHAPTER 14

Four calls from Barrett Fairburn and two desperate messages from Dean Haslett greet Nikki on her office answering machine. She punches in the dean's number first and is put through to his office.

"Reverend Barnes, I've been trying to reach you." He sounds indignant, as usual.

She answers calmly, as she sits in her highback leather chair. "I was going to call with a report as soon as I had some definite information."

"It seems to me the assault in your office is definite information, Reverend Barnes." He's long past excited. "A second murder, this time one of our own students, is definite information."

"What I mean is...," Nikki tries again, "the police don't have a solid suspect yet."

"I don't care who the murderer is," he cuts her off. "My concern is negative publicity for St. David. And this should be your major concern. Do you understand, Reverend?"

Nikki keeps her thoughts about his callous approach to human life to herself, as she reassures him. "The publicity surrounding the murder of Dr. Sullivan remains low-key. The Medical Center can't afford bad publicity, either. Their publicist is controlling it," she says, trying to sound soothing and composed.

"They may be trying to control the publicity, but their efforts aren't working. Someone leaked the whole story. Didn't you see this morning's *Daily Examiner*? St. David's campus on the front page and yearbook pictures of Edmond Long. Someone is trying to sabotage this university. I expected more from you, Professor Barnes."

Her status sinks from Reverend to Professor, a demotion she prefers. Her loyalty is not to Dean Haslett or the university, but to her students. This realization makes her think about her philosophical disagreements with Edmond Long, and she makes a mental note to offer condolences to his widow.

She tries to continue the conversation. "Anyone could have called the newspaper. There were a lot of people milling around last night. Security might have leaked the story."

"That's unfortunate, Professor." Haslett now uses a more formal tone. "As of this moment, you no longer represent the university in this matter. We are disowning this whole situation. We don't want anyone thinking we're in any way involved. Is that clear?"

"Perfectly clear." But she is involved and has no intention of leaving the case.

"I'd like to see you in my office, Professor, as soon as possible." Haslett carefully pronounces each word.

Nikki feels no need to rush, assuming her employment is going to be terminated. She isn't sure she wants to return next year anyway. "I can be there after lunch. Is 1:30 convenient?"

"That's fine," the dean says curtly. "We'll review your status evaluation, so bring any documents you wish included in your personnel folder." He abruptly hangs up.

Nikki has a strong urge to clean out her desk. Instead, she gathers the notes needed for her year-end evaluation and works intensely for almost an hour.

"KNOCK, KNOCK. HELLO, Professor. Thought I'd find you here," Lisa Holt says seductively from her position in the office doorway.

Nikki is startled by this unexpected visit. "Lisa? What can I do for you?"

"Well, Professor, you're so smart—I knew that the first day of class. I don't mean just book smart, but smart like a man. You figure things out so quickly." She sits down in the chair next to the desk, facing Nikki.

"If that's a compliment, I don't care for the comparison." Nikki puts down her pen and straightens out some papers.

Lisa leans toward Nikki, her arm on the corner of the desk. "No. You wouldn't like being compared to a man. You're such a liberated woman, aren't you?"

Nikki is annoyed by Lisa's attitude and impromptu visit. "What's your problem, Lisa?"

"You are, Professor." She suddenly sounds angry and almost snarls, "I want you to stop accusing Sheldon Peterson of these horrible crimes. Stop humiliating him in front of the police. I know you're siding with that bitch wife of his, but she's really no damn good. She's slept with half the Medical Center staff and constantly bleeds Sheldon for money. He loves me, but she won't divorce him. I'm warning you, Professor, I want you to stop twisting his words."

This outburst pushes Nikki to near explosion. She tries mentally to count to ten but only gets to seven. "How admirable of you to defend Dr. Peterson, but he doesn't need your protection. This may surprise you, but he gets himself in trouble without any help from me. The police can question him anytime they want. He's a viable suspect."

Lisa's plastic smile returns. "It's her, isn't it? Susan got to you, too. Have you slept with her yet?"

Nikki shoots up from her chair. "This discussion is over. You will leave my office right now!"

Lisa rises slowly, glaring at Nikki, and points her finger. "I'll do whatever I must to protect him from anyone who tries to hurt him, and that means you, too."

"Are you threatening me?" Nikki controls her anger, trying to remember this is a young student obviously in love with a married man. "Are you so much in love with him, you're willing to make threats and false accusations?"

Lisa stops smiling. "Nothing I say is false. I love him, and I'm going to share his work and his life. And I'll fight anyone who tries to interfere with our plans."

"Are you so sure he has the same plans?" Nikki's grey eyes are blazing. "Did you know he could have gotten divorced a long time ago? He won't because he's afraid of losing his father's money."

"That's a lie!" Lisa is almost screaming.

Nikki's on a roll. "Maybe he's a good choice for you. You can believe each other's lies and play games forever."

"What about your games, Professor? Your tutorial student? The Asian woman in Vietnam? Tell me you don't love women," Lisa hisses back.

How did she know about Trang? Nikki hadn't told anyone at the university about her. The photograph of Trang and her baby always stays in her briefcase—a hope or reminder that maybe they did escape to America. Nikki's anger builds again, but she doesn't respond.

Lisa continues her assault, "You hate men. That's why you're after Sheldon."

Nikki deliberately sits back down, exasperated by the foolishness of this situation. "I know this is hard for you to understand, but I don't hate men. I usually like them. Dr. Peterson, however, is not one I like."

Lisa's flirtatious smile returns. "I think I understand. You don't like my relationship with him, do you?"

"I don't care about your relationship," Nikki answers matter-of-factly, "and I don't care about Dr. Peterson."

Lisa picks up her purse and starts for the door. "I see it's useless trying to explain what Sheldon is really like. You can't understand." She half turns back. "I'll let you get back to your work. But remember—I'll do anything for Sheldon." She leaves, slamming the office door.

Nikki stares at the closed door, perplexed over how Lisa entered the office unheard, how she knew about Trang's picture in her briefcase, and why she said Susan Peterson slept with everyone. Did this mean Ginni, too? This wasn't the first time this had come up. Last night with Max, now in Lisa's insinuations. Would Ginni lie? And why would Nikki be so upset if they did sleep together?

Suddenly Nikki is aware that she misses Ginni, wants to call her just to ask how her day went, what her favorite color is, or if she's busy tonight. But her promise to Max was not to contact Barrett or Ginni until he cleared them. Hard as that was, she'd stand by her promise.

CHAPTER 15

The open food court is by the university duck pond. Spring is acting more like summer, with sunshine and temperatures of seventy degrees. Nikki takes her time crossing the grassy slopes, enjoying the sunshine. Max is sitting on a bench, munching a hot dog and studying the ducks.

After stopping at one of the kiosks for french fries, Nikki joins him. "None of Rosa's special food today?" she asks, sitting next to him.

"Told her forget it today. I'm hoping I'm home early. She's making spaghetti. I'll snack for lunch and save my appetite for dinner. You're invited too."

"I have to meet a deadline with my year-end paperwork." Nikki tries to decline gracefully.

"We're eating lasagna Sunday. What about then? I'll keep hounding you 'til you come. Might as well give in," Max says lightly.

Nikki stops avoiding what will probably be a pleasant time. "Sunday's fine," she finally says. "I'll be there."

"Great." Max perks up. "Rosa'll be surprised. Told her all about you. She'll put on a spread you've never seen."

Nikki nibbles two french fries but can't wait any longer. "So, Max, what've you found out about the Long murder?"

Max finishes his hot dog in two big bites and wipes the mustard off his fingers with a thin napkin. He takes out his little notebook and flips through the pages. "Bullet was a thirty-eight caliber. Pretty common gun." He stops reading and looks up. "You bring back any guns, Rev?"

"Officially...none." Nikki gazes blankly out at the pond. "Unofficially, I've got my forty-five and the twenty-five Browning I bought over there."

"Kept my forty-five, too. Even with the police hardware, I've got the forty-five as backup. Tough gettin' rid of 'em. It's like a survival mechanism."

Nikki moves them back to the case. "If the thirty-eight is an army issue weapon, maybe we need to talk to Eugene Blake again."

"Already thought of it, but he's taking an all-day exam to update his physician's assistant certification." Max catches her eye. "Questioning him tomorrow at nine. Wanna be there?"

Nikki nods. "By the way, I had a visit from another sweetheart, Lisa Holt. She came into my office so quietly, scared the hell out of me. Then she reamed me out for picking on the saintly doctor, Sheldon Peterson. She said I'd been putting words in his mouth, humiliating him. Then she accused me of sleeping with his wife." Nikki blushes. "According to Lisa, everyone is. She even had the audacity to threaten me." Nikki pauses and picks at the fries. "I'm not sure, but I also think she's been in my office, going through my briefcase."

"Threatened you, huh?" Anger shows in Max's voice. "So, Lisa Holt is not the naive school girl she appears to be?"

"She's mean and mixed up." Nikki's angry too.

"I think Holt just made it to the suspect's list," Max adds.

Nikki isn't so sure. "Protecting Peterson may be her present goal in life, but she was already sleeping with him while Shari was with Susan Peterson. What reason was there for her to kill Shari? If she was going to kill anyone, I think it would have to be

Susan. You know, get rid of the perceived threat, or competition."

"Maybe not." Max tosses the dirty napkin into a nearby garbage bin. "Still missing a piece to the puzzle, the one with a glimpse of the whole picture."

He flips another page of his notebook. "Detective Ostrow checked out Barrett Fairburn. He found out from, as Henry puts it, 'somebody who knows somebody with access to certain information,' that Fairburn does have a juvenile record. And, of course, it's sealed. But Henry's unnamed friend can arrange for him to talk to an officer connected with her case."

Nikki shakes her head, about to protest, but Max quickly adds, "I know. I know. It's a long shot. But, Fairburn does seem to be around whenever there's a murder. For now, keep away from her 'til Henry has more information about her juvie record. Okay?"

"Don't worry," Nikki says with a smile.

Max closes his notebook. "I'm talking to Clayton later this afternoon. What are you up to?"

Nikki wants to be at that interview but knows Max won't go for it. "I'm going to see Mrs. Long later, but first I have to see Dean Haslett. He summoned me to his office."

"Haslett? What does he want? I hope he's not gonna blame you for leaking that front page story to the press. He always blames someone for the negative publicity the college gets. What he doesn't know is the leak comes from his own office. One of his secretaries calls the newspaper whenever anything happens. Been a confidential source for years."

"Perfect, his own secretary." Nikki rolls her eyes to the sky. "Yeah. He blames me. I'm probably going to get the axe. It's that time of the year—annual evaluations—which means I may not be back next year." Nikki bites her lower lip.

Max gets very serious. "What will you do?"

Nikki tries to reassure him. "Don't worry, Max. I'm still somewhat employable. Maybe I need to get more flexible." She pauses, wanting to say one more thing. "Let me know how the interview goes, okay?"

Max leaves for the Medical Center with the promise to call if anything pertinent comes out of his meeting with Dr. Clayton. Nikki's to do the same after seeing the dean. Otherwise, they'll meet at his office in the morning.

Nikki departs from the tranquil scene at the duck pond and returns to her office. She reaches for the clean, black clerical shirt she stores in her desk drawer and puts it on. She adds the white plastic collar, then slips on her black jacket, which matches her slacks. This full uniform seems rather fitting, since Dean Haslett prefers her as a professor, not a priest.

"This outfit should at least make him uncomfortable while he fires me," she mumbles to the mirror on her wall.

STERLING HALL IS the recently renovated administration building for St. David University. Most of the classrooms and offices at St. David's are painted dull yellow and are dirty. In contrast, the administrative offices have thick grey carpeting, tasteful reproductions hanging on the walls, and bright track lighting overhead.

Reverend Barnes enters Dean Haslett's outer office, and three secretaries look up from their desks. Nikki can't help but wonder which one is Deep Throat. Secretary Number 1 gives her the signal, and she enters the large inner office.

Dean Haslett doesn't get up. "Please take a seat, Professor Barnes." He waves her to a chair across from his desk and steeples his fingertips. "First things first. As I mentioned earlier, you are not to be involved with the murder investigation at the Medical Center."

Nikki isn't surprised. He waits until a student is killed, then disowns the situation. His disinterest in the very people he's supposed to serve is less than admirable. She says nothing.

"Secondly," Haslett continues, "as you know, we evaluate our faculty and course offerings at the end of each academic year to see if they warrant continuation. We've received several complaints from students about one of your courses, Modern Moral Ethics. And we have complaints from your colleagues."

"Really?" Nikki is surprised but realizes not everyone will like a course or colleague. "How many complaints were there?"

"Several." Haslett is poker-faced and evasive.

Nikki gets up and sits on the arm of the chair, placing herself slightly above Haslett. "I hope you don't mind—bad back, the war, you know. Now, how many complaints did you say there were?"

"I said several." Haslett holds his ground.

"I'm entitled to have specific information as stated in the faculty handbook." Nikki is textbook now. "I have a right to know everything but the student's name."

Haslett is seething but gives in. "There are three. Three definite complaints."

"And they are?" Nikki tugs at her pant legs, freeing them from the tops of her loafers as she presses on.

Haslett opens a folder. "This one talks about your unchristian attitude toward social problems. You must agree that is a heavy charge to place against a reverend."

Nikki guesses who made this complaint and, though not wanting to speak ill of the dead, feels she has to defend herself. "Is the social issue in question abortion? Because even you are aware of the dual position of Christian churches on that issue. Many Christians, a label which you must admit has become difficult to define, are not against abortion. That sounds like the complaint of an antiabortion activist."

"That's not the only complaint." Haslett shuffles another paper. "This one talks about loud laughing and talking in your office with a student, which disturbed a colleague who was trying to work in his own space."

Nikki knew the "Barrett thing" would come back to haunt her. But, she never expected it to bring out the jealousy of a petty academic who couldn't just ask her to be quiet. A man again, who has to file a formal complaint in order to elevate his own status. A man who waits and listens to all the conversation first and then files a "too much noise" complaint.

"I was tutoring Barrett Fairburn...at your request. My contract also states that I will schedule time to meet the academic needs of students outside of class hours. If our conversations were too loud, the faculty member should've come to me at that moment and complained. Why do you suppose he didn't come to me?" she asks, controlling her tone and diction.

"Perhaps he felt you should be more sensitive to his need to work in quiet." Haslett has all his answers ready.

"And the last complaint? What was that?" Nikki asks.

Haslett's in control again. "This implies that you pay more attention to the women students than to the men and that your grading reflects your bias." He looks up. "Can you comment on that charge, Professor?"

"I think you have a complaint by a disgruntled male student who got a lower grade than one of the women. I don't think I'm intentionally biased. I think I'm fair, but if I'm not, I'm glad I grade in favor of female students. After all, they've been getting screwed for years." She takes a deep breath and stands. "I'm very willing to turn over my grade book, if you'd like to pursue this complaint."

The dean frowns. "Complaints are not the only thing we consider in this review. We need to look at the cost effectiveness of any program or course. Because of budget constraints, the board is considering dropping some courses next year. No decision will be made until the end of June." He stands and offers Nikki his hand, not in friendship but in dismissal.

Nikki ignores his hand and leaves his office, feeling momentarily useless in terms of the investigation and her employment. But maybe she can be of some help to Edmond Long's widow.

CHAPTER 16

Polly Long lives with her two little girls in a housing project next to the chemical plants in Steel City. Nikki takes off her sunglasses as she drives down the narrow road between the buildings and parks her car in a space perpendicular to the row houses. The late model Cadillac parked in the space next to hers strikes her as an odd choice for this low-rent area. She knocks on the weathered door of number 36 but gets no answer. Hearing muffled yelling inside, she knocks harder. She slowly opens the unlocked door. Two men in their late sixties, wearing expensive, dark blue suits, are in the living room forcing an exhausted Polly Long to lift her arms into the air. They are shouting, "Renounce the devil! Pray harder! Amen! Amen!" Two young children are crying as they cower in the kitchen doorway.

"What's going on here?" Nikki shouts over the din.

The men abruptly stop yelling and turn to her in unison. Polly runs to the two children.

"And just who are you?" the church elder to the left asks.

Nikki stands her ground. "I'm Reverend Barnes, the university chaplain. I was one of Edmond's professors."

"And what are you doing here?" the second church elder demands.

Nikki turns to Polly Long and lowers her voice. "I've come to offer condolences, Mrs. Long, and to see if you or the children need anything." She shoots an authoritative look back to the men and asks, "Just what are you doing here?"

The first elder, with the bushy eyebrows, answers, "We're elders of the Pentecostal Fellowship Chapel. Mrs. Long is a sister in our congregation."

The second, sporting a close-trimmed beard, continues, "We came to give our sister and her children our support."

By this time, Polly Long has her youngest child in her arms and the other one by the hand. More composed, she now has some control back, but is barely audible when, in a tired, hoarse voice, she says, "That's not my church. Eddie was the only fool in this family. I need some money and food for my children. I need to bury Eddie...and buy some milk." Sobbing now, she buries her face in the baby girl's dress.

Nikki steels herself again and addresses the men. "Did you bring money or food for the children?"

Trimmed Beard answers, "We don't have funds to provide those kinds of services."

Nikki tries again. "Did you make arrangements for the funeral?"

"We never said we would make those arrangements," Bushy Brows replies.

Nikki is about to lose her temper. "Then I suggest you get the hell out of here and don't come back, or I'll call the police."

Bushy Brows takes a few steps toward Nikki. "And what makes you think you can speak for Mrs. Long?"

Nikki senses a standoff coming, but Polly raises her voice. "Get out of my home!"

The men don't move. Trimmed Beard says, "Mrs. Long, that's the devil talking, you're upset. We'll pray, and you'll feel better."

Polly slowly and deliberately puts her baby down next to

the other child. Then, mustering her remaining strength, she runs at the men, slapping and punching both of them, all the while screaming, "Get out! Get out! You hypocritical bastards. You're the devils!"

Nikki joins the melee and tries to pull Polly back. Polly keeps yelling, "Make them go away! I don't want them in my house!"

Nikki holds Polly back and glares at the men. "I told you I'd call the police, and I will."

The men look at each other and nod gravely. They start to exit, but Bushy Brows turns back. "Because of this behavior, we will no longer be able to help you, Mrs. Long. You will be dropped from our church rolls." They slam the door behind them, and Polly runs to her children.

Nikki looks at the young mother. She's about twenty years old and wears a washed-out, cotton house dress. Her long brown hair is pulled back in a ponytail held with a rubber band. Her eyes are red and puffy from crying. The baby in her arms is less than a year old and is holding a slimy-looking pacifier in her hand. The other little girl, about two years old, hangs on to her mother's dress, sucks her thumb, and whimpers.

Nikki moves closer to Polly and the children. "I'm sorry about Edmond's death. What can I do for you and the children?"

Polly sits almost trancelike on the shabby parlor sofa, one child on her lap, the other next to her. Several toys are piled in one corner of the room, and a drying rack full of baby clothes is in another corner. Polly looks up at Nikki. "Eddie told me about you." The baby in her arms starts fussing, and Polly starts crying.

Nikki bends down in front of the sofa, trying to comfort Polly. "Is anyone helping you at all, Mrs. Long?"

Polly answers through her tears, "There's no one. My folks are back in Ohio. It's just me and the kids."

"Can I get something for you?" Nikki asks as she stands upright again.

"The elders came last night, but all they wanted to do was pray. I told them I needed food for the babies. I don't have any money. I don't know if I'll even get Eddie's pay this week." She gets up and walks the whimpering baby back and forth.

Nikki listens as Polly talks about her husband. She met Edmond as a freshman at the university, fell in love with his charismatic ideals, and gave up her educational goals for Edmond's. "I'm so tired, really tired." The frequent repetition of this phrase reveals her physical and mental exhaustion.

Polly stops talking and looks directly at Nikki. "Eddie prayed for you a lot, Reverend. He thought you were misguided."

"I didn't always agree with Edmond. I thought some of his ideas were...," she hunts for the right word, "...too conservative."

"He thought you were lost. I never imagined you coming to see me. You know Eddie gave half of everything he earned to the Pentecostal Chapel. Even when we needed the money. I called them last night and wanted someone to go with me to identify the body. When I saw Eddie, I almost fainted. The elders grabbed me, told me not to give in to the devil. I just wanted to touch Eddie one last time, but they dragged me away."

She sits back down on the sofa. "They kept asking about money. I said we didn't have any. Eddie even cashed in his insurance for the building fund. They got mad, made me pray with them. The kids were crying. They said it was the devil's work. We prayed and prayed and you know what? They weren't praying for Eddie; they were praying for money."

Nikki goes into the kitchen and warms the last bottle in the refrigerator for little Beth. She finds a small juice pack in the cupboard for Sarah and makes a cup of tea for Polly, who then puts the children into the bedroom for a nap.

Nikki pours Polly a second cup of tea and waits for an opportunity to ask some questions. Sipping her own tea, she calmly asks, "Do you know of anyone who wanted Edmond dead?"

Polly takes another swallow before answering. "He wasn't well liked, especially when he got into one of his righteous moods. But most people ignored him."

"What about at work? Did he fight with anyone there?" Nikki asks cautiously.

"Maybe, Dr. Sullivan. Eddie was always forcing pamphlets on her, preaching to her. And there was Eugene Blake. He always teased Eddie. Telling him about dead babies just to upset him. Once, Eddie told me he couldn't turn the other cheek anymore. He told Eugene he was going to tell Lisa Holt what a perverted person he was. They had a fight in the common room."

"Why would Edmond threaten to go to Lisa Holt?" Nikki hides her surprise at this revelation.

"Eddie knew her from classes they were in together. They were friends. She even came to chapel with us a few times," Polly continues nonchalantly.

Nikki can't believe what she is hearing. "Why would telling Lisa anything make Eugene back off?"

"Lisa works for Dr. Peterson," Polly tries to explain. "He's sponsoring Eugene for medical school. A wrong word and he could lose his sponsorship. But, she'd never say a wrong word. Eddie knew Eugene and Lisa had been dating. They've been going together for almost a year."

"Did you say Lisa and Eugene were dating?" Nikki can't imagine Edmond not knowing about Lisa's affair with Sheldon Peterson. Maybe it was too unchristian to repeat to his wife.

Nikki doesn't want to burden Polly with any more questions but does want to help her. She phones Helen Wheeler at Episcopal Charities and explains the situation. Helen will make funeral arrangements and get Polly and the children back to Ohio. In the meantime, she promises to send over a grief volunteer and a food voucher to see them through the crisis.

At nine that evening, the volunteer arrives, and Nikki drives home. Her main agenda for the rest of the evening is emptying her mind of everything. However, she does wonder what Max learned when he questioned Ginni.

Ginni is in her thoughts now. Whenever her mind is at rest, she sees her face, feels her lips, and yearns for her company. She hasn't felt this longing to be with someone since Mo. The ghosts of Vietnam are in their last skirmish in Nikki's head.

CHAPTER 17

Max arrives early for his appointment with Virginia Clayton. He introduces himself to the suite secretary and continues down the hallway and into the common room. "Dr. Clayton." She looks up from her work, and he continues, "Like to ask a few more questions."

Dr. Clayton closes the patient record she's working on and gives Max her full attention. "Is this about Edmond Long's murder, Sergeant?"

Max nods, smiles, and takes the seat opposite her at the worktable. Pausing to take out his notebook and pen, he asks, "Where were you last night around 7:30?"

"I am sure you already asked...," she stops abruptly, not changing her facial expression. "I am sure you have already talked to Professor Barnes, and she told you we had dinner together at the Checkered Table. From there, I went directly to Mercy Hospital and had a consultation that lasted until after eleven, then I went home."

"Who was the doctor you consulted with and the patient's name?" Max keeps writing. "Anyone see you enter your apartment? Someone who could vouch for the time?"

Ginni doesn't show her annoyance but quietly answers, "I was called in on the consultation by Dr. Anna Muscato. The patient's name is Spencer Shaw." She thinks for a moment before continuing. "Mrs. Fister, a woman in my building, walks her dog every night at 11:30, right after the 11 o'clock news. I saw her last night, and we said hello. You can ask her."

"Count on it. You're pretty exact about your times," Max says, still not looking up from his writing.

"Doctors are scheduled people. We try to be exact. Sometimes scheduling means the difference between life and death," Ginni says softly.

Max seems to ignore this last comment and stares at Ginni. "You said you and Shari Sullivan were friends." He flips some notebook pages. "The last time we spoke you admitted having some loud arguments with her here at work."

Ginni maintains her soft, even tone. "There was only one argument, and yes, the argument was very loud. I felt she was making a fool of herself and told her so. Shari was ready to sell out everything she believed in for someone she didn't know very well. I was angry, and we argued about it."

"That wasn't very professional," Max criticizes.

"We're human. We get frustrated with our friends and their lack of judgment, just like anyone else." Ginni is still unruffled.

"What about Susan Peterson?" He looks for a reaction and doesn't get any. "How do you get along with her?"

Ginni stares back at him. "I don't really know her. I only see her at formal gatherings with her husband."

"How'd you feel about her affair with Dr. Sullivan?" Max asks.

Ginni can no longer hide her feelings. "I'm trying to tell you, I thought it was professional suicide for Shari. But it made her happy, so I never brought up the subject again after that argument."

"So, you fought about her affair." Max lays on the pressure.

"No." Ginni bites at her lower lip and breaks the rhythm of her answers. "As I said, the argument we had was a result of my concern for her." Ginni begins to fiddle with her pen.

"Were you jealous of Mrs. Peterson?" Max keeps pushing.

"No," Ginni says quietly but firmly, as she tries to end the questions.

Max plays a hunch, suddenly asking a question he didn't plan to ask. "You own a gun, Dr. Clayton?"

Ginni hesitates. "Yes. I have one..." She nervously rubs her right temple. "As you probably already know."

"Is it a thirty-eight?" Max asks.

Ginni stops rubbing her temple and explains, "I really don't know. The gun could be a thirty-eight. My father sent it to me after I told him about several rapes on campus. He was worried and thought I needed protection."

"Where's the gun now?" Max asks.

"I'm not sure." Ginni feels a flush on her face. "In my apartment somewhere. I put the gun away as soon as I got it."

"I'd like to see the gun." Max pauses. "I can get a search warrant if I have to."

"That won't be necessary." Ginni's voice has a slight shake now. "I'll find the gun, and you can pick it up tomorrow. Or, I can bring it to your office."

"Bring it in tomorrow." He makes some lengthy notes in his notebook again, forcing Ginni to sit in silence and wait. As he finishes writing, he doesn't look up but asks, "You friendly with Dr. Peterson?"

"We are not friendly." She's exact with her choice of words. "We have a business relationship. He is chief of medicine, which means he is my boss."

"You ever friendly with him?" Max pushes.

Ginni measures each word again. "Not that I think it has any bearing on the case, or that it is any of your business, but I would have to say Dr. Peterson and I were never friendly or even politically compatible."

"If your relationship with him is less than compatible, why's he naming you chief of family medicine at the Medical Center?" Max fires his questions. "Why isn't he getting someone who agrees with him politically?"

Ginni is momentarily taken off guard by this latest revelation. "As far as I'm concerned, that's just a rumor, and it has gone around before. Shari and I used to joke about who he might pick." She stops, noticing her last comment caught all of Max's attention.

"If the rumor is true," she continues, "the main reason Peterson would pick me is because I'm a good doctor. I have a large, established practice at the center, and I am board certified. I don't feel a need to do abortions, which seems to be what Dr. Peterson prefers for the center. He incorrectly interprets my position to be anti-adoption, which I am not. But then, Dr. Peterson is somewhat baffling himself, since the center will no longer do abortions, but I hear that his private clinic will do them."

Max listens attentively, then asks, "If Dr. Sullivan was alive, would you be competing with her for the position of chief of medicine?"

"Probably," Ginni says flatly, not knowing what to expect next.

"How badly do you want the promotion?" Max asks.

"Not enough to kill a friend." Ginni feels her throat tighten on the words.

Max puts his notebook and pen away and sits back in his chair. He links his fingers together and rests them on his stomach. "You're an intelligent woman, Dr. Clayton, and quite resourceful."

Ginni sits back also and puts her pen in the pocket of her white lab coat, but doesn't smile. "Those should be compliments, but I get the feeling they are more like concessions."

Max speaks slowly, thinking before each word. "Maybe they are concessions. Reverend Barnes is a personal friend of mine."

Ginni's taken aback by the change in direction. "Yes. She told me you were together in Vietnam."

"Yeah, we went through some bad times together. She's quite a woman, and quite a priest." He looks again for a reaction, then continues, "Nikki had a tough time in Nam. Did pastoral care work with the dying. Not just the soldiers, but the civilians too. The Rev wanted to help the women. Vietnamese women had it bad. Kept trying to help, but could only help 'em die."

Ginni listens with interest and responds, "She hasn't said much about Vietnam. We don't talk much about her life."

Max reminisces, "No. She won't. I tried to find her when I came stateside, but she disappeared. Even made formal inquiries, but no luck. Then she turns up here, tells me she's on leave from the priesthood. But, she's still a priest. Ya know what I mean?"

Ginni feels the barbs in his voice again. "No. Just what do you mean?"

Max shoots back, "Nikki loses perspective sometimes and gets overly involved in people's problems."

Ginni curbs her rising annoyance. "What does this have to do with me?"

Max sits up straight, putting both hands on the table. "Nikki Barnes is a good friend. I don't want her hurt. So I think you should back off."

Ginni glares at Max but still doesn't raise her voice. "My relationship with Nikki is none of your business, Sergeant Mullen. And if you are really her friend, you will talk to her, not me." She stops, knowing how easy it would be to say something she doesn't want to share at this time. "If you don't have any other questions about the investigation, I do have a lot of work to finish."

Max stands up. "I'll see you tomorrow. Don't forget the gun." He leaves abruptly.

As he walks to his car, he realizes he's glad he told Nikki to stay away from Ginni Clayton. He doesn't trust the doctor's motives, or her seemingly perfect alibi. He wouldn't choose

Clayton to be Nikki's *friend*, not that he was asked. Nikki wouldn't like him butting into her business, but he owes her for saving his life in Nam. He wants to repay her, even if it only means running interference in her personal life.

CHAPTER 18

Nikki feels utterly frustrated. Why did she promise Max she wouldn't contact Ginni? She takes a long hot bath and puts on her favorite pajamas—white cotton with blue stripes. Right out of the Penney's catalog of men's fashion. They hang loose all over, and wearing them without underwear makes her feel free and relaxed.

She sits cross-legged on the sofa, with Fluffy on a nearby chair. After a while, she puts down the reports she's working on and clicks off the lamp. The room is dark except for a smaller lamp on an end table and the lit candle in the dove-shaped terra-cotta candle holder on her personal altar.

Feeling small and useless in relation to the events that have happened in the last few days, she seems cut off from anyone interested in her life or thoughts. She huddles into a corner of the sofa, wrapping the cushions tightly around herself in a hug.

The doorbell breaks this momentary embrace. She isn't expecting Max but in her present mood welcomes the company. There's no need to cover up her odd pajamas since Max has seen her in worse, and less. During surprise attacks at the base hospital, the tropical heat made the bunkers feel like steam ovens and forced everyone to strip to as little as possible.

She pads to the door with bare feet, thinking Max might

even get a laugh out of her outfit. After checking the peephole and starting to unlock the deadbolt, she knows it's too late to run for a robe. She opens the door.

"Don't you ever ask who it is before you open the door?" Ginni quietly asks, smiling as she enters the house.

Nikki steps to the side. "I saw you through the peephole and was afraid you'd disappear when you realized you were lost."

"I'm not lost." Ginni wears her trenchcoat over a mauve, long-sleeved, tailored dress. "I'm actually feeling great, now that I'm here with you."

Nikki's smile is warm and welcoming. "I'll take your coat. Come into the living room."

As Ginni hands over her coat, she asks, "Has anyone ever told you that you have interesting clothing?"

"I'll turn on the light and get my robe." She crosses in front of Ginni, who steps into her path.

"Forget the lights," Ginni whispers, "and you don't need the robe. I like the cut of your pajama top." The oversized top is loose and open down to Nikki's breasts.

They're only inches from each other now. Nikki takes a deep breath and wraps Ginni in her arms. The space between their eager lips disappears, as their mouths meet. Nikki tightens her embrace as she feels Ginni's hands move across her shoulders, over her neck, and through her hair.

Their eyes and thoughts are fixed only on each other.

Nikki's open mouth moves to Ginni's. Soft lips pressing harder, tongues sliding and searching. Time...even life itself... stands still, as they continue to inhale each other...kissing deeply, like lost lovers finding each other after a long separation.

Ginni is first to loosen her embrace and move slightly away. "I could use something to drink."

"I have just the thing. Make yourself comfortable and don't mind Fluffy. She'll probably just ignore you."

Ginni enters the dimly lit room and gives Fluffy a gentle

pat on the head. Seeing the candle-lit altar, she walks over to it. The small, pine pedestal table, made by Nikki's father, was given to her when she returned from Nam. The white flower-patterned silk scarf that covers the table belonged to her grandmother. Her Uncle Louis, who was custodian of the scarf, left it to her when he died. He was an Episcopalian priest and probably the most influential person in Nikki's growing-up years. It was his old worn Bible that she considered her most valuable possession. His Bible was with her on all the trips to the EVAC hospital and the civilian hospitals, whenever she was requested or needed to pray for, or with, someone. The Bible was her companion when she was alone, or frightened, or suffering the unbearable pain of grief.

Ginni moves away from the altar and sits on the sofa. Nikki returns with glasses and a bottle of homemade red wine. "I've been saving this for a special occasion. One of my old parishioners handpicked the grapes and made the wine. A very unique blend, he told me."

Ginni, who's sitting at the opposite end of the sofa, takes a long sip of wine. "So, this is what good communion wine tastes like."

Nikki also takes a drink and sits down. "Not communion wine, just good wine."

Ginni's face reflects a new seriousness, as she slides closer. "Is this relationship going to be a problem for you, being a priest, I mean? I need to know now, before it goes any further."

Nikki smiles. "Being a priest is my vocation, my job. I made a choice years ago to help people connect to their own spirit. I love the job. It brings hope and purpose into a sometimes crazy world. But I learned a long time ago that being a priest doesn't exempt me from pain or joy. Did you know the Holy Spirit is traditionally the feminine side of God? That's the side I try to serve. I know She wants me to live life fully. My job isn't a problem for me...what about for you?"

Ginni's green eyes sparkle as she takes another sip and

says, "It's not a problem now. But, I suppose you'll always be running around in that funny collar, with candles lit all over the house. And I suppose you begin...everything...with a prayer."

They both laugh as Nikki puts her glass down. "I guess I'm always praying for something." She reaches behind Ginni to turn off the light. Ginni touches her arm and stops her. "Your friend Max came to visit me today."

"I know." Nikki sits back, giving Ginni her full attention. "He had some questions to ask about the murders."

"Don't you want to ask me those same questions?" Ginni fingers a fold in her dress.

Nikki's silent for a moment. "Okay..." Then she blurts out, "Did you ever sleep with Susan Peterson?"

Ginni does a double take. "What? That's what you want to ask? I thought you wanted to know about Peterson supposedly planning to name me chief of family medicine. Or maybe about the gun I own, since it might be the gun that killed Long."

"You own a gun?" A shiver runs down the back of Nikki's neck, but she ignores the warning. "The only question nagging me all day is did you sleep with Peterson's wife?"

"No! I never slept with her. Where did you get that idea? I told you the other night, I haven't been with anyone in years. I thought you believed me." Ginni raises her voice, a noticeable contrast to her usual calm demeanor.

"I *did* believe you. I just...I don't know." Nikki sips more wine, beginning to feel its warm effects. "Lisa Holt paid me a nasty little visit and said Susan Peterson slept with everyone at the Medical Center."

"Lisa Holt's a tramp." Ginni is almost at half-smile. "And she is probably the only one who sleeps with almost everyone at the center. I hardly know Susan except to say hello to at mandatory staff cocktail parties."

Nikki looks into her wine glass, avoiding eye contact. "I'm sorry, I guess I was jealous."

Ginni runs her finger around the rim of her glass. "Your friend Max wants me to stay away from you. Should I worry about him?"

Nikki, relieved at the change in subject, starts to laugh. "My God! He must think he's Humphrey Bogart or something. He's got nerve. Old Max can't help it. Ever since Nam, he's been my guardian. He just doesn't realize what he's protecting me from, or maybe he does. Maybe that's what he's worried about."

"Then maybe we should give him something to really worry about." Ginni puts her glass down and moves toward Nikki. She cups Nikki's pale face in her hands. They kiss long and passionately. Ginni's tongue traces Nikki's lips and moves farther into her mouth. She puts one arm around Nikki's neck and slides her other hand into the opening of Nikki's pajama top, caressing her breast.

Nikki's heart is pounding as she pulls Ginni closer. The women lean back against the lumpy, uncooperative sofa, trying to get comfortable. As Ginni shifts from an awkward position, she accidentally knees Nikki in the stomach. "Sorry."

"I'm all right, really." Nikki laughs and rubs the sore spot. "This poor excuse for a sofa came with the rental."

Ginni doesn't want to lose the mood. She almost whispers, "Is the bed as bad as the sofa?"

Nikki bolts upright, answering more with her movement than her words. "The bed is great! I mean, the bed works fine. You'll like the bed." She laughs nervously.

Nikki leads Ginni by the hand into the sparsely decorated bedroom. The only furniture is an old brass bed, a chest of drawers, and an army trunk with a small ginger jar lamp on it.

She turns on the lamp, which casts a soft light over the bed. Nikki turns into Ginni's arms, her eyes filled with desire. As they kiss, Nikki slowly runs her hands down Ginni's back to her butt, where she lets them rest. The two women sway to music only they can hear. Nikki pulls Ginni's hips tight against her.

Suddenly there's a loud meow, and Fluffy jumps up on the bed. Both women laugh and take a deep breath. Ginni pulls away gently. "Would you like to help me get my dress off?"

Electricity pulses through Nikki's body as she slowly unbuttons the dress. She doesn't look at Ginni's body. Her eyes are transfixed by Ginni's eyes...and mouth. The rhythm of her pulse quickens, as Ginni reaches over and unbuttons the rest of Nikki's white and blue pajama top. The top falls open. Ginni's eyes move slowly down to Nikki's breasts. She smiles, then tries to concentrate on slipping out of her own dress, pushing it over her hips to the floor.

Nikki's eyes follow the dress now. She quickly picks it up, folds it neatly, and places it on the chest of drawers—an automatic response from rigid army and seminary training.

Ginni sees humor in this inappropriately timed neatness, but uses the few moments to remove her lace-trimmed black slip, bikini panties, and skimpy bra. When Nikki turns back, her heart beats a passionate rhythm in her ears, shutting out all other sounds. The sight of Ginni's nude body releases a flood of new feelings — paralyzing and mesmerizing at the same time.

Ginni is more in control. She reaches over and removes Nikki's pajama top, letting it fall to the carpeted floor. Nikki takes Ginni's hand and kisses her fingertips, all the while drinking in the beauty of this lovely woman—who could, nevertheless, be a murderer. Moving closer now, Ginni slowly pulls down the baggy pajama bottoms. Something primal—a raw passion —stirs their hungry spirits. Holding each other—breast to breast—they watch the soft light playing off their shadows—bouncing off the sheen of Nikki's white skin and Ginni's darker hue. Their bodies merge.

Moments pass and Ginni urges Fluffy off the bed. She pulls down the bed covers and quickly slips under. Never taking her eyes off Nikki, she pats the bed, and Nikki slides in next to her. Slowly, deliberately, Nikki moves on top of Ginni...kissing her shoulders...neck...ear lobe. Lips skimming across Ginni's cheek to her waiting mouth...wanting more. All senses are reduced to touch, electric and white-hot. She caresses Ginni's breasts with her lips. Nipples respond, hard and erect.

Ginni shudders...quickly searching for Nikki's breast. Uncontrollable waves of pleasure ripple down Nikki's body...small explosions thrust her hips forward. She slides across Ginni's moist body, wanting to know and feel every inch of her. Hands, mouths, bodies intertwine, moving in unison like a quickening tide.

Nikki loses track of where her body begins and Ginni's ends. No longer separate...just a mass of hot, sweet wetness. Nikki can't hear or speak.

Nikki enters Ginni...slowly, creating sweet waves of pleasure. She listens to Ginni's short, shallow breaths, sees the pleasure on her face. Ginni kisses Nikki harder, then pulls away almost screaming, as her body grows taut, finally exploding in bursts of orgasmic fireworks.

Nikki holds her tenderly, though lost in her own burning, undulating desire. Minutes later, her breathing quickens, her hips arch upward and begin to move rhythmically. Ginni reaches down between Nikki's legs, exploring her...teasing ever so gently...then harder...then slipping inside, matching Nikki's rhythm with her own. Cosmic waves of pleasure wash over her and suddenly, Nikki hears herself scream, as she is catapulted to the crest of ecstasy.

"Nikki? Ginni asks in a panicky voice.

Nikki opens her eyes to Ginni's worried expression and practically coos, "I'm fine...and you're wonderful."

"It's been so long, I was afraid I'd forgotten how. I thought I hurt you." Ginni starts to cry. Big sobs shake her body as tears roll down her cheeks.

Nikki leans up on an elbow. "Don't cry, please, Ginni. What's the matter?"

Ginni now laughs and cries simultaneously. "I don't know. I just need to cry, I guess. The feelings are too much." She snuggles into Nikki, pulling the covers up over them.

Nikki takes a moment to think about how perfectly God created woman—each curve, mound, and valley a flowing line of endless beauty.

A deep contentment envelops them as they lie together, Ginni's head resting softly on Nikki's chest.

CHAPTER 19

Nikki wakes first and stares at the sleeping Ginni, very aware she's falling hard for this woman. She'd never expected to feel this sweetness again. She'd resigned herself to a life of painful reminders of lost love, not this overpowering joy. She wonders if her grieving is finally over, and she can share her heart again.

After showering, Nikki reenters the bedroom and finds Ginni awake but still in bed. "Good morning," Ginni grins. "Come here for a minute. There's something I want to ask you."

Nikki can't help herself—she smiles broadly and walks to the bed. Ginni starts untying the sash on Nikki's robe, but she stops her, gently holding her hands. "Just a minute. I've got a nine o'clock appointment, and I'm sure you have early patients."

Ginni sits up, keeping the covers around her body. "This is strictly medical curiosity. I noticed something last night, and I want to ask you about it. As your doctor, I think you should cooperate."

Nikki thinks this is funny and lets Ginni untie the sash and push off the robe. In doing this, Ginni drops the covers and bares her naked breasts. Beautiful breasts, Nikki thinks, feeling an electric charge surge through her.

"These scars...," Ginni touches a three-inch oblong-shaped scar on the left side of Nikki's chest and a smaller one by the right side of her waist. "I've never seen surgery like this. And there's another scar on your back. What are they?"

Nikki leans in and hugs Ginni, kissing her cheek. "And I thought you were concentrating on something besides medicine last night. What a romantic!"

"Well, you said you're always praying, maybe I'm always examining." Ginni gets serious. "Please, tell me about the scars."

Nikki fastens her robe again and sits on the edge of the bed. Ginni wraps the covers back around herself. There's an awkward silence in the room, and Nikki finally speaks. "They're bullet holes, Doctor. You probably haven't had the opportunity to see many. They're plain old bullet holes, though nicely mended."

"Did you get them in Vietnam?" Ginni persists.

"Yeah, a long time ago." Nikki dearly wants to end this conversation.

Ginni moves closer. "This one came close to your lungs and heart." She puts her hand on Nikki's chest.

Nikki puts her arm around Ginni. "I guess I'm lucky. I'm fine, Doctor, really. I can have my x-rays sent over."

Ginni leans in and kisses her gently, then leans back. "You don't want to talk about Vietnam, do you?"

Nikki gives her a quick kiss. "No. I can't talk about it right now." She turns away but doesn't leave the bed.

Ginni reaches over, turning Nikki's face toward her. "I want you to share your past. Your past is part of who you are."

Nikki avoids her eyes, her face suddenly steels into the protective mask of the surviving vet. She softly touches the wound on her chest. "This was my ticket out. I'm not sure I would have left Vietnam unless they carried me out...Max was with me."

She stares at a blank spot on the bedroom wall. "I had three months left until the end of my tour of duty. I'd already decided to go stateside for a month or two and then request another tour. We both had the day off, and I promised Max I'd help him take some 'borrowed' medical supplies to a civilian hospital in

Xuan Loc. A friend of his with the Agency for International Development was working at the hospital.

"The temperature was over a hundred degrees again. We decided to take a rather desolate dirt road, considered one of the main highways in that part of the country. Max was driving, his automatic rifle next to him on the driver's side. I was wearing my forty-five, even though we women weren't supposed to be armed in Vietnam.

"A tree's down in the road." Nikki talks as if she's there. "Not unusual, but my body goes on alert. In-country, your instincts take over. Max has to stop the jeep...we'll try and move the tree. But before we can get out of the jeep, a dozen Viet Cong rush out of the adjoining field, shooting. They're wearing camouflage grass and brush on their hats. The field brush is alive and moving.

"Max is hit before he can reach his gun. He slumps over the door and falls to the ground. I practically jump over him, grab the rifle, then try to drag him out of the open. I pull him to the wooded area on the opposite side of the road from the fields...from the Viet Cong...from the living brush that's shooting at us.

"The gunfire is deafening. I'm terrified. I pray. Holy God Almighty protect... Suddenly, I feel this pressure on my back. It turns into a fiery pain as the first bullet hits me. I almost have Max moved into the cover of the underbrush, but I must stop and return fire. I squeeze the rifle trigger and spray the whole area of the field where the Cong are.

"I smell my fear. Then I feel a second bullet hit my side. Suddenly, there's movement behind me...in the wooded area...where I thought Max would be safe. I hear more guns firing. I try to position myself over Max. I want to be a bunker for him, to protect him. But when I kneel down...the third bullet hits its target. This one sends a searing pain into my chest, like a hot poker stuck in and never taken out."

Ginni holds Nikki's hand, tears flood her eyes.

"Before I lose consciousness, I see the men behind us. They're soldiers, American soldiers, stepping out of the woods and firing at the Viet Cong. They're our men, a recon unit out on patrol. They heard the gunfire...they radioed for a chopper...they saved our lives.

"I vaguely remember being flown back to the 90th. Father Gambino praying over me, Max crying. A longer flight to Fort Derussy, Hawaii, where I finally come out of the stupor created by pain killers. I receive a Medal of Commendation. There's another flight to Fitzsimmons Army Hospital in Denver, where I get some physical therapy and an honorable discharge. Due to the severity of my wounds, I can't return to active military service." Nikki stops talking, hearing her voice cracking. She rocks back and forth.

Without saying anything, Ginni leans over to hold her again. Nikki slowly pulls back from the embrace. With effort, she pushes back the memories and finally changes back to her earlier cheerful behavior. "I really do have an appointment at nine."

"And I have to get home, change, and then see my patients." Ginni squeezes Nikki's arm. "Will I see you tonight?"

Nikki smiles back. "Absolutely!"

"Let's meet at my place, just for equality's sake." Ginni pauses. "And maybe because this secondhand mattress nearly killed my back."

They both laugh, and Nikki tries to remember the last time she started a day with laughter. This morning feels so good, she has to hold back tears.

They're about to leave for their various appointments when the phone rings.

"Good morning, Nicolette." Barrett's voice is loud and clear. "I couldn't wait any longer. I miss you."

"Barrett. I can't talk. I'm late for an appointment." Nikki

doesn't want to be rude.

"But, I've been thinking of you all night." Barrett is settling in for a long chat. "Have you been thinking of me?"

"I have to leave now." Nikki ignores the question, trying to rush the goodbye.

Ginni walks over, puts her hand on Nikki's shoulder, and kisses her on the cheek. "See you later."

Barrett obviously has sensitive hearing. "Who the hell's that? Is somebody there with you? That doesn't sound like a fat cop."

Nikki shakes her head and answers, "It's a friend who's just leaving, and I am too."

"Some woman's with you! I'm not allowed to see you, but you've got some other woman with you! I love you—I told you I did. So, I'm feeling sorry for you being all alone, and you're with somebody else!" Barrett is near screaming now.

Nikki's heard more than enough. "Maybe you need to meet some new friends. People more your age. I have to go—goodbye." She hangs up the phone, still hearing Barrett's protests.

CHAPTER 20

Though she drives faster than she likes, Nikki is late arriving at Max's office. She goes directly to the interrogation room. The oversized Eugene Blake sits at an old, scarred, wooden conference table, which bears the marks of many suspects. His face is a mixture of hate and sarcasm. Max sits across from Blake and motions for Nikki to sit next to him.

"Thank you for voluntarily coming down to answer some questions that might help us with this case," Max begins, then abruptly adds, "You own a gun, Mr. Blake? Maybe an army pistol?"

Blake spits back a response. "I worked in a Texas army hospital. I didn't need a gun, and I don't own a gun."

Max continues his questions. "Where were you Tuesday night around 7:30?"

"With a friend, studying. We were in my apartment from six to at least eleven."

Nikki jumps in. "What's your friend's name?"

"I didn't know you were still playing cop, Professor." Blake turns to Max. "Do I have to answer her questions?"

"Answer mine!" Max raises his voice. "Who's the friend?"

Blake glares at Nikki. "I was studying with Lisa Holt. Just ask her."

Nikki looks at Max. Blake smirks and says, "She's a helluva

lot smarter than both of you."

Ignoring the barb, Nikki calms her voice and asks, "Did you get along with Edmond Long?"

Blake shoots back the answer. "Long was a sniveling little fundamentalist shithead. He was only good for cleaning up garbage."

"Did you get along?" Max repeats. "You ever fight, throw punches, anything like that?"

Blake smiles. "He told me every day that I would burn in hell, and every day I laughed in his face."

"Why the hatred?" Max asks.

"I like helping with the abortions. Gynecology is going to be my specialty. I kept telling Eddie about it because it made him crazy." Blake laughs as he says, "I'd even make up stories about the fetuses gasping for air. That really drove him wild."

Nikki decides to change course with the questions. "Did you know there won't be any more abortions at the Medical Center, that Dr. Peterson will be making some significant changes at the Medical Center?"

Blake seems puzzled by the question. "Yeah, I know."

"So what's going to happen to your specialty interest?" Nikki asks.

Blake's smug again. "Dr. Peterson is taking good care of me. Eddie Long had nothing to do with ending abortions at the Medical Center. That's part of a larger plan."

Nikki wants more information. "How is Peterson taking good care of you?"

"It's none of your business. I'm proud of my relationship with Dr. Peterson. While he runs the alternative clinic at Memorial Medical Center, I'll run the private clinic on the East Side, under his supervision, of course."

Nikki has one last question. "What do you think of Dr. Clayton? Did you know she may be put in charge of family medicine."

Unsure of why she's asking this, Blake replies, "I don't have any problem with Clayton. She's a little full of herself, and her practice is pretty boring. But, I agree with Dr. Peterson, she's a good choice."

Nikki turns to Max. "I don't have any more questions, except...," she turns back. "Do you always wear Cool Water?"

"Why? Is it a crime to wear aftershave?" Blake is obviously annoyed. "This is getting ridiculous."

Max takes over the questioning, saving his last volley until now. "We know about the assault charges in Texas, Eddie, and the hospital stay. You used a gun to beat that woman."

Blake's face flushes red. "That was a long time ago. I was suffering from a lot of stress, which led to a substance abuse problem. The United States Army put me in a hospital and cured me. No civil charges were ever brought against me." He holds out his arms. "See, I was rehabilitated. It was a fuckin' miracle, Reverend." He takes a few minutes to calm himself. "Besides, she was a Mexican whore. The army confiscated the gun." He takes a deep breath. "Anything else from you wizards?"

Max breaks eye contact with Blake. He stands and walks calmly around the table. He bends down and suddenly grabs Blake by the collar, lifting him a few inches. "You're free to go now, but we may have more questions, so don't even think of leaving town, Mr. Blake." With that, Max shoves Blake back in his chair.

Blake ignores Max and says nothing. He rises slowly from his chair, snickers, and swaggers out of the interrogation room, patting down his collar.

Max leans back in his chair and opens a folder containing Blake's military records. "Says here, the military police found him in his apartment, high on peyote, with stockpiled weapons, explosives, and *Soldier of Fortune* magazines. They locked him in a hospital for eighteen months and gave him a medical discharge. And here's the kicker, he went to college on a GI loan."

Nikki shakes her head. "And no one checked his history,

not the university, not the Medical Center. And he's certified to see patients."

"Legally, he's right. No one pressed charges. He suffered from an illness. When they thought he was cured, they released him." Max closes the folder.

Nikki looks at Max. "So, is Blake our man? How does he connect to the two murder victims?"

"I'll bet money he was the one that cracked your head open," Max says. "He could even be the killer, but he's awfully casual and open about hating both victims."

"But why attack me?" Nikki rubs the cut on her head. "He hardly knows me. I couldn't be that much of a threat."

"Someone thinks you are." Max slaps the table for emphasis. "They might think you can figure something out, or maybe you know something already. My money says Eugene Blake is the guy who attacked you in your office."

"I can't imagine what it is he thinks I know." Nikki slides back in her chair.

Max pats her shoulder. "Don't worry. It'll come to you. You need to be really careful, Rev. We've stirred up Blake. He could get nervous and dangerous. Be on guard. Speaking of which, I'm glad I told you to stay away from those two women."

Max opens another folder. "Henry jotted down a coupla notes from his unofficial peek at Fairburn's juvenile record." Max pauses for a moment. He's grateful that Henry has a contact with access to sealed documents, and he feels no remorse about using the information to solve a case. He moves his finger down the sheet of paper as he reads.

"She was picked up at fifteen for trespassing. Some kinda rowdy party when the parents were out of town. Later that same year, she's picked up for assault. She hit two officers with a pipe when they tried to question her in her car at three in the morning. Broke a finger on one guy."

He looks at Nikki, who shrugs her shoulders. At this

point, nothing about the outrageous Barrett surprises her.

Max has one more comment. "As for Virginia Clayton, did you know she owns a thirty-eight? Says her father sent the gun for her protection. Supposed to bring it in today, so the lab can check it out. Now, why do I think she won't be able to find it?"

Nikki ignores his last remark.

CHAPTER 21

Later that afternoon, Max is behind Nikki as she starts to open the side door to her house. She nudges the door gently—it's already unlocked. Did she forget to lock it? It's possible, her mind was probably in the clouds this morning. Pushing the door all the way open, she enters, and Max follows her in. On the floor in the small entranceway is a new vase full of spring flowers and a note. She doesn't have to read it; Barrett strikes again!

She picks up the note, and Max reads over her shoulder. *My dearest Nicolette, a beautiful woman deserves beautiful flowers. I put the flowers in the house so they wouldn't get droopy. The chocolate cheesecake is in the refrigerator. These gifts are just because we're still friends. Please call me. I have an important favor to ask you. Friends forever, Barrett.*

Nikki turns to Max and shrugs again. Max looks at the letter. "Sounds like she's got the hots for you. Don't like her coming in here when you're not home, Rev, so don't even think about staying here tonight."

Max moves into the parlor and turns on a lamp. He bends down and picks up Fluffy, then sinks into the lumpy sofa. Nikki joins him. "I don't think she means me any harm. I must have left the door open, but I don't remember doing it." She pauses, getting his attention. "Max, before we talk about tonight, I want to go over a few details with you."

"There's no discussion about tonight." Max gets out his notebook. "And by the way, while you were at your office, Clayton called. Says she can't find her gun. I'm getting a search warrant. My gut tells me her gun's the murder weapon."

At the moment, Nikki's not fond of his gut. She's a little unnerved by Ginni's inability to find the gun but pulls her thoughts back to the present discussion and says, "The only people we know of who hated Long were Shari Sullivan and Eugene Blake. And both Blake and Long attended the university, worked at the Medical Center, and were friends of Lisa Holt."

"Circle of suspects keeps going around," Max adds.

Nikki agrees. "Something's going on at the center, and I think Shari and Edmond tried to throw a wrench into that larger plan that Blake keeps talking about."

Max picks up her train of thought. "I still say Blake attacked you in your office, but I can't figure why. And Holt might be involved. Ever have any problems with her at the university? She get attached to you like that Barrett?"

Nikki gives him an annoyed look. "No! She didn't. The only time I ever shared anything with her was when she worked on a class paper on Contemporary Gender Ethics. We touched on abortion, adoption, and surrogacy. As I recall, she kept asking for my personal opinion about abortion versus adoption, and I think I avoided answering."

"Abortion," Max says thoughtfully. "Must be connected to Peterson's new abortion alternatives clinic." He struggles to piece things together.

"Lisa never struck me as conservative." Nikki shakes her head. "People do things for love and money, but how much additional money can be gained by restructuring the clinic? The clinic's still part of the Medical Center, and Peterson's father still runs it all. Junior can't get that much of a pay raise. He might get more prestige, but he's already the doctor in charge."

Max flips pages backward, checking an old entry. "Maybe it isn't the clinic that's gonna make him his fortune."

"What do you mean?" Nikki asks, unconsciously rubbing her healing stitches.

Max looks up. "Remember, Blake told us Peterson sponsored him, so he could supervise the new private clinic that Peterson's opening."

"Why would Peterson do away with abortions at the Medical Center but open a private abortion clinic?" Nikki asks, trying to solve one part of the puzzle.

"To force the abortion business to his private clinic," Max answers. "He's probably desperate to be a financial success and get out from under daddy. And there's the wife and the girlfriend, Lisa Holt...both want Sheldon to be a success. Either of 'em might want to get rid of anyone standing in his way. And for some reason, you might be some kind of roadblock for him, too."

"Maybe." Nikki twists a flaxen curl around her finger. "I'm out of my league here."

Max places a purring Fluffy on her own cushion and closes the notebook, tucking it in his side pocket. "For inspiration, I'm getting a piece of that chocolate cheesecake. Barrett may be a little strange, but she sure can bake."

Max goes into the kitchen, where he begins rattling plates and silverware. Nikki stands up and stretches, ready to join him, when she hears the refrigerator door open. Suddenly, a deafening blast shakes the house on its foundation, sending Nikki and Fluffy flying across the room. Seconds after landing on the floor, she jumps up with one thought in mind.

Nikki races from the living room to see the kitchen exploding in flames. "Max! Holy God! Max, where are you?" Smoke and flames are everywhere. An old familiar fear engulfs her.

Thick black smoke begins to fill the house. Electrical

shorts pop from room to room, spurting plumes of sparks. Part of the refrigerator is wedged in the doorway. Mustering her strength, Nikki pushes it aside. A blast of heat hits her full force. Her throat burns, her breath comes in gasps. Finally, she locates Max on the floor, blood running from his mouth.

At least he's breathing. Have to get him out of here! The mortar shells are landing everywhere. Adrenaline surges through her. She grabs Max's lapels and drags him across the kitchen floor, straining every muscle in her body. But the weight of his unconscious body combined with her smoke-filled lungs cause her to stumble and cough.

In the hallway, her breath is short and shallow. The entire house is blackened. The crackling explosions continue. She manages to open the side door, pulling Max down the steps and across the narrow yard. She kneels beside his unconscious body and calls his name while checking to see if he's still breathing.

The scream of sirens grows louder, filling the quiet neighborhood with a sense of tragedy—thank God someone called the fire department. Her gasping breaths can't cool the burning in her lungs. Suddenly, she remembers Fluffy. "Can't leave Fluffy." The house is steaming smoke from every crack and crevice. "Gotta get Fluffy." But the door closed behind her; there's no way for the cat to escape. She jumps up and runs to the door. Jerks it open. A gas explosion hurls her back across the yard. Nikki falls into a black void.

Some time later, she wakes up in the back of an ambulance, breathing pure oxygen, which cools her lungs. She strains to get up, but is held down by a paramedic. "How's Max?"

The attendant tries to be reassuring. "They took Sergeant Mullen ahead of us in another ambulance. We'll be at the hospital in a few minutes, Reverend."

She tries to relax her breathing. There's no sense asking about Fluffy. Warm tears well in her eyes and wash down her face.

CHAPTER 22

The emergency room doctor bandages the burn on Nikki's hand. In the confusion of the blast, she hadn't felt it. Now, it sends stinging messages up her arm.

She's finally released and begins searching the long hallway for Max, who's in a cubicle surrounded by doctors and nurses. Technicians are scooting various machines next to his bed.

A nurse directs her to the waiting room, where she finds Detective Henry Ostrow. Even seated, his thin body towers over her. "Has anyone called Max's wife, Rosa?" she asks as she shakes his hand.

Henry stands. "She's on her way. Did they tell you anything about Max's condition?"

Nikki shakes her head, her emotions choke her for a moment. "He took the blast full in the face."

Henry motions for the two of them to sit, then calmly says, "We're waiting for the report from the crime lab and bomb squad experts."

"The bomb must have been in the refrigerator," she says. "Max went for some cheesecake. I heard him open the refrigerator, and then the blast went off."

"Any idea who or why?" Henry asks in his slow cadence.

Her mind searches for an explanation. "Barrett Fairburn

left a note and some food while I was out. I might have left the side door unlocked, but I don't think so."

"Barrett Fairburn again?" Henry asks quietly. "Did Max tell you about her juvenile record, the assault charge?"

"He told me, but I can't see her going this far," Nikki says. "She's not really linked to the murders."

Henry touches her arm briefly, then continue, "You're not linked either, but someone bombed your house, Reverend."

"Max's pretty sure Eugene Blake attacked me in my office," Nikki offers. "He had some army demolition training, which he probably hasn't forgotten. I'm not sure why he thinks he has to get rid of me."

"The bomb squad is sifting through the ashes," Henry explains. "In the morning, I'll pay a visit to Eugene Blake."

"I'd like to come along, Detective Ostrow." Nikki sits up straighter, her determination to find answers apparent in her request.

"Call me Henry, please. I know Max trusts you." Henry nods a reply. "If you feel up to it, it's okay with me."

The door to the waiting room swings open, and a petite, olive-skinned woman wearing a long denim dress enters. Her medium-length dark hair frames a pretty face. A worried Rosa Mullen goes directly to Henry. "What happened, Henry? Is Max all right? They didn't tell me anything over the phone."

Henry rises, his height accentuated by Rosa's diminutive size. He puts his arm around her. "Rosa, why don't you sit down?" Reluctantly, she does. "This is Nikki Barnes."

Before Rosa can say anything, Nikki moves to her and says, "I'm sorry, Rosa. I didn't want to meet you this way, but Max's tough." She holds Rosa's hand and fights back tears.

"Was he with you?" Rosa asks, trying to get information. "He was worried something might happen to you. Guess he was right again."

Nikki gains some composure. "The bomb was in my house."

"Bomb?" Panic spreads over Rosa's face.

Henry fills in the details and is sure to tell Rosa how Nikki saved Max's life. "He's breathing on his own, but, so far, he hasn't responded."

"What does that mean, Henry? He hasn't responded? Is he unconscious?" Rosa asks, her voice trembling.

Henry's searching for the right explanation when a doctor wearing surgical greens enters the waiting room. "Is Mrs. Mullen here?"

"I'm Rosa Mullen. How's my husband?" She stands quickly.

The doctor approaches Rosa. "He's a lucky man. He has a broken left wrist and forearm, a couple of cracked ribs, a broken nose, multiple contusions and burns, and smoke poisoning. According to Reverend Barnes, the refrigerator door must have afforded your husband some protection. He's lucky to be alive."

"I want to see him. Now," Rosa demands, stepping closer to the doctor.

"That's the good news, Mrs. Mullen." The doctor puts a hand on her arm. "The problem is your husband hasn't regained consciousness. He's in a coma. But we're hopeful that he'll come out of it soon."

"A coma? My God! I've got to see him!" She starts moving around the doctor, heading for the door.

He stops her. "We're having him moved to the intensive care unit, where he'll be closely monitored. We try to encourage family members to talk to comatose patients. We think it helps them regain consciousness."

Nikki feels weak. The word comatose sticks in her mind.

The doctor leads them to a waiting area across from the intensive care unit.

"Patients do hear what you say when they're comatose," Henry says in his slow, quiet way. "I'd like to talk to Max before I leave, if it's okay with you."

Rosa puts her fingers to her lips, hoping to hold back her tears. "Of course, Henry, of course."

Nikki moves close to Rosa. "The guys talked about it in Nam. Many of them woke up from comatose states. Frequently, it took a while. Sometimes a few days or weeks, but they woke up." She hesitates, awkwardly changing the subject. "Max wanted me to spend the night with you and the boys."

"Max hates when I'm out alone after dark." Rosa gives a small nervous laugh. "And he *is* going to be all right. I'll make him be all right. Like you said, he's tough."

All three enter Max's cubicle. He appears peaceful in spite of the IVs in his arm and an oxygen mask that covers his broken nose and mouth. Several monitors are beeping and humming. Nikki never gets used to this scene, everything white and stainless steel, eerie and inhuman. Henry and Rosa step closer to the bed.

Rosa takes Max's free hand and motions Henry to talk. He clears his throat. "Max? I know you can hear me. I'm rooting for you, partner." Henry is clearly uncomfortable. "We've got some good leads, and I'll keep you posted every day. I'll need you to put the pieces together, so wake up soon, okay? I'm going to leave now, but I'll be back in the morning, partner."

Rosa stares at Max's face, tears filling her eyes. Nikki moves to the other side of the bed and puts her hand on his forehead. She prays silently.

There's no response from Max. His barrel chest moves up and down with each breath.

Rosa lets go of his hand and takes a long, deep breath, letting it out slowly. She then stands on her toes, leans across Max's chest, and shouts into his face, "You wake up, Max Mullen! You wake up this minute! What do you think you're doing! I will not be left with those two boys. That was the deal. I take care of the girls; you get the boys. Now wake up!" Rosa kisses Max's cheek and prays.

Nikki can't believe what she's hearing. Rosa must be losing

it. Wait just a minute! Max moves! First his legs, then his arms. He groans. Monitors whine and beep, and suddenly nurses swarm into the cubicle as Max begins to open his eyes.

Rosa refuses to move for the nurses as they check on Max and is still leaning over him as she starts crying. "You big Irish lug. You gave me a scare." Almost on top of his chest, she hugs and kisses him.

Max tries to speak, his voice raspy. "Rosa, what's wrong, sweetheart? Why ya yellin'?"

Rosa kisses him again. "I'm yelling because I love you, and you scared me. I never want you to leave me." Her crying starts again. This time Nikki goes over to her.

Max struggles to regain his full senses. "Nikki, you all right? I was worried."

Rosa gives a laugh of relief. "She's fine, and she saved your butt, again. Thank God. You'll never even that score, honey." The tiny woman reaches up to Nikki and gives her a grateful hug.

While Rosa stands by the bed, patiently explaining to Max all that has happened, a nurse comes up to Nikki and tells her someone is waiting for her at the main desk in the lobby. Nikki leaves the room hurriedly, thinking it might be Henry, and she is eager to tell him the good news about Max.

CHAPTER 23

Nikki reaches the main reception area and sees Ginni Clayton standing in the dull light of the hospital entrance doors. Ginni forces a small smile, while both hold back from running into each other's arms. They walk quickly to each other. Ginni holds out her hand awkwardly. "Thank God, Nikki! You're all right!"

Ignoring the hand, Nikki gives her a little more than a polite hug. Several late night visitors leaving the hospital take no notice of the two women. "I'm so glad to see you. How'd you know I was here?"

Ginni's smile disappears. "Well, not because you called to let me know."

"There wasn't any time in all the chaos." Nikki struggles for an excuse. "Max was in a coma."

Ginni keeps her hand on Nikki's arm. "When you didn't call by eight, I tried to call you. The operator said your phone was disconnected. I drove over to see if you were hiding in a dark house again."

She notices the bandage on Nikki's hand and asks, "Is this a burn?" Then she touches Nikki's face carefully. "You have some abrasions and a few burns, here."

Nikki grins. "Thank you, Doctor. You can keep your hand

there all night."

Ginni takes her hand away slowly as Nikki tries to explain what happened. "Max took the brunt of the explosion. I managed to drag him out of the house."

"Can you leave now?" Ginni asks quietly. "I want to take you home with me."

"I can't." Nikki struggles with her desire to be with Ginni and her loyalty to Max. "I can't come to your place tonight."

"You have to. I went by your house. Have you seen it?" Ginni speaks quickly, almost pleading. "Your house is almost totally gone. The police cordoned off the area. No one can get near it. I tried. I was terrified when I saw it." Ginni's voice gets more muted. "I thought...I thought, I lost you. I was screaming for you when the police told me you were taken to this hospital." Ginni takes a few moments to compose herself after this emotional confession. "I did pick something up outside your house. Come over to the car."

With a lump in her throat, Nikki follows. Ginni points to the back seat. There, stretched out in the full luxury of the Honda, is Fluffy. She looks resplendent, except for a makeshift hankie bandage halfway down her tail. Nikki opens the door and slides in next to the cat. Fluffy meows, not wanting to be disturbed. "You unbelievable cat. How many lives can you have?"

Ginni offers reassurance. "She's fine. Lost some hair on her tail, but she's not even bleeding. Fluffy had no qualms about coming with me, which is more than I can say for her mistress."

Nikki gives Fluffy another hug and puts the wiggling cat back on her comfy seat. "I promised Max I'd stay with his family tonight. I feel I owe him. I don't want any more guilt over this."

Ginni wraps her arms around Nikki. Her cheek brushes Nikki's forehead. "I don't want you to have any guilt, but none of this is your fault. I know you and Max are friends, and I won't pressure you." She stops. "Tonight, that is. I'll plan to see you tomorrow night, unless I'm in jail."

Nikki breaks the embrace. "What do you mean?"

"I can't find the damned gun." Ginni shakes her head. "I don't know where it is. I remember putting it in my desk drawer, but it's gone. And I don't think your Sergeant Mullen believes me. I understand the police will have a search warrant by tomorrow morning. I sure hope they can find the gun." Ginni looks down at her feet and quietly says, "Nikki...Nikki...I'm not a murderer. Please believe me, darling." She looks up at Nikki and smiles weakly.

"Don't worry." Nikki tries to exude confidence as she looks up into those green eyes. "You're not going to jail. I'll see to that." In her mind, Nikki adds, *darling.*

Ginni still has her hands on Nikki's shoulders. "Be careful and don't take any chances. There's a lunatic out there. Remember, I want you at my house tomorrow night and in my arms." She squeezes Nikki's shoulder.

She gets her keys out of her coat pocket. "I guess it's just me and Fluffy tonight. Maybe she'll share some family secrets."

They don't care who's watching this time. They hug again, not wanting to part. Then Nikki makes the separation and returns to the intensive care unit.

Max is almost asleep, so she quietly kisses him good night on the cheek. Just as she's tiptoeing out of the room, she swears she hears him say, "And stay away from the Clayton woman."

She smiles and leaves the ICU with Rosa.

CHAPTER 24

Rosa drives them home, taking advantage of the opportunity to get to know Nikki. "Max talked about you for years. Even wrote to me about you before we were married. His letters from Vietnam were full of the 'Rev.'"

Nikki's only half listening. The motion of the car and the letdown of adrenaline are sending waves of exhaustion over her. She sinks lower in the seat as Rosa continues talking. "You're not what I expected. I've pictured you so many ways over the years. I mean...I saw all the photos from over there, but I thought maybe you'd look like a female Rambo or something. Or I sometimes thought you'd look like St. Theresa, angelic, with a certain glow."

This gets Nikki's attention. She pulls her blazer tighter around herself and sits up. "Where were you getting these wild ideas?"

"Max." She shoots a quick glance to Nikki and then watches the road again. "Every time an old buddy came to visit or every Memorial Day, we had to hear the exploits of the Rev, who saved his life. He's always so serious about it."

Nikki can't hold back a burst of uncontrollable laughter. It takes a few minutes for her to quiet down. Then Rosa starts laughing, making her laugh again. "I know it sounds crazy, but for years after we got married he spent a lot of time trying to find you. He used to call veterans' hospitals, asking if you were, or ever had been, a patient there."

Nikki realizes there's a seriousness behind these stories which needs to be addressed. "I never knew I was so important to him. I was very into myself for those years, I had a lot to work out. I didn't contact Max or anyone from my unit. Guess I wasn't ready to see anyone then."

Rosa's tone turns serious also. "I know, it was pretty hard for Max and me, too. He went through six jobs before trying college. We fought almost every day. He finally saw a counselor…I blamed you sometimes." She takes another quick look at Nikki.

"Of course, our problems weren't your fault. I knew that even then, but you were the only other thing I knew about Vietnam, so I blamed you. First I was jealous, then I blamed you."

Nikki is surprised at Rosa's honesty and tries to explain. "Max and I supported each other in Nam. He was so different from the other guys because he was in love with you, and only you. He wasn't into drugs or booze or the bar girls. Most of our time was spent in the hospitals, giving pastoral care to the guys and civilians who needed it. That's how we became friends. For a while, I thought Max wanted to be a priest, but then he'd take out his picture of you and go over every plan you two had for your future together. He'd read your letters. I'd listen. On bad days, he'd read them twice. Your letters helped him to survive."

Rosa giggles. "You mean he'd read everything? He'd read the whole letter?"

"The whole thing." Nikki's smiling again. "Even when I protested that they were too personal."

The women are laughing as they reach Max and Rosa's home. Nikki puts her hand on Rosa's arm. "There was never any romance or sex between Max and me. I love him as a brother. He was one of the few soldiers who didn't condone the torture and the raping of native women. He cried when napalmed children were brought to the hospital and went to visit the orphanage almost every week. He came out with my respect, and I think his own self-respect. He's just a little too...," she hunts for a descriptive word, "proper. I've been trying to break the news to him that even though I'm ordained, I'm a human with faults and a sex drive."

Rosa jumps in. "Oh, he'll never go for it. He's having trouble with you being on a leave of absence, maybe losing your job. No. I'm afraid sex is out of the question, except under the blessing of marriage. He is, however, willing to give the wedding and still thinks there's time for you to have children."

Nikki shakes her head in exasperation, hoping Rosa is really only kidding. "There won't be any children. There won't even be a partner Max likes."

Rosa starts to get out of the car. "Don't be too sure of that. He's a little stuffy, but he believes in love and wants to see you happy. He might grumble, but he's happy if you're happy."

As they enter the house, they're greeted by Mario, the eight-year-old, and Max Jr., the twelve-year-old, who is upset. Max Jr. blurts out, "Is he okay? He's coming home, right? How long before he's home?" The questions tumble out one after the other.

Rosa hugs her sons and tries to quiet them down. "Shush! Shush. You'll wake your sisters."

Mario asks the same questions in a loud whisper, only with more directness. "Mom...Daddy's not dead, right? Right, Mom?"

"No! No. Your father's doing fine. He has a few broken bones, and he broke his nose again. All in all, he's doing great. He'll be home in a few days." She messes up Max Jr.'s hair and hugs both boys. Rosa then introduces Nikki. "There was a bomb at Nikki's house, and she saved your dad's life by dragging him out of the burning house." She gives Nikki a quick hug. "Thanks

for all the times you looked out for my Max. I need that guy."
She hugs Nikki again.

Nikki never thought about the logistics of staying at Max's
house. He made it sound so convenient, but she realizes now
she'll have to displace one of the children from their bedroom.
Embarrassed, she says, "I can just sleep on the sofa."

"That's not necessary." Rosa's in command in her house.
"We thought you might come over one of these evenings. Mario
and Max will share a room. They always do when family or friends
stay over."

Nikki's led by the silent Mario into what appears to be
another Jurassic Park. Dinosaurs are on the bedspread, on the
wallpaper, and on the pillow case. Dinosaur books spill out from
shelves, while various plastic, steel, and stuffed replicas hang and
sit in every available space of the room. "I guess you like
dinosaurs," she says, trying to open a conversation.

"And football, like Dad. He was a quarterback. You have
to be smart to be a quarterback." Mario is barely audible.

"Well, your dad's really good at that. He can figure things
out better than most people. He's the one who's going to solve
the case we're working on," Nikki offers.

"I know," Mario says with confidence. The miniature Max
looks up at Nikki and very seriously says, "I heard him tell mom
that a lioness protects her cubs—just like dinosaur mothers." With
that, he grabs his pajamas and runs out of the room.

Nikki falls asleep quickly, but her dreams are frightening.
She's screaming at Max. First, about how happy she is to be a
lesbian, then how she's madly in love with Ginni, who is not the
murderer. She's also happy with her cat and can't imagine wanting
children at her age. Then she is fighting a lioness and being chased
by a dinosaur. The night is very tiring, and before awakening, she
finds herself ablaze, fleeing from her burning house with Fluffy
in her arms. Finally, Nikki wakes up, feeling more tired than when
she went to bed.

BY 8:00 THE next morning, Nikki and Rosa are back in Max's cubicle in the ICU. He's complaining about the small portions at breakfast. The doctor promises to release Max soon, if he promises not to return to work for four weeks.

Henry enters as the doctor is leaving. He requests a private briefing with Max. Obligingly, Rosa leaves to find a bathroom, and this gives Nikki time to find a phone and reserve a room at the Maple Leaf Motel. She doesn't want to stay at Max's or at Ginni's until the murders are solved. Nikki momentarily, allows herself to think about the missing gun. *Ginni can't be involved in the murders—impossible.*

Twenty minutes later, Nikki returns to Max's cubicle just as Henry announces that Barrett Fairburn is coming to the station for questioning. "I didn't get a warrant, didn't have to. I just told her Reverend Barnes and I wanted to talk to her. She said she'd be there."

Max looks at Nikki. "Could've guessed she'd cooperate, knowing you'd be there, Rev." He forces a grin despite his bruised cheeks.

"Sure, sure," Nikki smirks. "And I'll ask her to make another cheesecake—just for you, Max."

CHAPTER 25

At last, the police inform Nikki that the investigation at the bomb site is completed, and she can retrieve what remains of her smoke-damaged, but salvageable, belongings. She asks Henry Ostrow to have them delivered to the Maple Leaf Motel. He doesn't question her choice of lodgings but guesses Max will be angry at her decision.

LATER THAT DAY, Barrett catches a glimpse of Nikki walking in her direction and barrels down the first floor hallway of the Sheridan police station. "Nicolette! I was so worried! You could've died." She throws her arms around Nikki.

Nikki fights off the hug, noticing Henry makes no attempt to intercede. Finally, she peels away Barrett's arms from around her neck. "Barrett! Barrett, listen to me. Calm down. I wasn't hurt." Barrett takes a deep breath. "Good. Now, we have some serious questions to ask you."

"But your hand, Nicolette." Carefully, she links arms with Nikki, who rolls her eyes heavenward.

They enter the interrogation room, and Henry requests that Barrett sit across from them. Barrett appears a little frightened; she begins to drum her fingers on the scarred table.

"Barrett, would you mind keeping your fingers still?" Nikki smiles apologetically. She is tired and in no mood to coddle Barrett. "Why'd you go to my house yesterday?" Nikki asks, placing both hands on the table. The white bandage on her burned hand is a reminder of the attempt on her life.

Barrett keeps the same grave expression on her face. "I wanted to bring you flowers and the cheesecake. You said you never tasted chocolate cheesecake."

"But why did you bring them without calling first?" Nikki is quick and curt.

"Because we had a fight on the phone, if you recall. I didn't want you mad at me." Barrett answers, as she begins to shake her leg.

Nikki feels foolish. "Barrett, we didn't have a fight. But that doesn't explain why you didn't wait until I was home to come over."

"But Nicolette, you're never home lately, and I had something important to ask you. I wrote it in the note." Barrett is almost pleading.

Nikki is somewhat afraid to pursue what Barrett wants to ask her in front of Henry. She's pleased when he takes over the questioning. Her shoulders relax, and she sits back in her chair.

"Miss Fairburn, how did you get into Reverend Barnes' house?" he asks in a firm voice.

"The door was unlocked," Barrett says nonchalantly. "I put the flowers in the hall and the cheesecake in the refrigerator. It's in the note. Don't you have the note?"

Nikki speaks slowly for emphasis. "The letter and everything else was destroyed in the explosion, Barrett. Did you know that Max almost died?"

Barrett's eyes widen; she shakes her head.   "No."

"Furthermore, I always *lock* my doors. So how did you get in?"

"The door was open, I swear, Nicolette," she repeats,

gesturing with her long arms for emphasis. "I walked right in. I went into the kitchen and put the cheesecake into the refrigerator. Then I found some paper and wrote the note. I put the flowers and the note right by the door, so when you came in they'd be the first thing you saw. Then I went into the bedroom..." Barrett's gaze never leaves Nikki.

Nikki gets a nervous knot in her stomach. Not really wanting to hear, nor have Henry hear the rest, she quickly asks, "Did you do anything in the bedroom related to the explosion?"

Barrett looks confused. "I had nothing, whatsoever, to do with the explosion." She slaps her hand hard on the table. "How many times do I have to tell you—I care about you, Nicolette. I...I love you." Barrett's eyes plead with Nikki as she reaches for her hands, but Nikki pulls away. "Okay, I went into the bedroom...to...kiss your pillow."

Nikki sinks further into her chair, embarrassed by this public declaration of affection. If Henry is shocked or mildly surprised, he doesn't let on, but saves the moment by asking, "Was anyone in the house while you were there, Ms. Fairburn?"

"I don't know." Barrett flips her long, dark hair off her shoulders.

Henry pushes further. "Could someone have been in the house?"

"Someone could've been there." Barrett tries to think. "They might've been hiding. I wasn't aware of anybody. Do you think they were watching me." Barrett shudders at the thought.

Nikki picks up Henry's line of questioning. "Did you notice anything? Did you hear or see anything unusual?"

Barrett looks at her and says sincerely, "I wasn't concentrating on anybody but you, Nicolette. I was thinking about what I need to ask you. So no, I didn't see or hear anything. Please believe me, I could never hurt you. I...I...love..."

Henry interrupts. "By any chance, did you smell anything unusual?"

Barrett starts to laugh, hoping to break her own tension. "Did I smell anything? Like what? Like maybe a man? Maybe I smelled testosterone?"

Nikki asks, "Well, did you?"

"Did I smell testosterone?" Barrett giggles. "Don't be silly. What the hell...," she stops mid-sentence. "Wait a minute. Now that you mention it, I thought I smelled perfume in your kitchen. Didn't you once tell me you never wear perfume? But I thought I smelled some."

"Barrett, do you think you would recognize that fragrance again?" Nikki asks excitedly.

Barrett nods, "I...think so."

Nikki looks at Henry, who raises his eyebrows, remembering that the perfume and aftershave fragrances had been traced back to Lisa Holt and Eugene Blake. She asks, "Detective Ostrow, don't you think Ms. Fairburn can go now?"

Henry stands. "All right, Ms. Fairburn, you're free to go, at least for now. But don't leave town."

Barrett stands, gives Detective Ostrow a quick smile.

"Nicolette, can you drive me home?" She takes a step toward Nikki. "Please. I need to ask you that favor."

Nikki thinks it's a blessing to hear the word favor. A proposal, a proposition, an embarrassing request is not called a favor. "I can't drive you home, but I'll call you later."

"You promise? You'll call? It's really important." Barrett is steadfast. "My whole future depends on it."

Nikki is curious but cautious. She's also anxious to settle a score with Eugene Blake. "Promise. I'll call."

"Thank you, Nicolette. You're a good friend." This is said so quietly, Nikki looks twice to make sure she heard what Barrett said.

CHAPTER 26

Henry leafs through a second folder on the table in the interrogation room. "We can't get an arrest warrant for Blake, yet. What we have is pure conjecture, no proof."

"Can we at least question Blake? Or question Lisa Holt?" Nikki asks. "She did threaten me."

Henry thinks for a minute. "I don't think she's above doing any dirty work herself. But, from what I remember of the two, Blake's the likely one. I'm sure Barrett Fairburn would've noticed if a woman was in the house. That dumb student look can't hide the fact she knows exactly what's going on. The only reason I ruled Fairburn out is too many clues were left proving she was there. Plus, I think she's sincere about your welfare and has no reason to hurt you, that I'm aware of."

Nikki appreciates his diplomacy but wonders if Barrett knows about her relationship with Ginni. "Then, let's go see Blake and try to shake him up—put some pressure on him."

"Reverend, you know I can't force him to answer my questions." Henry pauses, still looking at Nikki. "But he won't be expecting us to come back to the Medical Center. He'll be off guard, but...he could be dangerous if we push him. I'm bringing backup, just in case."

THEY ARRIVE AT the Medical Center, and Henry stations two officers in the outer hallway. He and Nikki sit in Suite B's waiting room. When Ginni Clayton brings a patient file to the reception desk, she is surprised to see Nikki and smiles. Then she notices Henry, and her expression changes to one of concern. She walks over to Nikki and whispers, "Interesting clothes."

Nikki's still wearing her black slacks from the day before and an oversized pink knit sweater, compliments of Rosa.

Ginni takes a look at Nikki's burned hand and examines the bandage. "You should keep your hand immobile." She shares a knowing glance. "And you need to keep burn ointment on your face. I can get some for you, or do you want to pick it up later?"

"Right now, we're here to talk to Eugene Blake." Nikki lets the formality drop. "But, I'll stop by later." Her eyes twinkle.

Ginni leaves the waiting area, as Blake enters, carrying a folder. He doesn't notice them until Henry says, "Mr. Blake? Like to have a few words with you." Henry holds out his police ID.

"If you're the police, forget it," Blake growls. "I'm not answering any more questions without my lawyer."

He turns and starts down the inner hallway. Henry and Nikki are in pursuit. Henry raises his voice. "Blake, we can do this the easy way or I can get an arrest warrant and come back and haul your butt down to the police station. I'm sure the local papers would love to run the story."

Blake swings around to face them. He stabs his index finger at Detective Ostrow. "If you could get a warrant, you'd have one now. You don't have anything on me. So you'd better stop harassing me." He begins walking away.

Nikki speaks this time. "We know you put a bomb in my house last night, Eugene. There's a witness who can place you there just before the explosion."

He whirls around again. "You're a goddamn liar, Miss Barnes." He emphasizes the Miss. "There's no witness. And there's no way you can place me there." He laughs.

She recognizes Blake's tone and his wild look, a madness she's seen before—it's fast and unpredictable. Some guys got that look before they ate grenades or stomped on a mine pin. "You wear too much aftershave...," she says hesitantly, as he waits for the rest. "It smells, and the smell is with you wherever you go...even in my house."

Henry's behind her, taller than Blake by about eight inches, but outweighed by almost a hundred pounds. "Now, would you like to answer some questions?" he prods.

Blake panics. "Absolutely not!" Suddenly, he punches Nikki right in the solar plexus. She falls to the floor, gasping for air.

Henry shouts for the other officers, and then he wrestles Blake against the wall. Blake uses his weight to advantage and swings Ostrow around, then against the wall. Nikki looks up and sees Blake squeezing Henry like a tube of toothpaste.

A sharp pain in her stomach muscles prevents her from springing into action. She fights to push the pain to the deepest recesses of her mind. For the moment, Blake ignores Nikki, giving her an advantage. Cautiously, she approaches Blake from behind, then moves to his side. She takes a breath and assumes the stance. Without warning, she lets loose a deafening yell and snap-kicks Blake's right kneecap into the next universe. He screams with agonizing pain, then drops to the floor.

The two officers arrive in time to see Henry cuffing Blake's hands behind his back.

Henry straightens his suit jacket and adjusts his tie. "Now we *don't* need a warrant, Mr. Blake." Blake mumbles incoherently.

"Mirandize him, boys," Henry says. "And make sure he understands his rights." The two officers pull Blake up from the floor. He's favoring his right leg.

Henry, still huffing hard, examines a tear in his jacket. He goes over to Nikki, who is leaning again the wall, bent over. "Now I know what Max is talking about. You can play on my team any time," he says, with admiration.

Nikki lets out a low moan, still trying to catch her breath.

Henry looks concerned. "Can I help you, Rev? I mean, Professor Barnes." He blushes. "Maybe you ought to see a doctor. You took a nasty poke in the stomach."

"I'm a little sore, but I don't need a doctor. I think we've got our man. I'm sure Blake blew up my place." With effort, Nikki straightens up and brushes off her slacks.

"Why is Eugene handcuffed?" Unexpectedly, Lisa Holt makes a grand entrance into the hallway. "What's going on?" she asks in her petulant manner."

"Assaulted three police officers," Henry answers.

"Ridiculous!" Lisa fires back. "You're harassing him."

Nikki's anger takes over. "He blew up my house and almost killed Sergeant Mullen. That's attempted murder in my book." She steps in front of Lisa, blocking her view of Blake. "And I think you're involved in this, too."

"No! No! She's not involved!" Blake starts screaming hysterically, trying to break loose from the officers' grip. "She had nothing to do with it. I admit it. I blew up the damn dyke's place! I did it, all on my own!"

Henry steps in front of Blake, takes his chin in his hand and squeezes. "Shut your filthy mouth, unless you want to swallow a few teeth, you worthless piece of human manure."

Lisa looks right at Nikki. "Guess you just got your confession, Professor." Lisa walks over to Blake. "Don't worry, Eugene. I'm going to call Sheldon's lawyer. You'll be free in a few hours. I promise." She pats his cheek and walks away.

Nikki stops her. "What did I ever do to you, Lisa? I'm not the enemy—I'm not sure who is...but when whoever you're in this with goes down, they'll probably give you up in a second to save their own skin. Why not help us now, before it's too late?"

Lisa snickers. "Going down. You'd know about that, wouldn't you, Professor?" She walks away with a smirk on her face.

CHAPTER 27

Nikki is exhausted and gratefully returns to the Maple Leaf Motel. The room is musty and the carpet well-worn, but the bed is relatively comfortable. After locking the door, she closes the faded blue curtains and turns on a small lamp, which illuminates the shabby room. Nikki is pleased to see that the police have delivered her salvageable belongings.

She flops on the bed, closes her eyes, seeking just a few minutes of peace. Slowly a vision takes form: Ginni is in her arms. She feels her full breasts pressed against her. She kisses her neck, her lips, she slips her hand between her legs... Suddenly, the TV in the room next door blares, abruptly blasting her into the present.

Now that the sweet fantasy has been interrupted, Nikki tries to clear her mind and get back to focusing on the case. What were the key motives in these murders? Who would profit?

Let's see, first, there's Shari Sullivan's murder. Who'd profit from that, except maybe Blake? So now Shari's out of the way...she can't file any formal complaints against him. But that doesn't seem like enough of a motive for even a loose cannon like Blake. And why didn't Shari's murderer also kill Peterson's wife? After all, she was Shari's lover.

As for Edmond Long's murder...maybe wrong place, wrong

time. Blake's hatred of Long, and his daily presence at the Medical Center make him the best suspect. Bingo! Motive and opportunity. But how's Lisa Holt involved with Long and Blake?

And why attack me? Was it my work at the university? Long, Holt, and Blake are all students there. Can't think what else connects me to the Medical Center or the murder victims. True, I'm pro-choice, but I never tried to influence my students. And, anyway, freedom of choice would most likely make Sheldon Peterson's new private clinic successful and serve both Lisa Holt and Eugene Blake. So why am I a target?

Damn! There are too many contradictions. Peterson fights to get rid of abortions at the Medical Center but plans to build a new clinic to perform them. And then there's Barrett Fairburn— who is always where she shouldn't be.

Thoughts of the love-sick student remind Nikki that she promised to call her about the favor. As she slowly gets up, her body feels like something run over by an enormous bowling ball. She punches in the phone number. "Hello, Barrett?"

"Nicolette. You sound funny." Barrett is ecstatic that Nikki is calling as promised. "I'm worried about you. Where are you?"

Nikki decides not to tell anyone where she's staying. "I'm working with the police. What was the favor you wanted to ask me, Barrett?"

"I've finally got a bitchin' plan." Barrett gets into the mood. "The plan's got to work, but I need your help, Nicolette."

Nikki thinks to herself, *Do I want to be involved in a bitchin' plan?* "This plan isn't about the two of us, is it?" she cautiously asks.

Barrett laughs loud enough for Nikki to move the receiver away from her ear. "This isn't a sexual proposition—unless you've changed your mind, dear Nicolette." She waits, gets no response, and goes on in a more serious tone. "The plan's for my future. What I'm gonna do and what I'm gonna be. I've got it all worked out. The Dragon Lady is out of the country for four months, setting up one of my father's firms in Southeast Asia. I'm going home to Buffalo next week, right after I get my grades.

"Now, here's the plan. I told my father I want to have a small dinner party just for the family and maybe a friend from the university. That's where you come in. I want you to come and wear your death suit with the white collar. He loves titles and positions. He'll think it's awesome that my friend is a priest."

"Barrett...," Nikki interrupts. "I'd like to impress your father for you, but I have more important things to do."

"No!...Wait! Please don't hang up!" Barrett is getting frantic. "That's not the whole plan. I'm going to cook an outstanding meal. I'm going to tell my father I can be a great international celebrity chef...if he'll just let me go to the Culinary Institute. Then you jump in and tell him how good it'll be for my attitude and maturity and self-confidence and all that other bullshit. We've just got to convince him. Then I can start classes next month. Once I'm enrolled and my grades are good, he can convince the Dragon Lady to let me continue. Please, Nikki. I need your help."

Nikki's mouth falls open. "Did you just call me Nikki?"

"Yeah." Barrett lowers her voice. "I'm a desperate woman. Will you do it?"

Nikki doesn't have to think very long before answering. The Culinary Institute will help Barrett's emotional well-being and get her out of town. "Okay. I'll come to the dinner wearing my clerics, and I'll try to convince your father that your choice is the best one."

"Oh! Nicolette...I mean, Nikki, that's bitchin'! I'll leave the details and a map in your faculty mailbox. Do you see why I love you?"

Nikki doesn't want to get into this discussion again. "That will be fine, Barrett. I have to go now."

Barrett doesn't hang up. "I understand, Nikki. I think you have a new girlfriend, an older woman. You were probably afraid of our age difference. It happens, but age won't always matter. I'll wait for you."

Nikki's brain is silently screaming, *It's not age! Please don't wait!* But she calmly says, "I think the Culinary Institute will be good for you. Goodbye, Barrett."

Nikki hangs up and tries to shake away the stray thoughts left from Barrett's conversation. She focuses on her immediate needs, namely her belongings that were rescued from her house. She makes a mental note to thank Henry for sending them over to the motel.

Her army trunk is intact, but the only clothes in it are old dress uniforms and fatigues. Green plastic bags filled with clothes are piled against the wall. She starts going through them, hoping to find a pair of jeans. Most of the clothes from the dresser seem to smell of scorched drywall. Suits and slacks from her closet haven't fared well either. She sorts clothes that can be washed from those going to the cleaners.

Just as she finishes changing into an old but clean army tee shirt and a pair of jeans, the phone rings. Henry invites her down to the station. Blake's about to crack, and the lawyer Lisa Holt promised to send never showed.

CHAPTER 28

Nikki follows Henry into the interrogation room and quietly takes the seat next to him, across from Blake. Eugene's face is blotchy red and puffier than usual. He fidgets with a well- used hankie and looks up when she enters. "What do you want, bitch? I thought I was getting some dinner."

"Watch your mouth, Mr. Blake, if you want that dinner." It's getting late, and Henry wants to move this case along. "Now, Eugene, all we want to do is record what you told us earlier. Cooperate and we'll talk to the D.A. on your behalf. Then things will go much easier for you."

Henry nods to the officer sitting at the other end of the table, who turns on the tape recorder. "I want to remind you of your rights, Mr. Blake." He takes a card from his pocket and reads Blake his Miranda rights. "Do you understand these rights?"

Blake covers his huge face with the hankie. He wipes away perspiration and talks at the same time. "I understand. I understood the first time your cops did the Miranda thing, and I understand it now. I've answered all your questions."

"Eugene, I understand your lawyer has not contacted you," Henry says.

"Something must be wrong. I'm sure Lisa'll send a lawyer."

"Mr. Blake, would you like to call a lawyer to represent you now?" Henry asks. He doesn't want this case thrown out of court on a technicality. "Just a reminder, if you can not afford one, the court will appoint a public defender."

"No! No! I don't want any damn lawyer. Let's just get on with it all."

Henry keeps his voice soft and soothing. "According to your previous statement, you admitted to me and the other officers that you put the explosives in Reverend Barnes' house." Henry looks at his notes. "You said that you weren't trying to hurt her, that you just wanted to scare her, like when you attacked her in her office at the university. " Henry raises his eyebrows. "Is this correct, Mr. Blake?"

Blake cracks his knuckles. "Yeah, right. I planted the explosives. But I didn't want to hurt anyone." He looks at Nikki, his voice jittery. "I just wanted you to leave this case alone. I didn't want you coming back to the Medical Center and poking around."

This sounds like two confessions, but Henry knows he has to make it official. He asks, "So, you're admitting to the attacks on Professor Barnes, both in her office and in her home?"

Blake looks past them at the dirty green concrete wall. "Why don't you send one of your cops out to get me a hamburger and fries? Don't forget the Pepsi."

Blake looks pathetic. Henry pushes on. "No problem, Mr. Blake. You'll get your burger, but first we need some answers."

"Okay...yeah!" Blake suddenly shoots back, "I clobbered her in her office, and I planted the bomb. But I just wanted to scare her." Blake drops his head back and stares at the ceiling. "Guess the device did more damage than I planned for. You gotta believe me."

Henry signals the detective working the tape recorder. He nods an affirmative and keeps the machine running. "Why did you want Reverend Barnes out of the way?" Henry asks.

Blake looks at Nikki now. "She was nosing around too damn much."

"Eugene, I want to help you, but you got to give a little more information. Who put you up to attacking Reverend Barnes?"

Blake's agitated. "No one!"

Henry turns to Nikki and says, "I think Mr. Blake is protecting someone. I sure hope this person is worth protecting..." He looks back at Blake, "Because you, Mr. Blake," Henry points his finger, "will spend the rest of your life in prison for the two murders."

Blake's head snaps up. "Murders? What the hell are you talking about?"

Henry answers, "It's simple, you'll be charged not only with the assault on Reverend Barnes and Sergeant Mullen, but also with killing Shari Sullivan and Edmond Long."

"Are you crazy? You can't pin their murders on me." Blake's fighting his growing panic. "I tell you, I didn't kill anyone. I'm a healer, not a killer. You don't give a damn who you set up for these murders." Blake starts to get up, but an officer moves quickly behind him, pushing him back down. Blake's shouting now. "But I never killed anyone. *We* aren't murderers!"

"Who, Eugene, who?" Nikki demands, leaning over the table.

Henry places his hand on Nikki's arm, silencing her. Then he turns to Blake. "Eugene, I thought you were smart, being you're almost a doctor, and all." Henry shakes his head in disapproval. "Are you gonna go to prison for someone who doesn't care enough to even get you a lawyer? Come on, Eugene. Get smart, man." Henry gives Blake a few minutes to think, while he gets up to get some water.

Nikki thinks Blake is a pathetic weasel. Not feeling very Christian, she would like to kick his ass into hell.

Henry comes back to the table and remains standing.

"Eugene, you're gonna feel a whole lot better when you tell me who you're protecting. I gotta have something good to tell the D.A. about you. You're not making it easy for yourself. So who is worthy of your protection?"

"Stop pressuring me!" Blake looks at the ceiling again.

Henry's tone becomes more adamant. "I'm trying to help you understand your situation. These are the facts, Eugene. You're going to be charged with both murders, and you don't even have a lawyer. Ms. Holt has no intention of helping you. Why should she?" Henry knows Blake's weak spot. "She's sitting pretty, now that you're out of the way." Henry laughs.

"You're wrong! She wouldn't lie to me! She loves me!" He's pounding the table.

Nikki sits back in her chair and, with a mean laugh, says, "You're a fool! Do you really think she loves you? Get serious! She's probably sleeping with Sheldon Peterson right now." Nikki lets this sink in. "Get smart, Eugene, if she cared about you she'd be here, along with your lawyer. Do yourself a favor and make a deal with the police while you can."

"She doesn't love him!" Blake mumbles. "She just wants to keep her job and for me to get my promotion. She never loved Peterson." Blake collapses in his seat. "I don't know where she is," he whines.

"It was her idea, wasn't it?" Henry asks. "Clear your conscience, Eugene. Why'd she want Dr. Sullivan killed? And why'd she want you to kill Long? Come clean and we can help you."

Blake looks at his watch as if he's going someplace. "We didn't kill anyone!" Blake slams his hands on the table. "Why aren't you listening to me? Lisa and I are not murderers."

"She asked you to get rid of me, didn't she? You dumb turd." Nikki hammers at him. She leans across the table, gets right in his face. The white bandage on her burned hand is a reminder of how terrified she was. "She's the one who told you to scare me off. Right, Eugene?"

"Yes! Yes!" Blake yells back at her. "I did it for Lisa. I'd do anything for her, but not murder. We never murdered anyone."

"Why'd she want Reverend Barnes scared off?" Henry asks, again putting his hand out to silence Nikki.

Blake puts his elbows on the table, resting his forehead in his hands. "I don't know. It didn't matter to me."

Henry nods again to the other detective, who switches off the tape recorder. They know they have as much as they're going to get from Eugene Blake. "Okay, fellows, book him for the murder of Shari Sullivan and Edmond Long. And don't forget all the other charges."

HENRY CLOSES THE interrogation room door behind them. "Well, we know who committed the assault and the bombing. Now, we'll pick up Lisa Holt. She's officially an accessory to those crimes, unless Blake changes his story. And I bet once he sees her, he will. He'll deny she's involved."

They walk down the hall in silence. Then Henry adds, "Reverend, we still haven't found the gun that killed Long, and there's no sign of the Clayton woman's gun."

Nikki feels that familiar uneasiness again. "Have you searched her apartment?"

"A thorough search was made—no gun. As long as her gun is missing, she remains a suspect." He pauses after a few more steps. "By the way, Max wants to see you at the hospital. I'll call and tell him about Blake's confession."

CHAPTER 29

On her way to the hospital Nikki has a strong urge to telephone Ginni. She fights the impulse and again reassures herself that Ginni is innocent. But what about the gun? Maybe Max has some answers.

As Nikki enters Max's room, she stops to witness an emotionally moving tableau. Max is sitting up in bed, reading reports held awkwardly in his injured left hand. He holds Rosa's hand with his right. She sits on a chair next to his bed, reading a magazine. They're happy and content, and Nikki hates to interrupt this quiet moment but finally says, "You look well enough to go home."

Max puts the report down and quickly drops Rosa's hand. "Didn't hear you come in, Rev."

Rosa puts her magazine down with a smile. "Max can't wait to leave. Too much rest might kill him. I don't think we've spent this much time alone since our honeymoon."

"What about that weekend in Detroit?" Max feigns indignation.

"How can I forget that!" Rosa laughs. "Of course, we had a long weekend together just last year. We attended a "forensic litter" conference in Detroit. I did sight-seeing while Max learned how to evaluate a criminal's trash."

Nikki hugs Max. "How's the nose?"

Rosa jokingly answers for her husband, "Don't worry about his nose, a break can only improve it. This may actually help his snoring."

Max looks at Nikki's bruised face. "What happened? Henry told me no one got hurt during the arrest."

"I'm not hurt," Nikki says seriously. "I just got too close to a raging bull."

Rosa makes a face. "Sounds painful to me. Sure you're not hurt?"

Nikki looks at her. "Only my pride, as they say. Fortunately, I have a doctor as a personal friend."

Max's eyebrows go up. "What doctor is a personal friend?" His voice is biting.

"Doctor Clayton is a friend." Nikki grits her teeth.

"Clayton again, huh. We need to talk about her." Max sifts through papers in a folder, looking for one in particular.

Rosa taps his arm. "Before you get back to work, I'm going to say goodbye. Since the surgeon is keeping you here another night, I don't want to leave the boys alone. How about a kiss?"

They kiss and Rosa holds him for an extra moment, then says, "Call me in the morning before they release you. I'll bring fresh clothes and take you home where you belong." She kisses him again and picks up her things to leave, then walks over and gives Nikki a hug. "When are you coming for that lasagna? I'm making it by request tomorrow night."

Nikki doesn't hesitate this time. "I'll be there. I hear your lasagna heals what ails you."

"Of course it does. Wait 'til you see Max's nose after dinner." Rosa smiles again. "Goodbye, you two."

She walks out of the room, and Nikki points to Max's folder. "I see you're keeping up with the case."

"Henry called—told him I'd be down if he didn't. He

brought over a few files I wanted."

"So, what do you think of Blake's confession?" Nikki sits on the edge of the bed.

"I'm sure he attacked you and set the explosives." Max looks pensive. "Almost blew us to kingdom come."

This last comment touches something unspoken in Nikki, and she moves closer to Max. "I'm sorry about what happened at the house. The bomb was meant for me. You probably saved my life."

He smiles and grabs her arm for just a moment. "Finally. It's taken years to pay back the debt from Nam. Thought I'd never see you again, or ever have the chance. Then, when we do meet again, thought maybe you didn't need me around." He takes a long pause. "Thanks for saying it, but I know you dragged me out of the burning house."

Embarrassed, Nikki quickly changes the subject. "Do you think Blake committed the murders?"

"What's his motive? He told everyone, he hated 'em both. Too obvious." Max rubs the two-day bristle on his chin. "I have my doubts about Lisa Holt, too. Oh, she got him to attack you and probably masterminded the bombing, but Blake has the mean streak."

"I'm not so sure." Nikki gets off the bed and faces him. "I think Lisa is capable of many things. Can she at least be arrested as an accessory?"

"After Blake gets some food and sleep, he'll change his story. Remember, he loves this woman. He'll protect her. Look what he already did for her. We may get her in for questioning, but an arrest is something else. We're not gonna get anything out of her, just like Clayton." He watches to see if she changes expression.

She tries not to but, "What about Ginni?"

"Didn't Henry tell you? Can't find the gun. They called her father for a description. It's a thirty-eight Smith and Wesson.

Consistent with the murder weapon. Of course, she's cooperative, even volunteered to come in for more questioning."

Nikki clenches her teeth again. "Maybe she cooperates because she has nothing to hide. So, I don't see the comparison to Lisa."

"Can't make anything stick to either of 'em." Max holds his stance. "We get Clayton in for questioning but can't find the gun. She says she has a gun, then reports it missing. Smart woman, covers herself well."

Nikki responds pensively, "I don't think she did it, Max. I don't see a motive."

"I'm not so sure." Max keeps his voice analytical. "We can't prove there wasn't a bad...," he searches for the right word, "...personal relationship between her and Shari Sullivan. As for Long, maybe he stumbled onto something about her sex life, maybe wanted to make a buck for his family. Blackmail can be good money. Either way, what some people think is love can be dangerous. Like I said, people commit murder and cover up in the name of love." He waits for her response.

"I don't think she committed the murders," Nikki says flatly.

"Why? 'Cause you like her? Or 'cause you have facts I don't have?" Max asks.

Nikki softens. "Probably because I like her in a very special way. The reason doesn't matter. The truth is, we don't have enough evidence to charge anyone."

Max jumps in. "Which means we still have a killer out there, and she may be getting nervous and desperate."

"Or, he may be feeling safe and confident," Nikki counters.

"Okay. I give up with you and this woman. Just remember, no one is ruled out yet. You have to agree with that." Max closes the folder.

"I'm careful, Max. Look at me, the vision of caution."

He looks at her bumps and bruises. Finally, he lets out a belly laugh.

Nikki says, "I'm getting suspicious of everyone, too. I want this case over, so I can relax again. As for tonight, I have my entire wardrobe waiting to be sorted and washed. I may have to break down and buy some new clothes. And if you remember, that's one job I hate."

"Never noticed." Max is smiling now. "Just thought you were crazy about black and army green."

"Enough already! I get the picture." Moving closer to the bed, she adds, "I'll check with Henry in the morning about Lisa Holt's interview."

"Henry knows I want you there. Maybe Holt will say something that triggers that mind of yours and slides the puzzle pieces in place." He lightly puts his hand on the side of her head.

She gives him another hug. "I'll be over if something comes up. Don't forget to rest. We need you back on this case...and I miss you."

Max is flustered by this display of emotion. "Don't forget. Lasagna. If you're late, I can't guarantee there'll be any left."

CHAPTER 30

From the pay phone in the hospital lobby, Nikki dials Ginni's number. She waits anxiously for Ginni to come on the line.

The now-familiar quiet voice answers, "I thought you might call. You heard about the gun and...you're not coming over, right?"

"Wrong! I've heard about the gun and...I'd like to come over." Nikki leans her body against the wall. "I want to talk and...I...uh...miss Fluffy."

"Oh, you miss Fluffy. I see." Ginni hesitates. "Well, don't worry, she's comfortable, feels right at home, and thinks I'm visiting." The lightness of Ginni's remark breaks the tension.

"I really appreciate your keeping her for me. They don't allow pets at the Maple Leaf Motel." Nikki speaks without thinking first.

"Why are you staying in that dump?" Ginni is noticeably irritated. "I thought you were staying with your friend Max. You don't need to stay in a motel. I have more than enough room...unless it's unprofessional to stay with a murder suspect. At least Fluffy doesn't discriminate."

"I have what's left of my things at the motel," Nikki says lamely. "They all smell like smoke. I need to sort and wash the whole bunch. The motel's a good place for that."

Ginni is calm again. "Most people use cheap motels for other things, not laundry. And, by the way, I have a laundromat in the basement of my building."

There's another long silence, then Nikki offers, "What if I bring a pizza? I haven't eaten yet."

"I'll make a salad so we can justify it as a meal." In a softer tone, Ginni adds, "I'm glad you're coming over. I'm sure Fluffy misses you. I know I do."

Nikki stands up straight. "I'll be there in twenty minutes, but you'll have to excuse my clothes." She smiles ear to ear.

"I always excuse your clothes," Ginni says softly. "Maybe you'll let me help you pick out some new outfits. That's not too obvious, is it?"

"I don't know," Nikki continues the teasing. "I'm pretty fussy about my clothes. I don't think anyone could quite come up to my standards, but thanks for the offer."

GINNI NO SOONER hangs up the phone when her doorbell rings. Hoping it's not the police again, she opens the door to Susan Peterson, wearing an Oriental long-sleeved tunic over black silk slacks. The red-and-white print pattern in her tunic matches her red heels, and her long black hair is pulled back loosely, so it hangs to her waist. Her dark brown skin gleams in the dull hall light.

"Susan!" Ginni's surprise shows in her voice. "Come in." She opens the door wider and gestures toward the living room.

"Thank you. I'd like to talk to you." Susan sits down on an easy chair across from the sofa.

Ginni immediately takes on a professional stance. "How are you, Susan?"

Used to this medical approach to conversations, Susan is anxious to get to the point. "I know you were Shari's friend. And...well...I wondered if she ever spoke to you about us?"

Ginni doesn't know the purpose of Susan's visit but is getting used to being interrogated. "Often. She talked about you often... Can I get you something to drink?"

"No. I can't stay long. I'm sorry for coming unannounced like this, but I need to talk about Shari. She didn't trust many people, and my living with Sheldon...well you can understand why. But, I always felt she trusted you, perhaps confided in you."

Ginni is uncomfortable, unsure why. "She did confide in me the last few months. She didn't have anyone else at work she could trust."

Susan's shoulders relax slightly. "I know. I've always respected your professionalism from the time I worked at the Medical Center. Can you tell me what Shari said...about us?"

Ginni reasons that perhaps this overture is part of Susan's grieving. Sheldon wouldn't allow them to have many friends, and she certainly couldn't discuss her loss with him. "Shari told me how much she cared about you and the children. She talked about your vacation plans."

Ginni's finding it hard to retell these events without feeling emotional. But nothing betrays Susan's emotions except a growing sadness in her eyes. "She told me the vacation plans were a secret. Shari was happy in her relationship with you. I never saw her so happy." Remembering these details releases Ginni's repressed feelings about Shari's death. She stops talking to swallow tears.

Susan sits expressionless. "Thank you," she says quietly.

Ginni wonders if the rumors about Shari and her had reached Susan. Maybe that's really what Susan wants to know. "Shari and I were friends and working associates, but we never shared a romantic relationship."

Susan doesn't hesitate in responding, "I know Shari was faithful to me. We discussed fidelity. Being married to Sheldon convinced me I would never get into another relationship unless it was totally exclusive. Shari knew that from the beginning. I never worried about her. I knew when she left at night that she hated leaving the children and me at home, but there was nothing we could do."

Ginni feels tears welling again. "I'm sorry she's gone, and I do miss her. Is there anything I can do for you?"

"The children and I are managing. I still have plans." She pauses, changing the subject. "Did Shari talk much about the children?"

Ginni never had the maternal desire of many women and never understood what people wanted to hear about their children. Nonetheless, she does not want to offend Susan. "Shari loved the children and was very excited about the upcoming trip."

"Did she ever talk about how I got the children?" Susan asks, sitting forward.

Ginni's perplexed. "She told me your daughter was deserted by Sheldon's first wife, or he pressured her into leaving the child. Shari never trusted Sheldon."

"And my second child, what did she say about him?" Susan asks.

"To be perfectly honest," Ginni measures her words carefully, "I don't remember what she said about your son. I think she said he was your baby with Sheldon. Isn't that right?"

"Yes. He's our baby." Susan sits back a little. "That's why Jason is so precious to me."

"I'm sure he was precious to Shari, too," Ginni adds. "I remember she called him special all the time." Ginni can feel the strain of trying to be positive.

"Just one more question," Susan says. "Did Shari ever give you any...important papers or letters to keep for her? She told me there were some, and I thought she might have mentioned them, or where she kept them."

Ginni is puzzled. "Like insurance policies or personal letters? No. She never asked me to keep anything for her. They're probably in her apartment or her file cabinet at the Medical Center. We each have a locked file cabinet in the common room."

"What I'm looking for is not in her apartment," Susan says, preoccupied.

Ginni knows Shari gave Susan a key to her apartment.

Susan becomes agitated. "I'm sure she wouldn't just leave these papers just anywhere. The letters, in particular, were important to us. I wouldn't want them made public. I've checked the file cabinet. She has no record of a safe deposit box. You know Shari kept excellent records and was compulsive about that sort of thing."

"I could try to discreetly ask around work," Ginni offers. "But Shari wasn't friendly with too many people."

Susan suddenly stands up. "That won't be necessary. I just felt I had to check with you and make sure. I hope you don't mind my asking so many questions, Ginni. This is quite important to me."

Ginni walks her to the door. "I don't mind. I'm glad we could talk about Shari."

As they reach the door, the bell rings again. Susan looks more worried than surprised. "Were you expecting someone?"

Feeling awkward, Ginni decides there's nothing she can do about the coincidence. "I am expecting someone. She's a little early."

She opens the door and finds Nikki standing behind a large pizza box, looking disheveled and bruised, though clearly identifiable. "Hi. I'm early."

Susan takes a long look at Nikki. "Professor Barnes...I was just leaving." Nodding to Ginni, she gives a knowing glance to Nikki. "I hope you enjoy your evening." Her eyes fill with tears as she steps around Nikki and leaves.

Nikki enters the apartment, and Ginni closes the door, laughing. Nikki smiles because of the laughter. "What's so funny? And may I ask what Susan Peterson was doing here?"

"Are you jealous?" Ginni teases. "Will it take more women visitors to get you over here?"

"I look awful." Nikki lowers her voice. "I'm surprised Susan even recognized me."

Ginni starts laughing again. "You do look terrible!"

Nikki's insecurity is evident. "I said I looked awful. But do I really look terrible?" Nikki looks at herself and grimaces.

Ginni throws her arms around Nikki. "Not to me, darling. You look perfectly wonderful. Much more attractive than Susan, and far less serious." Laughing again, she buries her face in Nikki's shoulder. "I love the macho shirt and the perfume. What do you call it, *On Top of Old Smoky?*"

"If I wasn't so hungry, I'd leave," Nikki jokes. "Can you compose yourself long enough to eat this pizza while it's still hot?"

Ginni kisses her on the cheek and finally stops laughing. "I think I'm composed now. Come into my kitchen, Reverend Barnes." Ginni makes an exaggerated bow and, with a sweeping gesture, motions the way to the kitchen.

CHAPTER 31

Nikki pours wine while Ginni details Susan's visit and prepares the salad. "I thought she wanted to share her feelings about Shari, but it seems she was trying to locate some papers and personal letters that appear to be missing."

Nikki senses a piece of the puzzle floating just at the edge of her grasp. "I guess she was surprised to see me?"

"I think anyone would be," Ginni says, moving close to Nikki while she puts the salad on the table.

"She gave me a funny look," Nikki says naively as she sits down.

"Beware of funny looks," Ginni says, smirking. "You never know what they mean." She returns with the pizza on plates.

Nikki looks at Ginni, realizing how comfortable they seem together. There is no forced conversation. Several times during the meal, she wants to talk about the gun but doesn't want to spoil the serene mood.

As they finish eating, Ginni asks, "Are you ready to see the queen?"

"Where is Fluffy, anyway?" Nikki asks.

"The queen does not come out of her throne room until midnight. At that time, she appreciates fresh food and water, and no one touching her throne. I'll show you." Ginni leads the way to her bedroom. Fluffy is stretched out in the middle of the bed. "She claimed my bed her first night here. I didn't know enough about cats to protest."

Standing close to each other, they look into the semi-dark bedroom. "You have to be assertive with Fluffy, more assertive than she is," Nikki whispers as she feels the heat of Ginni's body next to hers.

"I just crawl in the other side," Ginni explains, moving close enough to touch Nikki's shoulder with hers. "Last night, I thought the cat would move. She didn't. She just gave me a look of disdain and held her ground."

Nikki reluctantly moves into the room, sits on the bed, and pets the aloof Fluffy.

Ginni moves close again. "She doesn't seem very excited to see you."

Nikki smiles, drinking in Ginni's deep green eyes. "Nothing can move Fluffy when she makes up her mind."

"Like her owner, I see." Ginni sits next to Nikki, their thighs touch. "I wonder if she'd move if two people got into the bed...and started thrashing around?"

"I doubt it," Nikki says. Though the idea of thrashing around in bed is appealing, she is distracted by thoughts of the missing gun. "I think I would enjoy another glass of wine."

They return to the living room. Ginni brings two glasses of wine and sits next to Nikki on the sofa. "What is it, Nikki? Something is eating at you tonight. Is it my missing gun?"

Nikki is unnerved at Ginni's directness. "Are you sure you don't know where the gun is, Ginni?"

"The gun was here last week," Ginni tries to explain. "I remember seeing it in the back of my desk drawer. But I've checked the desk several times, along with every inch of this apartment. I'm baffled by its disappearance. Two police officers searched also. The gun is gone." She turns her earring nervously and looks at

Nikki. "I hope you believe me."

"I want to," Nikki says, pursing her lips together.

Ginni looks at her glass, circling the rim with her finger. "Someone must have stolen it. There's no other explanation."

Ginni pauses briefly, then continues, "You know, it was no secret at the Medical Center that I had a gun. After the rapes on campus became more prevalent, most of the faculty women talked about the morality of owning a gun. Many of the staff knew I had a gun. Anyone could have stolen it."

"Okay, let's be logical. Have you noticed anything else missing from here, or out of place?" Nikki puts her glass on the coffee table and looks around. "Ginni, who has a key to your apartment?" Nikki wants answers.

Ginni thinks for a moment. "I gave one to Shari in case of an emergency. I guess it's in her apartment, or maybe at the center."

"Is she the only one?" Nikki asks.

"As far as I know." Ginni sips some wine. "Wait a minute! A few weeks ago I lost my keys at work. Edmond Long found them... I suppose someone could have duplicated them. I did ask the apartment manager to change my locks, but he said he couldn't do it just yet. I'm sure he'd verify this."

Nikki finishes her wine. "You realize that your gun may have killed Edmond Long, and someone doesn't want the police to find it. Any idea why?"

Ginni reaches across Nikki to put her glass down. Very close now, she says, "Maybe I was scheduled to be the next murder victim, but with all the police around, the murderer decided to blame it on me."

Nikki sees for the first time how frightened Ginni is and puts her arms around her. Her desire to comfort changes to something quite different. As she holds Ginni in her arms, the embrace becomes heated and intense. Ginni runs her fingers through Nikki's curly hair. Their lips meet in a soft yet passionate kiss. Then, suddenly, from the floor in front of the sofa, Fluffy gives a loud, elongated meeeow! Ginni starts giggling, and the spontaneous flow of ardor ends abruptly.

Nikki laughs too. "And she won't even stay for a little attention. I think she's heading back to your bed."

"That doesn't sound like a bad idea," Ginni says seductively. "We could join her."

Nikki is tempted but beginning to feel all her bruises again. She also needs to mentally sort through more of this case. "I'm going to have to leave."

Ginni's disappointment is apparent in her face. "Why can't you stay? Is the gun still the reason? Do you think I'm the murderer?"

"If I thought you were a murderer," Nikki says, touching Ginni's face, "I'd never let you keep my cat."

Ginni hugs her. "I know you're leaving and nothing will keep you here. I don't suppose if I took off every stitch of clothing and started dancing on the table, you would stay?"

Nikki hugs back, but hers is slow and lingering. "Very tempting. I'd like to see that, but not tonight. Can I have a raincheck?"

"No rain checks." Ginni pouts. "The offer is for now or never."

"I guess I've lost another great opportunity." Nikki smiles, then gets a serious tone in her voice. "I'll see you tomorrow, and please double lock the door after I leave. And use the chain." She kisses Ginni tenderly.

Ginni pulls away slowly, looking deeply into Nikki's grey eyes. "I think I'm falling in love. Maybe if you stay around long enough, I'll find out for sure."

CHAPTER 32

Although she wants nothing so much as to stay with Ginni, a stronger force pushes Nikki to help solve the murders. She drives back to her motel room, and opens her army trunk. Under a small pile of fatigues is her forty-five automatic and several full clips. She picks up the gun and snaps a clip in place. Nikki has mixed feelings about having a gun. She removes the clip and puts the gun back into the trunk. Her attention moves to her clothes.

The laundromat is near the university, and students staying for summer classes are washing and drying clothes. Their study notes, spread out over a low table, trigger Nikki's memory. She dumps a load of wash in a machine and races over to her office to check some old class papers. Specifically, she is looking for Lisa Holt's work.

The building is dark again, but a security guard has been assigned to each entrance, a new university policy since the murders. She asks him to accompany her to her office and wait while she quickly goes through her student files. There's a copy of Lisa's term paper in the Modern Moral Ethics course file. Lisa's paper had focused on adoption and not abortion. Nikki thanks the guard for accompanying her and returns to the laundromat.

While waiting for her clothes to dry, Nikki reads Lisa's

paper, looking for anything that will shed light on the murders. Several students wrote about adoption. The arguments were mostly conservative and ethically traditional, focusing on the needs of the child. She glances through the beginning of Lisa's paper. It differs from the others—deals with the economics of adoption. Lisa investigated cost factors related to adoptions, and her basic contention was that the morality of adoption depended on everyone involved profiting.

Nikki reads her own penciled margin notes. She questioned if profit itself could ever be moral, pointing out that if the title of the paper were changed from "The Economics of Adoption" to "Baby Selling," the arguments might be viewed differently.

The class discussion following Lisa's oral presentation was heated, Nikki remembers. Most of the students didn't want to accept adoption as a profit-making business. They couldn't accept the fact that government agencies involved in adoptions are also driven by financial motives.

Playing devil's advocate, Nikki questioned the morality of baby selling, even though international networks of commercial brokers call it "private adoption."

Lisa argued back that everyone profits, in moral as well as material ways, by such brokers. The person giving up the child gains needed resources and peace of mind, while the new parents pay for a child they truly want and accept as a priceless commodity. And the intermediary, whether lawyer or doctor, makes enough money to continue business as a service organization.

As she continues reading, Nikki is again impressed with Lisa's academic astuteness. The paper shows good research and firsthand interviews. Replaying the arguments, she wonders if Lisa was already working at the Medical Center when the paper was written, and if the firsthand information wasn't in fact from Sheldon Peterson. Nikki had been so sure the connecting factor for the murders was abortion, she never thought of a second issue.

Suddenly, a question forms in her mind: if all the suspects and victims are connected by the abortion issue, are they also connected by the adoption issue? At last, the critical puzzle piece floats into focus.

After returning to the motel, Nikki tries to quickly jot down these fresh ideas. Too tired to think anymore, she goes to bed determined to sort through this new information with Max.

She falls into a deep restless sleep where the unconscious world of free mind personifies an eerie hallway with walls pulsing and rolling in waves. In this dream, Lisa, in a leather miniskirt, calls her and holds her in a sensual embrace. Nikki twists and pulls away. Lisa frowns and then brings her right hand out from behind her back. Wielding a Medical Center letter opener, she plunges the letter opener repeatedly into Nikki, who screams and falls backward so rapidly no words come out of her open mouth. Finally, she lands on a mountain of feather pillows in the middle of a huge bed.

The bed is too soft, and she falls back, landing spread-eagle. "Where am I?" The words bounce and rebound until they make no sense. Out of one of the pillows, the ghostly figure of a woman emerges, wearing a flimsy nightgown. Her shoulders bare, breasts exposed, she comes closer. The bed is now moving in an undulating motion. The woman falls on top of Nikki, smiling and kissing her. Then, she puts a thirty-eight Smith and Wesson to Nikki's temple and, still smiling...pulls the trigger.

EVEN A HOT morning shower can't erase the discomfort lingering from her dream. Nikki phones Henry, who explains that Lisa finally sent a high-powered lawyer. Blake's written denial of Lisa's involvement in the two attacks is already submitted. Henry's frustration is evident. "We're still looking at her as a suspect, but we've got no solid evidence to prove any connection."

"Maybe I have something." Nikki dries her wet, curly hair with one hand as she talks. "I found a paper she wrote entitled

'The Economics of Adoption' for one of my classes. Her firsthand source was probably someone at the Medical Center."

There's a short silence while Henry digests this new piece of information. "That's a long shot, but it's as good as the abortion angle. I'll have someone find out if the Medical Center ever arranges adoptions. Reverend, one more thing...this afternoon I'm questioning Dr. Clayton again, about the missing gun. Maybe you want to be there?"

"You bet! I'll be there, and, Henry, please call me Nikki." They hang up with Nikki hoping this round of questioning will absolve Ginni.

Feeling energized, she phones Max, eager to talk about the paper, but he cuts her off. "Where were you last night, Rev?"

"I went to see Fluffy," Nikki tries to explain. "She escaped the blast. A friend's keeping her for awhile. After that, I went to the laundromat, and I remembered a paper Lisa Holt wrote in my class. I've got some fresh ideas on the case."

"Just back up a minute." Max's voice gets sharper. "This friend who saved old Fluffy. She wouldn't happen to be a woman doctor by any chance?"

Nikki takes a deep breath. "It's Ginni Clayton."

"There's too many coincidences with that woman." Max is still agitated. "Like what was she doing poking around your place after the explosion?"

"I was supposed to spend the night of the explosion with her." Nikki blurts this out a bit too quickly.

"I thought you were going to spend that night at my house." Max tones down his voice.

"No, I wasn't, Max." Nikki is annoyed now. She pauses, knowing that Max is worried about her safety. "We spent the previous night at my place, and we were going to be at her place the night of the explosion. I never had a chance to tell you."

Max says nothing for a minute. "You're really hung up on her, huh?"

"I really like her. And I trust her, Max," Nikki says.

"With your cat?" Max asks.

"With my heart, too," Nikki answers.

"Then that's that, Rev. You know I want you to be happy. But you need to be real careful, at least until we apprehend the murderer." He takes another long pause. "So, what about this paper Holt wrote?"

Nikki explains the subject and tells him about the heated discussions on selling babies for profit. "Something else came to me. Lisa talked about her personal experiences. Seems she had an abortion as a teenager and got pregnant again in college. Once she learned a few details about the family who adopted her second baby, she had no remorse over giving the child up and taking the money."

Nikki relives all the angry classroom emotions again. "Suppose a doctor arranged the adoption, and he worked at the Medical Center. Maybe the doctor was Peterson, and he has a secret side business selling babies."

Max agrees. "Sounds like something Sheldon Peterson would do. This is getting interesting. Go on."

"The paper would be enough of a reason for her to want to discourage me from getting involved in this case," Nikki continues. "She knew, sooner or later, I'd remember the paper or her stand on the adoption business."

Max extends the logic. "Maybe Shari Sullivan found out about the adoptions and wanted them stopped, or wanted a share of the profits."

Nikki focuses back on the first murder. "I'm having a hard time believing she was involved. Dr. Peterson might have invited her to join his adoption racket. She probably refused, threatened to expose him, and then we have motive enough for him to want to kill her."

"So, you're saying Peterson is the killer?" Max scratches his stubble.

"I think Peterson and Lisa are somehow involved in this together." Nikki's still thinking. "I just can't figure out how the murders are connected to the baby selling. One doesn't necessarily lead to the other."

"You're getting too anxious to crack the case. Slow down. I agree that somehow, those two are involved, but I'm not sure they committed the murders. Not even sure the same person killed both victims. Why would Peterson kill Edmond Long?"

Lightly scratching the burn on the back of her hand, Nikki responds, "Maybe he got in the way, or found out something by mistake. Or, like you say, was at the wrong place at the wrong time."

"And that wrong place is always the Medical Center," Max finishes her thought.

CHAPTER 33

That afternoon, Nikki meets Henry at the police station, where he briefs her. "We've got a detective checking the Medical Center records concerning adoptions. No question doctors could arrange them privately, but if they use the center, it'll be in the legal records. We're shaking them up with the inquiries, so they'll try to hide something, or run, or..."

Nikki finishes for him, "Or they might try harder to get rid of me."

"For sure, Nikki, you're getting to be a big pain in the ass for Blake and Holt," Henry offers with a short smile.

They enter the interrogation room. Ginni Clayton is seated at the long table. She looks up, surprised to see Nikki. Feeling a little uncomfortable, Nikki joins Henry sitting across the table from her.

"I'm Detective Ostrow...and you know Reverend Barnes." Henry is also uncomfortable. "I need to ask a few more questions about your gun." He opens his notebook. "You said your father sent it to you for protection, and you misplaced it. You remember seeing the gun in your desk drawer a week or so ago, but it's not there now. So let's go over your story again. Can you explain what happened to it?"

Ginni fingers her earring. "Someone must have broken into my apartment and taken the gun."

"Do many people come to your apartment?" Henry asks.

"No, not many," Ginni says quietly.

"Who do you think took it?" Henry asks.

"I don't know." Ginni's voice is quivering.

Henry pauses, then says, "I'd like the names of the people who've been in your apartment in the last two weeks."

Ginni feels a need to hold back some information. "I think that's my private business."

"If we're going to find out who took the gun...," Henry is firm, "...and possibly used it to kill Edmond Long, we need to know who had access to your apartment."

Ginni avoids looking at Nikki. "Shari Sullivan was over. Dr. Peterson brought some insurance papers last week, and Mrs. Peterson stopped last night." She looks at Nikki for a quick second and looks back at Henry. "That's all."

"No one else?" Henry asks as he writes. "There's been no one else in your apartment. You're sure?"

She nods, but Nikki realizes what isn't being said and why and offers the information. "I was there last night," she says.

Henry glances up at Nikki, then back at the list he's writing. "Does anyone have a key to your apartment, Dr. Clayton?"

"My keys were lost last week. And a few days later, Edmond Long found them at the Medical Center and returned them to me. He said he found them under my desk, against the wall." Ginni's nervousness is apparent. "I can't believe he was murdered. You know, I looked all over for the keys, in my apartment and at work." Ginni stands and asks Henry for some water. After several sips, she says, "My apartment locks haven't been changed yet. You can check with the apartment manager. I did ask him to change the locks."

Henry makes a note of this. "Did you ever give an extra

key to anyone?" he continues.

"Shari Sullivan had a key." Ginni turns the small garnet earring again.

"Anyone else have a key, Dr. Clayton?" Henry again looks at Nikki.

Ginni doesn't wait for Nikki to answer. "No! She doesn't have one. And no one else has one."

Henry doesn't flinch. "Do you have any idea why someone might want to frame you for a murder? Do you have any particular enemies?"

Ginni rubs her forehead. "I can't believe I'm a suspect in a murder investigation. This is too bizarre. No less to think of anyone angry enough to frame me." Ginni is clearly trying to figure this out. "I get along with my co-workers. Well, most of them. No, I can't think of anyone."

"Perhaps someone who doesn't like your lifestyle?" Henry looks directly at her.

Nikki starts to protest, thinks better of it, and says nothing.

Ginni stiffens but answers softly, "If you mean my lifestyle as a doctor...people are always jealous of our supposed status. If you mean my being a lesbian, I try to keep that private. You know, Don't ask, don't tell."

Henry brings the questioning to a close. "Dr. Clayton, the thirty-eight caliber Smith and Wesson your father described as the gun he gave you was probably the murder weapon that killed Edmond Long. Since we can't find the gun, you remain a suspect. So, please don't leave town without letting us know."

Henry smiles and thanks Ginni for cooperating. He closes the folder and quietly says to Nikki, "I'll keep you posted." He leaves the room.

Nikki leans over the table toward Ginni, touching her hand. "What about dinner tonight?"

Ginni tries to regain some composure. "That's sweet, but

I'm on call tonight. I'm seeing emergency patients until eleven." Ginni wants to ask Nikki why she didn't tell her she would be present during the questioning, but doesn't.

Nikki wrinkles her brow. "Can I see you after eleven?"

"I don't know what shape I'll be in. I use night call to catch up on all the paperwork and mail I've tossed in my filing cabinet during the week. By the time I'm finished, I'm not always suitable for human companionship."

"I'll take my chances," Nikki asserts. "We can go back to your place."

"Don't try and tempt me," Ginni interjects with a smile. "If you come to my place, you spend the night, the whole night." A mischievous grin suddenly appears.

Nikki smiles. "I'll be back in my motel room by ten. Call. I like hearing your voice."

"I will call," Ginni says.

ON THE DRIVE to Max's house, Nikki begins feeling frustrated and lonely. Her relationship with Ginni reminds her of the joy associated with being a couple, as well as the pain of separation. She remembers this is the price of falling in love.

Rosa's dinner resembles a small feast, with only one thing missing—a strolling violinist. Max is in an up mood, proud as a peacock, surrounded by loving wife and children. *He finally made it out of Vietnam*, Nikki thinks to herself. *For Max, the war is finally over. Maureen made it out in a body bag. What about me? Will I ever make it out?*

She secretly hopes dinner will end quickly and begs off the rest of the evening to sort clothes and, as she puts it, "wait for an important call." She regrets this last slip.

Max walks her to the door. "Who's the call from, Rev?" He feels self-conscious. "I don't want you thinking I'm prying into your personal business, but this is about your personal safety, since Dr. Clayton is a suspect."

Nikki should be angry, but she isn't. "I understand. We're friends—we look out for each other."

She puts her hand on the door handle, but Max has more to say. "Clayton's involved in this case. I believe she may be able to lead us to the killer."

Again, a shiver goes down the back of Nikki's neck, but she answers steadfastly, "I don't think we have to worry about Ginni. We probably need to concentrate on Blake or Holt."

CHAPTER 34

On her drive back to the motel, Nikki has too much time to think. Briefly, she wonders if Ginni could be involved in Peterson's scams, then promptly erases the thought...Ginni's not the killer.

Just as she pushes open the motel room door, the phone rings. She grabs the receiver. "Nikki? Is that you?" Ginni's whispering.

"Yes. I just got in." Nikki sits on the edge of the bed. Cigarette holes adorn the bedspread.

"Can you get over here right away?" Ginni asks nervously. "I think I've found something important. Shari mailed it to me, and it's been in my backlog."

Nikki's alarmed. "Can't you at least tell me what it is?"

Ginni hesitates. "I don't want to discuss it on the phone. There is still one patient to see, and some staff are still in the building. Please come immediately."

Nikki's first instinct is to get to the Medical Center as fast as possible. But she thinks twice. "Maybe I better call Henry Ostrow for backup. That'll keep us both safe."

"No!" Ginni stops her. "I don't want the police or anyone else to see this unless it's necessary." Ginni's firm. "Come alone."

Nikki decides to take the risk. "Be there in ten minutes."

Nikki is unnerved now...like Vietnam before a major Viet Cong shelling. She opens the army trunk and takes out her forty-five automatic and a full clip. Snapping the clip in place, she puts the gun through her leather belt, behind her back and under the black blazer she's wearing. To be safe, she drops another clip into her pocket. Finally, she looks in the mirror, kisses the gold cross which hangs around her neck, and tucks it under her shirt.

NIKKI IGNORES THE Medical Center guard, who's busy chatting with departing staffers. So much for security! She walks briskly down the corridor to Suite B. The waiting area is dark and empty. She goes around the reception desk, past the first examining room, and heads down the inner hallway toward the common room, where she expects to find Ginni.

She feels her heart thudding. As she passes examining room B, she hears familiar voices, barely audible. She turns back, walking noiselessly to the examining room door. Her right hand automatically reaches around and grabs the butt of the forty-five in her belt, while her left hand quietly squeezes the door handle, twists, and cautiously opens the door.

The bright, overhead lights bounce off the stainless steel sink and exam table, giving the small room a sterile, unreal quality. Ginni, who nervously grasps the stethoscope draped around her neck, stands across the room, facing the door, her back to the wall. Two things separate her from Nikki, the empty examining table in front of her and Lisa Holt, her back to Nikki.

Ginni's eyes widen slightly as she sees Nikki, then they rivet back to Lisa, who's crumpling a large piece of paper in her left hand. "This is the only evidence that can link us to the murders. When I destroy Shari's letter, all the proof is gone. And unfortunately, Dr. Clayton, you're the only one left who knows what Shari found out. I really wish you hadn't found this letter."

Ginni steps toward the exam table, moving closer to Lisa, trying to reason with her. "Lisa, you don't want to shoot me. I can't hurt you. You're young. Why ruin the rest of your life? Please don't..."

Lisa turns slightly to her right and a horrified Nikki sees the gun in her hand. Nikki's forty-five slides easily out of her belt. Her instincts take over. She raises the gun, holding it in both hands.

"Lisa! Drop that damn gun!" Nikki barks.

Nikki steps into the room. Her voice is deep, tight. "Get out of here, Ginni!" she orders. "Get out of here! Right now!" But Ginni is frozen.

Suddenly, Lisa spins around. And Nikki stares down the barrel of a Smith and Wesson thirty-eight. "It's over, Lisa! Put the gun down!" Nikki stares coldly at Lisa, and the twisted sense of power she sees in Lisa's eyes tells her this is a standoff. Nikki realizes that she's ready to die to protect Ginni. She couldn't save Mo, but...

"I warned you, Professor." Lisa's voice betrays a nervousness, a moment's hesitation. "I told you...no one gets in my way."

Nikki watches Lisa, who holds the gun with one hand. Nikki's mind is an x-ray machine, looking for the weak spot. This might be her last chance.

"Lisa, you're really pissing me off..." The forty-five in Nikki's hands seems to have transformed her. She's no longer Reverend Barnes. "But I'm gonna give you one last chance before I blow your fucking head off." The former Lieutenant Barnes talks tough. Nikki is aiming the forty-five at Lisa's chest. "Now bend down and slowly place the gun on the floor." Nikki's voice is deadly soft.

Ginni can't believe what she is witnessing and realizes that she needs to distract Lisa, even if only for one second. Suddenly, she flings her stethoscope against the side wall. Instantly, Lisa turns her head. Time stands still. Nikki begins to squeeze the trigger.

"Holy God Almighty forgive...I...can't."

Abruptly, Nikki snaps a left hand blow to Lisa's gun hand, pushing it aside. Then, before Lisa knows what's happening, Nikki lands a hard punch with the heel of her hand to Lisa's nose.

Lisa screams and stumbles backward to the floor. Nikki momentarily loses her balance. Ginni stands paralyzed, not knowing quite what to do. Lisa has no intention of dropping her weapon and, as her hand hits the floor, the gun fires. The shot is deafening. Lisa and Nikki instinctively look at where the gun was pointed.

Ginni is hit! She bounces against the wall and collapses to the floor. Bright red blood begins to stain the upper right side of Ginni's white lab coat.

Nikki releases a heart-wrenching scream. "Holy God! No! Not again!"

Nikki takes a moment too long to look at Ginni. Lisa jumps up, pointing her gun at Nikki. Nikki's running on pure adrenaline. Now she's driven by the anger and fear she feels over Ginni being shot. Automatically, she swings her forty-five and smashes Lisa's gun hand. Lisa fires the gun as she cries out in pain and drops to the floor.

The sound of the gun explodes in Nikki's ears. She freezes. The past engulfs her...the room echoes like an empty bunker.

Lisa takes advantage of the moment and scoops up the gun with her uninjured hand. Nikki sees in her mind's eye the Viet Cong rising from the grass again. *They're close enough. She fires the forty-five and shoots the gun out of the enemy's hand.* Half of Lisa's hand is blown away. *Now it's hand-to-hand combat with the enemy.* She lunges at Lisa's throat and bangs her head hard against the nearby wall. Lisa's body jerks on impact and hits the floor with a nasty crack.

Ginni moans, her voice weak. Barely audible, she calls, "Nikki...Nikki...are you all right?"

Ginni's voice brings Nikki out of the in-country rice paddies. *It was a dream,* Nikki thinks, as she finds herself staring at the vision chart on the wall. But then she sees Lisa, unconscious, on the floor.

Ginni faintly calls her again, "Nikki...Nikki!"

Nikki shakes off the memories and quickly moves around the exam table. Ginni lies crumpled on the floor. Nikki immediately kneels next to her, watching in horror as blood stains the whole right side of Ginni's lab coat.

Nikki lays her gun down. Then she takes Ginni into her arms. "Ginni? I'm so sorry. Why? Why didn't you get out when I told you?"

Ginni can't open her eyes now. She licks her lips, already feeling parched from the loss of blood. "I...couldn't...leave you," she whispers.

Nikki fights back tears. Ginni's chest wound is dangerously close to her heart. Nikki knows she must do something quickly to stop the bleeding. Instinctively, she lays Ginni back down and grabs a clean gown off the exam table. She desperately presses the folded cotton gown against the wound.

"Nikki..." Ginni tries to talk again. "Lisa...killer...Shari found out...about the baby."

"Don't talk." Nikki touches Ginni's dry lips. "Save your strength. Everything will be okay. You'll be okay. You can tell me everything later."

Nikki lifts the now blood-soaked gown off Ginni's wound. More blood trickles from the wound, and she applies pressure again. Nikki is petrified. She screams, "Help! Help! Someone, please help! We need help!" She looks around the sterile, sparsely furnished room and sees a telephone on the wall, next to the sink.

The security guard must have heard the gunshots and called the police. But there is no sign of the guard. *The phone must have a line to the security desk*, she says to herself. Fearful that Ginni might lose too much blood if she lets up on the pressure, Nikki doesn't move. She looks at the phone across the room and mumbles, "911...911," as if the litany will automatically dial the number. This time, when she looks back at the bleeding Ginni, her mind flashes back to Xuan Loc...to Max dying in her arms. Max fades into the present and becomes Ginni. Nikki's whole body is shaking, tears well up in her eyes. "Please!" she screams again. "Someone help me!"

Suddenly, Sheldon Peterson appears at the door, pushing it open in a dramatic entrance. "What's going on? What happened?"

"Quick, call 911!" Nikki regains some of her composure. "Get the police and an ambulance. Ginni and Lisa both need immediate medical attention."

Peterson walks over to Lisa's limp body and kneels down with his back to Nikki. He feels for a carotid pulse, stands up, and turns to Nikki. He casually holds Lisa's Smith and Wesson thirty-eight.

"Is she all right?" Nikki asks, not looking at Peterson. She concentrates on stemming Ginni's bleeding. "Please, you need to call an ambulance right away." But when she looks up at him, she sees he is holding the gun.

Her mind drifts again...*the Viet Cong are firing. They're so close, she can smell the gun powder from their rifles. She can't drag Ginni behind the trees. There's no cover. They're both too far into the open...have to get away...*

Peterson jars Nikki back to the present when he sarcastically says, "Poor Lisa." He has Nikki's attention, and she watches in terror as he bends down, deliberately puts the gun to Lisa's temple—and fires. Nikki jumps with the blast of the gun and instantly moves her body over Ginni, trying to shield her as she had Max.

Peterson looks at Nikki and snickers. He walks over to the wall phone and yanks it out of the wall. "If I were you, I wouldn't count on being rescued by the security guard. Nothing but make-believe cops." Then he raises the gun again, pointing it at Nikki. "How convenient. I couldn't have planned this scene better myself."

Nikki breaks eye contact with him and forces her attention back to Ginni. *Gotta do something. Gotta get Ginni out of here...Must find a way to keep us both alive...Maybe I can talk my way out.* Nikki speaks without looking up at Peterson. "Please...put the gun down and help me. You're off the hook... Lisa confessed to the murders."

She looks at him, waiting for a response.

Peterson starts walking slowly toward Nikki. She looks at him and then at her gun, lying on the floor—just two feet away. If she moves quickly...

"Don't even think of going for that gun," he says coldly, coming up next to her and kicking it across the room. It lands next to Lisa's body. He's in control now. He turns his back on Nikki and walks to the door.

He's not looking at her. Here's Nikki's chance, but she's not sure what to do. She needs a weapon...something to attack him with...something to overpower him. She looks around...the stethoscope...a wastebasket, but it's too far away...scissors...a bottle of alcohol...a small stainless steel pan, a rolling stool.

She's too late...too slow. He closes the examining room door and turns back to her. "This is better than I hoped," he says smugly. "Yes, dear Lisa was useful, after all. And as far as the police are concerned, a distraught Lisa shot poor Dr. Clayton. Then, being the sensitive girl that she is, took her own life, but not before she shot you, too."

Nikki feels Ginni's life seeping through her fingers. She tries to stall the inevitable, to keep him talking until she can make a plan, think of a way out. "Why would Lisa shoot Ginni? And how is Ginni involved in all this?"

"You couldn't figure it out, could you, Reverend Barnes?" Peterson enjoys the power he has at this moment. "You and your cop friend's collective intelligence, and I fooled you all," Peterson gloats. "And by the way, there's no one here but us. I knew Clayton would be alone at this hour, so I told Lisa to come tonight and ask about the letter. I never did trust Clayton. She was always such a suspicious bitch. And I'm an excellent judge of character. I get that from my grandfather, the Right Reverend Gerald Peterson, a very self-righteous, holier-than-thou son of a bitch. Something like you."

Nikki wants to keep Peterson talking, but she knows how unpredictable borderline personalities can be. She's had enough psychotherapy training to know that a sociopath like Peterson loves the feeling of being superhuman, loves having the power to take what he wants when he wants it. He can go off at any time, for any reason. But she needs to keep him engaged, hoping something will come to her—a way to save Ginni. She looks at him and calmly says, "Susan's son was adopted through some secret enterprise of yours, and Lisa got nervous. She was afraid Shari might find out and go to the authorities about the adoption. Isn't that right, Dr. Peterson?"

Peterson sits on the small, rolling stool next to the exam table and starts to laugh. He rolls it closer to Nikki, still laughing. "You're so wrong. Excuse the pun, but dead wrong. Of course, Jason was adopted—I bought him for Susan. Did you know money can buy anything? Susan became such a bore after our baby died. It got to be so tiresome. A dead baby was all she could think of. She became totally useless. First, to me in my career. Then, to me in bed—dull, distant, passionless."

He gets up and kicks the stool under the table. "I married her because she looked good. She was impressive when I needed an impressive wife. But the miscarriage changed her. I thought a new child would bring back her sexual passions. And I was right again. It did. Unfortunately, there was no lawyer's sanction on that adoption, so Susan always worried. I, on the other hand, had been making money for several years on adoptions, money the IRS could never touch.

"That was until Shari Sullivan entered the picture. She

was a lot like you and my grandfather—extremely righteous and moral. So quick to criticize for even the smallest infraction." He points the gun at Nikki again. "I hated my grandfather, and I hated Shari Sullivan."

Peterson is starting to slip again, starting to feel out of control. Nikki knows she has to make him feel empowered. She has to calm him down.

"Shari wasn't really a threat to you," Nikki says softly, trying to keep her voice soothing and calm. "How did she find out about the adoptions? Was she in on them?"

"In on them," he laughs. "No one was in on them, unless I let them in." He calms down, crossing his arms with the gun still in his hand. "Stupid Susan told that dyke about Jason's adoption. Of course, Sullivan came to me for more information. She thought she was so superior—wanted to help Susan legally adopt the child. Even threatened to bring in the police and ruin my lucrative business."

He relaxes more now, letting his arms hang loosely at his sides, pacing back and forth, as if he's lecturing to a class. Nikki watches the gun as it swings back and forth. She needs to get that gun away from him.

"Do you realize that over fifteen students a year come to the Medical Center wanting to get rid of an unwanted pregnancy?" He pauses, making sure he has Nikki's full attention. He wants her to know how clever he is. "Out of those fifteen, I can talk at least half into going full term and giving the baby up for adoption. Do you want to know how I talk them into it? Money! Yes, money talks. I give them each five thousand dollars." He stops again, waving the gun for emphasis.

"You may ask how can I afford that. Well, my dear Reverend, I have an endless supply of barren couples, advertising in the back of college newspapers, who are willing to pay me forty thousand dollars apiece for an unwanted baby and a phony piece of paper saying they are parents." He gazes upward and adds, "It's amazing, really!"

Ginni tries to move and lets out a small moan. Peterson tightens his grip on the revolver but continues talking, in an almost manic way. "I tried to get Susan to persuade Sullivan to leave the Medical Center, resign, and stop snooping around. I also wanted an end to their sick affair. But Susan hasn't been herself since the miscarriage. Always blamed herself. During the first few months after the baby died, I tried to hire a companion for her, someone to console her and cheer her up. Lisa was pregnant and looking for a place to stay. But Susan wasn't really open to Lisa's support. But then they became bound by something stronger. After all, both are Jason's mother."

Nikki tries not to show her surprise at this revelation. She takes off her blazer and puts it under Ginni's head, feeling the extra clip in the pocket. She tries to find a dry area on the exam gown and applies pressure once again to Ginni's wound. Playing on Peterson's sick ego, Nikki asks, "So what happened to Shari Sullivan?"

"Reverend Barnes, I'm surprised and disappointed! You haven't figured anything out, have you? And Lisa thought you were so smart. Everyone always thought my grandfather was so smart, too. But he wasn't. He was a bastard, who belittled everything I did. He was never wrong." Peterson waves the gun again, making a point. "But he *was* wrong. I kept reminding Susan that the authorities could take her baby away. That kept her quiet and in line, but Shari Sullivan was not like Susan. That's where my lovely, sexy Lisa came in." Mockingly, he throws a kiss at Lisa's body.

He looks back at Nikki and begins his pacing again. "On that particular morning, Sullivan delivered an ultimatum to me. I don't like being threatened or told what to do. So I explained to Lisa our life together was in jeopardy. Lisa was very worked up by the time we entered the exam room. Sullivan was reading some mail, waiting for a patient to return. She was such a bitch, never would listen to reason. Just kept saying in that condescending way of hers, 'It's no use. I've made up my mind. It's the best thing for Susan and Jason.' Then she told us to get out. She turned her back to me and had the gall to dismiss us."

Peterson takes a few steps closer to Nikki. "That's when I grabbed Sullivan's letter opener and...I...I thought my problems were over. It was easy enough to get Blake to take the blame. After all, Lisa had been cultivating Blake's attentions long enough to incriminate him easily. But you posed another problem. We didn't count on a stupid woman priest, trying to crush everything that brings me joy!" He's shouting now, and Nikki is afraid he's going to crack and pull the trigger.

She turns her head away from him and leans over Ginni. She kisses her tenderly on the cheek...waiting for Peterson to fire the gun. Nothing happens. Nikki looks back at Peterson. He's staring at her. She knows he's evil personified. A parasite who lives off the pain of other people. A soul stealer, who enjoys bragging about his black deeds.

He shakes his head and says in disgust, "How pathetic you are. Just like my grandfather. Even on his deathbed, he belittled me." He leans over and looks at Ginni. Now, he and Nikki are only inches apart. "You do like those lady doctors, don't you? How sinful, Reverend. My grandfather never sinned like you. And, I imagine we have Clayton's charm to blame for your involvement in this whole affair." He gives a short laugh and backs away from Nikki.

"I'm not afraid of being a sinner," Nikki says, feeling the time has come to stand up for herself. "I accept myself as being human. And I'm not afraid to die."

"Oh, please!" Peterson mocks her. "You sound just like Edmond Long. 'I have sinned, but I have asked forgiveness.' What bullshit! And you'll never guess who that old sinner Edmond really is. None other than Jason's real daddy. That's right, Susan's store-bought baby is the love child of Lisa and Edmond. Mr. Religious

Right lost it one night with his college chum Lisa. Right in his own house, while the wife and kids were at church."

All the pieces of the puzzle are coming together. "Long found out about Jason, didn't he?" Nikki asks.

"Bravo, Professor. You finally made one connection. But Edmond was prying where he shouldn't. I warned him, but he wouldn't back off. Started ranting about God telling him to claim his natural child. I couldn't let that happen, could I? It wasn't hard for me to get the gun from Clayton's desk and use it appropriately on Edmond. I was even going to return the gun but never got the chance."

He waves the gun in his hand. "And what do you know, here it is again, almost back to its proper owner."

Nikki knows from Peterson's tone that her time is getting short. She stands, defiantly, showing him that he has no power over her. He can't control her or hurt her, because she has something he doesn't. Simple faith in herself, in other people, in something larger than life itself.

...Nikki hears the screams of the mortar shells just before they explode. Have to get Ginni into the bunker. More screams, then the pounding of the guns. The mortars are exploding closer and closer. She's afraid of the shrapnel...the fallout...

Nikki struggles to stay in the present. Time is running out for her and for Ginni. She steels herself, saying boldly, "No one will believe that Lisa had any reason to kill Ginni."

Peterson pensively puts the gun barrel next to his cheek. "I beg to differ, Reverend. Here's the scenario. Clayton killed Shari Sullivan in a jealous rage. Everyone knew how close they were. Long found out she was a murderer, so Clayton killed him, too. Then, she tried to blame the whole thing on Eugene Blake. This caused an unstable Lisa Holt to seek revenge by killing the good doctor. After all, Lisa was just protecting her lover, Eugene."

He starts to laugh, very pleased with himself. "Like the plot so far, Reverend? Let me see...oh yes...Lisa confronts Clayton, which costs both their lives."

"The police won't believe any of that garbage," Nikki says, shooting the words back, deliberately riling Peterson more. Then she takes a step toward him, trying to provoke him into some action, some movement that will leave him open, vulnerable to her. Her hands are rolled into fists. She's ready for the attack as she steps closer to the psychopath with a gun.

The exam room door slowly begins to open. Nikki stops. Her heart pounds harder and faster as her eyes dart from the door to Peterson.

"Too late for you to worry about what the police will or will not believe," he mocks. "Somehow, you just got caught in Lisa and Clayton's cross fire." Pointing the pistol at Nikki's head, he begins to squeeze the trigger.

...She has Max in the woods but now there's shooting from behind her as well as across the field. They're surrounded, but not by the Viet Cong. They speak English. They're our guys... a recon unit...and a chopper...we're safe...

Suddenly the door flies open and bangs against the wall. A flash of movement explodes into the room.

"Nicolette, I'll save you! Gimme that gun, you slimy bastard!"

Barrett takes Peterson by surprise. Spinning around with a block, slap, and twist, she grabs his gun hand, then knees him hard in the balls. He drops the gun as he begins to double over. Barrett's tall, muscular body is an easy match for Peterson's. She grabs his head with both hands and pulls his face down to meet her knee. He screams in pain as she breaks his nose. His face turns into a bloody mess. Peterson doesn't know whether to grab his crotch or his face.

"You fucking bitch, I'll kill you."

Barrett spins around and lands a flying kick to Peterson's solar plexus. "I don't think so," she says, smiling. He falls backward, doubled over in pain, sucking air.

Nikki can't believe her eyes. She dives, sliding across the floor, and quickly retrieves her forty-five. She holds the gun with both hands and points it at Peterson's face, hurling her words at him. "Don't move, you fuckin' bastard, or I swear, I'll fill you with every bullet in this clip!" She walks over to him and gives him several good kicks in the ribs. "Now roll over and lie face down!" she orders.

Barrett plants her booted foot on his back. Peterson whimpers, but lies still, his arms above his head like a beached swimmer.

Barrett huffs and puffs and grins triumphantly. "Nicolette, I've been waiting outside the center. I wanted to talk to you about the dinner. You don't have to wear a black shirt. You can wear one of those colored priest shirts." Her grin shows sparkling white teeth.

Nikki ignores Barrett's inappropriate craziness, never so happy to see her as she is right now. Her chef in shining armor. "Go call 911. Get the police and an ambulance, right away. Ginni's life depends on you. Hurry!"

As soon as Barrett runs out, Peterson starts to get up. "I told you to stay down!" Nikki points the gun at him, but he seems unafraid.

He continues getting up, his expression smug. "I don't think you'll shoot me. You're a priest, a woman of the cloth. You don't have the guts to shoot an unarmed man. What would your God think?" He moves toward the door, turning back only long enough to say, "I'm walking out of here."

"Don't, Peterson! Don't make me shoot you!" The dark side of Nikki takes over— something she pushed away years ago, a blackness she keeps locked up. It's free now.

Peterson turns back once again, long enough to say, "By the way, Shari Sullivan didn't write any letter explaining all about Jason and the adoption. I sent that letter to Clayton, just to set her up for Lisa." He turns, still laughing, and starts walking down the hall.

Nikki follows him into the hall. She raises her arms, aims the gun, and squeezes the trigger. The gun explodes, and the loud noise reverberates down the long hallway. Peterson screams in pain and falls down, clutching his shattered leg. He looks at her wide-eyed in disbelief. She walks toward him and squeezes off another round into his other leg.

Nikki hears the faint sound of sirens and walks quickly back to Ginni. She takes the unconscious woman into her arms. Choking on every word, she whispers, "Ginni. Please don't leave me. Don't die. I just found you, and I love you...I love you."

CHAPTER 35

Paramedics from Mercy Hospital are first to arrive. There's a flurry of activity in the examining room, and Nikki is urged out of the way and into the hall while they work. Ginni's unconscious. An emergency medical technician takes her vitals and reports them by radio directly to the hospital emergency room. At the same time, a second EMT applies a pressure bandage, stopping her bleeding. He also starts an intravenous infusion of glucose and saline to prevent shock. By the time he finishes testing the IV, the first EMT has her covered with a blanket and has moved the gurney in place for transport to the hospital.

Uniformed police remove Lisa's body. Henry Ostrow and the crime unit are on the scene, taking photographs and statements. One of the officers is assigned to guard Peterson. The EMTs treat his wounds and hook up an IV. Then they move Peterson onto a gurney and out to the second ambulance.

Nikki, exhausted and frantic over Ginni's critical condition, tells Henry about Peterson's confessions. Henry then shares his own recent findings. "There's an illegal adoption business going on here at the center. With a little persuasion, a couple of staffers were very happy to tell us what they knew. Seems Peterson would talk the girls from the college who came in for abortions into giving birth to the babies. Then he paid off the girls and sold the babies to desperate couples who wanted children. We're also calling in the FBI."

"He told me all about the baby selling," Nikki says, still shaking her head in disbelief. "He was taking a lot of money from those couples. And he wasn't giving much of it to the girls."

Now Henry is shaking his head too. "Only problem was, too many people were getting wise to what Peterson was doing. That's why he was getting ready to move the abortions to his new clinic on the East Side. He knew he could convince a lot of those girls into selling their babies. The man knows how to use money to make money."

Henry puts his hand on her shoulder and says, "With what we got from our interviews and Peterson's confessions to you, this adoption business is shut down for good. Peterson will spend the rest of his life behind bars."

Barrett is standing at the other end of the hallway, giving her statement to one of the officers. Nikki and Henry wait until she finishes talking. Then Nikki hugs her and thanks her for being there and saving her life. Henry also praises Barrett for her courage. As Nikki follows the gurney carrying Ginni, she leaves Barrett in the hallway with the policemen, basking in her new role as champion of justice.

Nikki gets permission to ride in the ambulance with Ginni. She sits away from the medical activity, watching Ginni's unconscious body. Ginni's face is covered with an oxygen mask— her breathing labored. Nikki can hear each tortured breath. She prays with all her heart. And in her mind, she holds Ginni close and tells her again she loves her.

AFTER THREE HOURS of emergency surgery and another two hours in recovery, Ginni is finally allowed visitors. Nikki quietly enters the room and approaches the bed. A heart monitor beeps in a steady rhythm, as green lines bump up and down on a monitor above Ginni's bed. Two long drain tubes snake from under the sheets to a container on the floor, and two different, colored IV bags hang from the same pole next to her right arm. The silent form on the bed frightens Nikki, but she leans over anyway and kisses Ginni on the cheek.

"Nikki." Ginni's voice sounds weak, sleepy, and slurred. "You...look...terrible...again. Do you ever look in a mirror?"

Nikki's clothes are now spotted with blood. But she's too happy about Ginni's predicted recovery to worry about anything else. "You have to take me as I am, a hopelessly sloppy dresser. Will that affect our relationship?" Nikki jokes rather than break down and cry.

Ginni reaches up with her unaffected arm and touches Nikki's cheek. "I will take you any way. I love you."

WHILE GINNI RECUPERATES in her apartment, which she now shares with Nikki and Fluffy, Nikki is in North Buffalo attending Barrett's carefully orchestrated dinner in the elegant Fairburn home.

Nikki sits at a long mahogany table, looking at her place setting—which seems to have too many forks—deliberately trying not to stare at Celine. But Celine is, indeed, as Barrett has often remarked, black, beautiful, and brilliant." When Nikki first arrived and Barrett introduced her to Celine, Nikki realized immediately that Celine is not African American. She's Amerasian—one of thousands of children fathered by American soldiers during the Vietnam War. Coincidences are making Nikki very uncomfortable again.

Throughout the eight-course meal, various toasts are made, several addressed to the missing mother. No one calls her Dragon Lady, however. She is referred to as mother, or as my wife, Tracy Fairburn. Another toast is made to the visiting priest and professor, Reverend Barnes. And the last toast is to the chef. As promised, Nikki takes every opportunity to convince Mr.

Fairburn of the wisdom of sending Barrett to the Culinary Institute. Her pink cleric shirt doesn't seem to add or detract from her conviction. The wonderful food is enough proof of Barrett's talent and justifiable goals. By dessert, Fairburn gives his permission and his blessings, and Nikki says a silent prayer of thanksgiving.

Nikki and Fairburn move into the parlor for coffee, while Barrett and Celine clear the dining room table. Douglas Fairburn is a tall, distinguished-looking man with grey hair and grey-brown eyes. His trim, muscular body belies his age, which Nikki guesses is at least late fifties.

"I'm sorry you couldn't meet my wife," Fairburn says, pouring the coffee from an ornate silver pot. "She's away on business in Southeast Asia. She's from Vietnam, you know. We lived in Malaysia for a time after the war."

The hair on Nikki's arms stands up at this last bit of information. "How did you happen to land in Buffalo?" Nikki asks, trying not to appear too eager for an answer.

"It was really Tracy's choice," he says, sitting on the sofa and crossing his legs. "I have company offices all over the world and in the four different time zones of the United States. Tracy said she had a friend in Vietnam who always talked about settling in Buffalo after the war. I guess that's why she chose it, but I don't think she ever did find that friend."

Celine pops her head into the room and tells her father the call he's been waiting for just came in. He excuses himself and leaves Nikki, confused now and alone, in the study. She gets up, distracted by what he has said and what it may mean. She walks over to the piano and looks at some of the family photos lined up across the top. Celine enters the room with a tray of cookies, just as Nikki picks up a picture of the daughters with their mother.

The mother is Trang! Nikki can't believe it. *So Trang did finally make it out with the baby. Celine's mother and Barrett's mother is Trang!* She repeats the name out loud. "Trang."

"No one's called her that since I was a child in Malaysia," Celine says in a hushed voice. She walks over and stands next to Nikki. "I think you know my mother. When Barrett was gushing over you one night, Mother said she thought she knew you before you became a priest."

Nikki is overcome with feelings. Tears well up in her eyes. "I knew her a long time ago...in Vietnam. I can't believe this!" She struggles to regain her composure.

Celine takes the picture. "During the war? She won't ever talk about that, but I think that's why she went on this business trip. She's going to visit relatives in Vietnam. I think to make some peace with herself and her past."

"We all have to," Nikki says quietly. "All of us who were over there—it takes so long to put it to rest." Nikki is starting to shake inside.

"My father was with the foreign service in Malaysia when he met my mother. They got married, and we lived there for three years. I can hardly remember it. When we came to America, she changed her name to Tracy. I haven't heard her called Trang since I was a young child."

Nikki isn't listening. "I'm not feeling very well. I think I better leave. Please thank Barrett and say goodbye to your father."

She practically runs to her car and drives blindly for the next ten minutes. At last, she pulls over to the side of the road and sobs softly. Memories surge forward and fill her mind. How, in her despair over Mo's death, she almost killed Trang. How Trang, as her Mama San, wrangled the money out of her, hoping it would get her to Malaysia. Sad memories from a dark time in her life. But now she knows Trang and the baby are alive. Trang's a successful businesswoman, a wife, and a mother. She made peace with the war. Now it's time for Nikki to put Vietnam to rest, too.

AFTER WEEKS OF planning, Nikki and Ginni are finally going to Mexico for a month's vacation. They're flying out of Buffalo, which gives Nikki an opportunity to stop at the Vietnam Veterans' Memorial located there.

Ginni waits in the car as Nikki crosses the small lawn leading to the back of the monument. She comes around the carved stone and finds Max waiting for her.

He gives a weak smile. "Ginni said you were stopping here. Thought you might want company."

Nikki says nothing but stares at the list of names. Hundreds of names, blurring with the pattern of the granite. She focuses her eyes, scanning the alphabetical list until she finds it. Then she puts her hand gently on the name, brushing her fingertips across the letters. Maureen Matthews. It's Mo. Nikki starts to sob, resting her face against the cold stone, her hand still on the name. Max puts his arm around her.

"She's okay, now. She's home. We're all finally home. You got to let it go, let it all go."

Nikki cries from the deepest parts of her being. She cries for all the friends, lovers, sisters, and brothers who are now names on granite stone. She cries not just for who she's lost but for what she's lost. Closing her eyes, she cries for forgiveness.

When there are no tears left, she pushes away from the stone and looks again at the monument. "In my heart, Max, I know we made a difference. The government did the lying and the destroying, but we tried to help. All that mindless savagery—can I ever forget it and be free?"

She doesn't wait for an answer, just touches the name once more and walks back toward her car. Max follows her.

He opens her door. "Anyway, I couldn't let you leave without saying goodbye." Max's face carries the sadness of their parting in Nam.

"I'm only going for a month. We're coming back." Nikki tries to keep it light.

"I know. I know. It's just...," he's stumbling. "We haven't talked much. What I'm trying to say is...I care about you...all the different yous." He's looking at his feet.

Tears are starting to choke Nikki again. "Max, you'll always be my friend."

He hugs her as close as he can. "I love you, Rev."

GINNI HOLDS NIKKI'S hand as the plane roars into the sky. She leans over. "Are you praying again?"

Nikki smiles, feeling a happiness she thought was lost forever. "It's taken a long time...but I think my prayers have finally been answered."

If You Liked This Book...

Authors seldom get to hear what readers like about their work. If you enjoyed this mystery, *Agenda for Murder*, why not let the author know? We are sure she will be delighted to get your feedback. Simply write the author:

Joan Albarella
c/o Rising Tide Press
3831 N. Oracle Rd.
Tucson, AZ 85705

About the Author

Joan Albarella is the author of four books of poetry and is an associate professor of writing at an educational opportunity center. She lives with two newly adopted older cats in the artist Charles Burchfield's house, which is across from a beautiful creek illuminated by Orion on clear nights.

She has a special passion for small towns with character, Sunday macaroni dinner, and a celebratory good cigar.

Don't Miss This Exciting Mystery

Deadly Rendezvous: A Toni Underwood Mystery
Diane Davidson

Back in the lodge, Toni began wandering among the people gathered there, her eyes frantically searching for Megan. She had a frown on her face when she turned to the sergeant in charge.

"Are you positive everyone is here? All the guests? You didn't miss anybody?" Toni asked, suddenly feeling a knife-like panic rip at her insides.

"Yes, Lieutenant Underwood, this is everyone."

Toni turned to Kelly. "What villa is Mrs. Marshall in?"

"Number three, down by the pool. Here's the key."

"Let's go, Sal." Toni was already halfway out the door, with fear consuming her, enveloping her in its clutches.

The room was dark and hot. *No one's been here all night.* Toni rushed through the living room area and into the large bedroom. The bed hadn't been slept in. Megan's pink cotton robe was lying in a heap on the floor.

"Her purse and car keys are gone," Sally said quietly, seeing the fear written on Toni's face.

"Megan! Megan!" Toni called out as she headed toward the bathroom.

"Toni." Sally put her hand on Toni's arm. "Toni...she's not here," Sally said, afraid to say what she really thought.

"What do you mean she's not here? That can't be. She knew we were coming to get her today; she wouldn't leave." Fear flooded Toni's face. "Where? Where would she go, Sally?"

Then her eyes narrowed; they were like daggers, her jaw set tight. She suddenly turned without a word, and ran out of the villa and toward the lodge.

"Toni, wait! Don't do anything stupid." Sally ran after her. Catching Toni by the arm, she spun her around and forced her up against the villa wall.

"Let me go, Sal." The look in Toni's eyes was terrifying. "That bitch Clark has her hidden away somewhere as a hostage. I'm gonna kill the mother-fucker if she doesn't tell me where Megan is, right now."

"Listen to me, please," Sally pleaded.

Toni was fighting to free herself. "I don't wanna hurt you, Sal, now let me go!" Toni was screaming, as tears filled her eyes. Fear and rage filled her heart. She knew she was out of control.

"All right, god damn it, go ahead and lose it. Lose the chance of putting Nicky away for good. Lose the chance of ever finding Megan. Go ahead, you damned hothead!" Sally released her grip and stepped back.

But Toni's sobbing was breaking her heart and she softened.

"Come back inside with me," Sally gently urged. She took Toni's arm and led her toward the villa. "Let's sit down for a minute and see if we can think clearly about this, okay?"

Perspiration and tears were streaming down Toni's face; she felt sick. Her shirt was drenched with sweat, her hair stuck to her forehead.

Back in the villa, Sally turned the air-conditioning on, went into the bathroom, got a glass of water and a wet towel. "Here," she said gently, handing them to Toni.

"What are we gonna do, Sal?" Toni sounded like a lost child. It took everything Sally had not to cry.

She sat down on the bed next to Toni and put her arm around her shoulder. "We're going to get Megan back. She's not stupid, you know. I'm sure she's okay. If Clark has her stashed somewhere, we *will* get it out of her, I promise." Sally was going all out in an effort to calm and comfort Toni. "We're going to conduct ourselves like professionals. We're NOT going to let Nicky get the best of us. No matter how hard it is, you are going to hang in there. For Megan's sake, you can't fall apart. You're a police officer, the best, and that's who Nicky Clark and the rest of the department are going to see."

Toni sat on the edge of the bed staring at the floor for a long time, not moving. Finally she sighed, and looked at Sally.

"Okay, Sal, we do it your way. I'll be okay, I promise. For Megan, I'll be okay." Toni took several deep breaths, then stood, pulling her tall body up straight. "Let's find Megan." Slipping on her Raybans, she walked to the door and stepped out into the bright desert sun.

—An excerpt from *Deadly Rendezvous* ($9.99), by Diane Davidson, author of *Deadly Gamble* ($11.99).

Another Exciting Mystery:

Rough Justice
Claire Youmans

Foaming green water tugged at Nic's boots. Her hands, stiff with cold, stung where the salt bit the cracks in her skin, but she couldn't lose her grip on the rail protecting the sailboat's mast. *Wayward* smashed into the sea and another wall of water crashed onto the deck, splashing into Nic's eyes and blinding her.

The seas lifted the stern and rolled beneath the keel. The wind howled in the rigging. Nic scanned the eastern horizon, searching the endless grey for the darker line of land. She breathed a sigh of relief: she saw nothing but endless waves and white foam merging into the stormy sky. Land, hard and unforgiving, on which a boat could smash to bits, was a danger far greater than the storm.

Wayward poised on the top of the swell, then began her giddy slide into the trough. Nic hung on to the mast guard and waited for the next wave to bring her up for another look. *It's getting dark fast,* she thought. *I won't get another look until sunrise.*

Nic had long since lost track of days or dates, but she knew she'd been about five hundred miles out when the storm began to move south. She had been sailing on a roughly northeast course, headed for the Strait of Juan de Fuca and the inside passage from Washington through Canada to Alaska.

When she changed course to get out of the path of the storm, she made what seemed like a prudent decision. She thought she had plenty of sea room. A summer storm, even an early one, shouldn't last long, she'd assured herself— a day, at most, two. But it had lasted longer than that by a full day. Now, Nic admitted to herself, she was frightened. Her safety margin of open water had to be just about gone. If the storm did not abate soon she was going to have to sail right into it.

As she turned to make her way back to the cockpit, a rag of blown foam slapped her across the face. As she reached to wipe it off, she lost her balance and slipped, barking her elbow on a stanchion base. "Damn," she muttered as she gritted her teeth and waited for the pain to subside. Head down against the wind, she began to crawl.

She concentrated on her hands — grip and wait, move and grip. The crawl seemed endless, her path riddled with obstacles. Finally, awkwardly, Nic slid down from the cabin top into the cockpit, switched her safety harness to its cockpit tether, and gave the cockpit a last once-over before going below.

The wheel held secure, lashed amidships. The heavy Manila ropes dragging off the stern might be old-fashioned, but they were still attached and still working. Then, without warning, one of the ties holding the boom secure came undone as she watched. Lunging for it, Nic caught it just as it blew free, re-tied it, then checked the rest of the ties. Finally, she decided, the deck and cockpit were as secure as she could make them.

It seemed to take her hours to lift out the hatchboards, tumble down the companionway, slip out of her safety harness, snap the harness tether to a pad-eye, and replace the hatchboards. She leaned against the hatch, exhausted. *It's just a storm,"* she reminded herself. *"It can't last forever. The point is to survive until it's over.*

Nic lurched forward, grabbing handholds, to the head, where she hung her red foul-weather jacket and pulled off her knee-high blue waterproof boots. She kept on the bib-topped pants that matched the jacket and her heavy wool socks. If she had to go on deck again, she would need to get ready quickly.

Wayward trembled and shook from the force of the seas, and the noise, that peculiar combination of rushing, crashing water and the whistling and roaring of the wind in the rigging, called up visions of disaster. The boots refused to stand up. Nic finally let them fall and clambered aft to the navigation table.

It was now fully dark. She was in 47 degrees of latitude. The June night would be short, about 8 hours between sunset and sunrise, 7 hours or less from last light to first. Though Nic had already decided to wait until daylight to turn into the storm, she leaned over the chart, as if it could somehow reassure her.

Nic's only light came from a waterproof torch, impossible to hold steady in *Wayward's* tumbling. There was no other electricity. Two days before, a wave had broken over the stern, soaking the cabin and shorting out the batteries. The radar, the satellite-activated Global Positioning System and depth-sounder were all useless, as were the lights and engine. The mechanical speed log had torn loose. She couldn't find a position from the sun or the stars if she couldn't see them. *Shit,* she thought. *I might as well pick a position by closing my eyes and pointing.* She was in the Pacific Ocean, somewhere off the state of Washington, about in the middle of the state's coast. But how far off? A hundred miles? Fifty? Five? Forty if all her guesses about boat speed were correct. Forty was enough. At five knots, she'd still be at least ten miles offshore when the first glimmerings of daylight appeared. If the winds had not died down, she'd turn back out to sea and the safety of open water.

"No storm beats me," she barked as she clambered over the leeboard into her sea-berth. A way of life could crumble in your hands, people changed before your very eyes, but a storm — a storm could be endured.

Suddenly the warps' drag vanished. Nic's eyes snapped open. *Wayward* took flight, catapulting Nic over the leeboard. "Holy shit, we're rolling," she screamed into the night, as she tucked her chin and tried to grab the mast. Her body bounced off the lockers like a ball in a pinball machine.

—An excerpt from *Rough Justice* ($10.99),
by Claire Youmans

These and other quality mysteries are available from Rising Tide Press, and from your nearest feminist or lesbian/gay bookstore.

Please see ordering instructions.

AND LOVE CAME CALLING
Beverly Shearer
The rough and ready days of the Old West come alive with the timeless story of love between two women: Kenny Smith, a stage coach driver in Jackson, Colorado and Sophie McLaren, a young woman forced to marry, then widowed. The women meet after Kenny is shot by bandits during a stage coach holdup. And love blooms when Sophie finds herself the unexpected rescuer of the good-looking wounded driver. $11.99

DANGER IN HIGH PLACES
Sharon Gilligan
Set against the backdrop of Washington, D.C., this riveting mystery introduces freelance photographer and amateur sleuth, Alix Nicholson. Alix stumbles on a deadly scheme, and with the help of a lesbian congressional aide, unravels the mystery. $9.99

DANGER! CROSS CURRENTS
Sharon Gilligan
The exciting sequel to *Danger in High Places* brings freelance photographer Alix Nicholson face-to-face with an old love and a murder. When Alix's landlady turns up dead, and her much younger lover, Leah Claire, is the prime suspect, Alix launches a frantic campaign to find the real killer. $9.99

PLAYING FOR KEEPS
Stevie Rios
In this sparkling tale of love and adventure, Lindsay West, a musician, travels to Caracas, where she meets three people who change her life forever: Rob Heron a gay man, who becomes her dearest friend; Her lover Mercedes Luego, who takes Lindsay on a life-altering adventure down the Amazon River; And the mysterious jungle-dwelling woman Arminta, who touches their souls $10.99

NIGHTSHADE
Karen Williams
Alex Spherris finds herself the new owner of a magical bell, which some people would kill for. With this bell, she is ushered into a strange & wonderful world and meets Orielle, who melts her frozen heart. A heartwarming romance spun in the best tradition of storytelling. $11.99

DREAMCATCHER
Lori Byrd
This timeless story of love and friendship introduces Sunny Calhoun, a college student, who falls in love with Eve Phillips, a literary agent. A richly woven novel capturing the wonder and pain of love between a younger and an older woman.
$9.99

HEARTSTONE AND SABER
Jacqui Singleton
You can almost hear the sabers clash in this rousing tale of good and evil, of passionate love between a bold warrior queen and a beautiful healer with magical powers. $10.99

SHADOWS AFTER DARK
Ouida Crozier
Fans of vampire erotica will adore this! When wings of death spread over Kyril's home world, she is sent to Earth on a mission—find a cure for the deadly disease. Once here, she meets and falls in love with Kathryn, who is enthralled yet horrified to learn that her mysterious, darkly exotic lover is...a vampire. This tender, beautifully written love story is the ultimate lesbian vampire novel! $9.95

TROPICAL STORM
Linda Kay Silva
Another winning, action-packed adventure/romance featuring smart and sassy heroines, an exotic jungle setting, and a plot with more twists and turns than a coiled cobra. Megan has disappeared into the Costa Rican rain forest and it's up to Delta and Connie to find her. Can they reach Megan before it's too late? Will Storm risk everything to save the woman she loves? Fast-paced, full of wonderful characters and surprises. Not to be missed. $11.99

SWEET BITTER LOVE
Rita Schiano
Susan Fredrickson is a woman of fire and ice—a successful high-powered executive, she is by turns sexy and aloof. And from the moment writer Jenny Ceretti spots her at the Village Coffeehouse, her serene life begins to change. As their friendship explodes into a blazing love affair, Jenny discovers that all is not as it appears, while Susan is haunted by ghosts from her past. Schiano serves up passion and drama in this roller-coaster romance. $10.99

SIDE DISH
Kim Taylor
She's funny, she's attractive, she's lovable—and she doesn't know it. Meet Muriel, aka Mutt, a twenty-something wayward waitress with a college degree, who has resigned herself to low standards, simple pleasures, and erotic fantasies. Though seeming to get by on margaritas and old movies, in her heart of hearts, Mutt is actually searching for true love. While Mutt chases the bars with her best friend, Jeff, she is, in turn, chased by Diane, a former college classmate with a decidedly romantic agenda. When a rich, seductive Beverly Hills lawyer named Allison steals Mutt's heart, she is in for trouble, and like the glamorous facade of Sunset Boulevard, things are not quite as they seem. A delightfully funny read. $11.99

AGENDA FOR MURDER
Joan Albarella
Though haunted by memories of love and loss from her years of service in Viet Nam, Nikki Barnes is finally putting back the pieces of her life, and learning to feel again. But she quickly realizes that the college where she teaches is no haven from violence and death, as she comes face to face with murder and betrayal in this least likely of all places—her college campus. $11.99

NO WITNESSES
Nancy Sanra
This cliff-hanger of a mystery set in San Francisco, introduces Detective Tally McGinnis, whose ex-lover Pamela Tresdale is arrested for the grisly murder of a wealthy Texas heiress. Tally rushes to the rescue despite friends' warnings, and is drawn once again into Pamela's web of deception and betrayal as she attempts to clear her and find the real killer. $9.99

NO ESCAPE
Nancy Sanra
This edgy, fast-paced sequel to *No Witnesses*, also set in picturesque San Francisco, is a story of drugs, love and jealousy. Late one rain-drenched night, nurse Melinda Morgan is found murdered. Who cut her life short, plunging a scalpel into her heart, then disappeared into the night? As lesbian PI Tally McGinnis sorts through the bizarre evidence, she can almost sense the diabolical Marsha Cox lurking in the shadows. You will be shocked by the secrets behind the gruesome murder. $11.99

DEADLY RENDEZVOUS
Diane Davidson
A string of brutal murders in the middle of the desert plunges Lieutenant Toni Underwood and her lover Megan into a high profile investigation which uncovers a world of drugs, corruption and murder, as well as the dark side of the human mind. An explosive, fast-paced, action-packed whodunit. $9.99

DEADLY GAMBLE
Diane Davidson
Former police detective Toni Underwood is catapulted back into the world of crime by a mysterious letter from her favorite aunt. Black sheep of the family and a prominent madam, Vera Valentine fears she is about to be murdered—a distinct possibility, given her underworld connections. With the help of onetime partner (and possibly future lover) Sergeant Sally Murphy, Toni takes on the seamy, ruthless underbelly of Las Vegas, where appearance and reality are often at odds. Flamboyant characters and unsavory thugs make for a cast of likely suspects... and keep the reader guessing until the last page. $11.99

CLOUD NINE AFFAIR
Katherine E. Kreuter
Chris Grandy—rebellious, wealthy, twenty-something—has disappeared in India, along with her hippie lover Monica Ward. Desperate to bring her home, Christine's millionaire father hires expert Paige Taylor. But the trail to Christine is mined with obstacles, as powerful enemies plot to eliminate her. A witty, sophisticated & entertaining mystery. $11.99

COMING ATTRACTIONS
Bobbi D. Marolt
It's been three years since she's made love to a woman; three years that she's buried herself in work as a successful columnist for one of New York's top newspapers. Helen Townsend admits, at last, she's tired of being lonely....and of being closeted. Enter Princess Charming in the shapely form of Cory Chamberlain, a gifted concert pianist. And Helen embraces joy once again. But can two lovers find happiness when one yearns to break out of the closet and breathe free, while the other fears that will destroy her career? A sunny blend of humor, heart and passion. A novel which captures the bliss and blunderings of love. $11.99

HOW TO ORDER

TITLE	AUTHOR	PRICE

- ❑ Agenda for Murder-Joan Albarella 11.99
- ❑ And Love Came Calling-Beverly Shearer 11.99
- ❑ Cloud 9 Affair-Katherine Kreuter 11.99
- ❑ Coming Attractions-Bobbi Marolt 11.99
- ❑ Danger! Cross Currents-Sharon Gilligan 9.99
- ❑ Danger in High Places-Sharon Gilligan 9.95
- ❑ Deadly Gamble-Diane Davidson 11.99
- ❑ Deadly Rendezvous-Diane Davidson 9.99
- ❑ Dreamcatcher-Lori Byrd 9.99
- ❑ Emerald City Blues-Jean Stewart 11.99
- ❑ Feathering Your Nest-Gwen Leonhard/ Jennie Mast 14.99
- ❑ Heartstone and Saber-Jacqui Singleton 10.99
- ❑ Isis Rising-Jean Stewart 11.99
- ❑ Nightshade-Karen Williams 11.99
- ❑ No Escape-Nancy Sanra 11.99
- ❑ No Witnesses-Nancy Sanra 9.99
- ❑ Playing for Keeps-Stevie Rios 10.99
- ❑ Return to Isis-Jean Stewart 9.99
- ❑ Rough Justice-Claire Youmans 10.99
- ❑ Shadows After Dark-Ouida Crozier 9.99
- ❑ Side Dish-Kim Taylor 11.99
- ❑ Sweet Bitter Love-Rita Schiano 10.99
- ❑ Tropical Storm-Linda Kay Silva 11.99
- ❑ Warriors of Isis-Jean Stewart 11.99

Please send me the books I have checked. I enclose a check or money order (not cash), plus $4 for the first book and $1 for each additional book to cover shipping and handling. Or bill my ❑Visa/Mastercard ❑American Express.

Or call our Toll Free Number 1-800-648-5333 if using a credit card.

CARD # _____ EXP.DATE_____

NAME (PLEASE PRINT) _____SIGNTURE_____

ADDRESS _____

CITY_____

STATE_____ZIP_____
- ❑ Arizona residents, please add 7% tax to total.

RISING TIDE PRESS, 3831 N. ORACLE RD., TUCSON AZ 85705